SIREN RISE

BETTINA M. JOHNSON

Aqua Raven Publishing

A WORD FROM THE AUTHOR:

While I cannot predict all the triggers that one may encounter reading my books, I included a list of some common ones that may cause distress. It is never my intent to do harm. Therefore, please use this as a guide:

Attempted Rape and Sexual Assault
Abuse (physical, mental, emotional, verbal, sexual)
Mild violence w/Blood/
Depiction of pornography
Death or dying/Murder/Killing
Drug Use/Alcohol
Sexual themes - consensual and non-consensual
The type of humor that might not be for all
Kinky or perverse situations

Siren Rise

Copyright © 2021 by Bettina M. Johnson
Don't be a pirate. Nobody likes them unless they look like Will Turner rising in all his glory in The Flying Dutchmen. This book is licensed for your personal enjoyment only.
All rights reserved.
This book is a work of fiction. Any resemblance to persons living or dead, or places, events or locales is purely coincidental and in the imagination of the author.
Some of the subject matter in this book may offend you; this is not my intent. I write what my characters dictate and never intend to upset or harm.

ISBN: 978-1-7365176-8-0 (paperback)

Cover art by Stefanie Saw (Seventhstar Art)

Remember this: I will take this secret to my grave...
For her - Logan

PROLOGUE

I used to think a home meant four walls, a picket fence, and all the trappings that go with it. It's crazy how quickly it changed to a tall, dark-eyed man with curly brown hair, a lopsided smile, and a wicked glint in his eyes.

But that was a long time ago.

I have no home now.

Drifting listlessly in my pond, I sought out the last vestige of leaves as they kept a tenuous hold on the tree branches above. Each color—yellow, red, orange—fading to brown then withering as they lost the fight. The wind took them then, cascading to the ground or surface of the water below.

I live a solitary life, so vastly different from the one I'd left behind, and I find myself often thinking of the past. A lot of good that does me.

Forty Seven. It seems like a long time to live and would be if I were human. I am not. But for twenty-five of them now, I have dwelled at the bottom of Nichols Pond on the border of North Carolina and Georgia. A stone's throw away from cousins who I haven't associated with in years, despite how close we used to be. Although I've met a girl recently—the daughter of one of my favorite cousins—and I gave her my tears.

This is no small offering, for my tears contain magic.

I am a siren.

Descended from murdúchann—merrow, or mermaids if you will, eons ago. And while I do not have a glistening tail made of iridescent scales, I can swim for miles and hold my breath indefinitely.

I also have a voice that can kill.

Perhaps I am being too harsh on myself. But I don't believe I am. Sirens can tempt, lure, entice with the softest of utterances. We can whisper sweet nothings that can topple nations and start wars. Or we can soothe the crankiest baby with a lullaby so tender, they can't help but relinquish their troubles and wander off to the land of Nod.

This ability is why all sirens—the females, anyway—have their vocal cords magically damaged as children, nullifying our voice. To me, it's a half-life not worth living.

Brutal. Invasive. Horrifying. Barbaric. And sanctioned by the ruling class.

There are very few males in our world. They seem to be dying out while the women thrive—if you can call a life subservient to the men thriving. Those few males remaining breed relentlessly, hoping to create sons; females outnumber them by one thousand to one. Our women have been so utterly brainwashed they never consider bucking the system—fighting for their rights. In fact, many of them work to keep the system running, choosing to remain in a patriarchal, orthodox vacuum.

Their blind obedience is nauseating.

The scarcity of males is why my father has had several wives—and I have more sisters than I know what to do with! It is also why I am in hiding from them and have been these many years. You see, I decided conformity and I would never be friends, choosing rebellion instead and going off on my own at nineteen to live among humans.

In my father's frustrating attempts at producing a son he hoped would be a powerful and manipulative force for world domination, it caused him to choose a highly unusual wife in my mother. For you see, my mother is a dark witch—with a bit of siren in her to make things interesting. Or she was. Father killed her after he found out she betrayed his people.

I am my mother's daughter. A dark witch.

A renegade.

There are many defectors in the paranormal world among all the various Breed. Witches that remained on a dark path performing foul magic, vampires who still fed on human blood and refused the modern way of having a volunteer host. Even minor demons have learned to tone down their natural tendencies for mayhem—although some of them have a hell of a time controlling the urge to cause chaos and break away occasionally to do just that. All are hunted.

A few of us have conveniently been lobbed in with those that would destroy all humanity in their quest for whatever power or dark purpose gets them going. These truly deserve to be hunted, their magical abilities suppressed.

For sirens, it is ten times worse—just because we possess the ability to influence so strongly. Our rebels are pursued with abandon because so many of my kind in the past had caused unimaginable devastation. Those that slip through the cracks usually wind up as top spies or assassins. Getting their charge to give up secrets is like taking candy from a baby.

When caught, execution is swift.

I do *not* plan on getting caught.

Perhaps I'm being dramatic when stating I have no home.

Especially since I have a large mansion not too far from this pond.

I lived in the human world and amassed a fortune. One that afforded me to hide among the Blue Ridge Mountains in an incredible house with a full staff of people to do my bidding. Notice I call it a house...not a home. But I digress. Magnificent it may be, but still, I would spend most of my time floating at the bottom of a pond to be close to the one item I treasure the most. The one thing I have that is his.

No one knows where I am. None of my people will ever betray me. I chose wisely those that would be my safeguard.

At least...I hope so.

My half sisters became hunters, determined to keep the siren world honest and free of renegades. They chose this path to temper my wayward father, who I was certain was still hell-bent on his task for world domination with a male progeny. Why my father believes a male is necessary for such a task is beyond my comprehension.

I could do it for him with ease.

I have already dominated the world and reached the heights of which most humans can only dream of attainting: fame, fortune, sex, power. I've had it all, until it came crashing down around me.

I'd do it all again if just to relive the time with the man I will always love...

Perhaps it is time I told my tale from the beginning.

My name is Tarni Vanderzee. And this is my story.

CHAPTER 1

Tarni, 1986

Running on the still-hot pavement with sneakers worn threadbare from misuse, Tarni quickly realized that she should have grabbed some with more substance. As it stood, she'd barely make it another mile before she'd have to stop and rest, hoping she wouldn't get sores on the bottoms of her aching feet. The grumbling in her stomach added to her misery, and she wished she had the guts to hitchhike instead of following the highway north on foot.

In the dead of night.

Tarni couldn't risk travel by day. Too many vehicles on the road, too many do-gooders who would see a teenager and stop to help—or stop to harm. There were plenty of perverts ready to take advantage of yet another runaway. At least at night, Tarni could jog along the pavement and when hearing a car or truck coming up behind her, have time to duck into the swampy woods waiting for them to pass.

Remembering the all too recent incident when, as an entering freshman in high school, senior Danny Kowalski pulled her into the boys' bathroom then shoved his hand up her skirt made Tarni grind her teeth. Even as she resisted, Danny pinned her up against a stall and grabbed her throat, crushing his lips painfully on hers. The revulsion and rage inside warred with the forbidden—use of magic against humans—until Tarni snapped, refusing to submit to such treatment. With her free hand she grasped Danny's wrist and slammed her magic into him. He went down, and she was rescued by a nameless boy who shoved her out of there and back to the relative safety of the hallway.

She never did thank that boy.

After one more confrontation where Danny all but accused her of being a witch, the lousy punk kept his distance—but so did everyone else in school. Word of her "strangeness" spread like wildfire.

"Hey, freak!" or "Here comes the spooky nerd!" shadowed her until she'd run home crying.

Her mom, Jenny, pulled Tarni out a week later, and she gladly homeschooled until she graduated. The novel and wonderful world of self-education opening her eyes to just how *Lord of the Flies* the unnatural, artificial environment of a public American high school truly was. It gave Tarni a jaded look on society she carried with her from that day forward. Especially the hypocrisy of it all. Pushing of agendas and expecting the kids to not shun authority, yet mimic the imagery pounded daily into their heads by movies and magazines and peer pressure to be popular. Society seemed like a slick, fake, corporate-sponsored march to create mindless minions who were obsessed with sex, money, college, careers, and getting ahead at any cost. Money, greed, power and the proverbial "sex sells."

"I'm not afraid of sex," she grumbled to herself. "I just want no part of it. Not yet. I have too much to do."

As a siren, she resigned herself to the fact she'd more than likely have to use her wiles to get things from men and figured somewhere along the way, losing her virginity would happen. Tarni didn't see it as the big deal humans seemed to make of it. She just couldn't imagine getting so excited over a guy that she'd willingly go "all the way." She had different plans.

I'm going to rule the world. If Madonna can do it, so can I, thought Tarni. *Sex would just be one tool to get there. But I will do it on my terms and to advance MY agenda.*

Right now, Tarni had other pressing matters with which to attend. She couldn't worry about sex or outlandish celebrities—or bad experiences from her past. She only had a small stash of money that she needed to be frugal with; it would be the only funds she'd have until she settled in a new place. She barely took anything, so quickly did she make her escape and decide to head as far away from Florida as her legs could take her. She had to hurry before someone in her family found her and dragged her back to her father's compound kicking and screaming the entire way—or worse—fighting to the death to remain free.

Tarni had been traveling for two full days.

She was still in Florida.

She couldn't risk buying a car in all cash...that would raise too many eyebrows. And how would she register it? The entire point was to run away, get a new identity, and remain hidden from discovery. So, for now, it's walking. Plus, she didn't have *that* much in savings that she'd be willing to blow on a car.

Another violent tummy vibration caused Tarni to pause. Removing the knapsack from her back, she grimaced as a rhinestone caught in her lengthy black hair. Rummaging around, she came up with a half-eaten Whatchamacallit chocolate bar that was a little mushy from her body heat. It would do, however.

It would have to.

She refused to spend a dime. For now, she'd steal candy bars and hope for the best.

Taking a bite brought her right back to her eleventh birthday and the first time she'd ever tasted her favorite treat. Jenny had brought home a birthday gift all wrapped up with a pretty bow, and sitting beside it, taped to the wrapping paper, was a Whatchamacallit candy bar. It was 1978, and Hershey had just premiered their new chocolate treat to accolades from the neighborhood children where they lived. Her youngest cousin, Adelaide, her favorite of all the cousins, came to visit the tiny North Carolina town where Tarni and her mom and little sister, Kimberly, had settled, from her neighboring town of Sweet Briar, Georgia, and gave her a taste one day. Tarni had begged her mother for the delicacy ever since.

The sensation of biting into that candy bar for the first time almost overshadowed the more significant gift her mother brought her. A tiny record player and a stack of used 45s—most of them disco—with the occasional rock and Top 40 single thrown in. They must've belonged to her mother's brother, her Uncle Buddy.

Tarni could remember playing "Hopelessly Devoted to You" and "Heart of Glass" over and over that year. She also remembered eating her body weight in Whatchamacallits—she has an overactive metabolism, and an entire box of those yummy bars wouldn't make a dent in her waistline. She could now easily subside on stolen chocolate from convenience stores and would thrive. Snickering a little, she realized her human counterparts would hate her for this.

As good as the chocolate was, however, the record player gave her the most joy. Tarni would sing her heart out while the 45 went round and round, but it never lasted long since her mother would rush in and beg her to stop.

"You know you cannot sing, child. Not here. Not where anyone can hear you!"

Tarni knew it wasn't due to a lack of keeping in tune or any other such nonsense. Hadn't she amazed both of her parents when she was barely four years old and did a grand job of imitating Judy Garland when the annual broadcast of *The Wizard of Oz* came on the television? Her father, for once, seemed pleased by his daughter... even if it was temporary. After all, he almost had an even dozen—and not a boy in sight.

No, singing was a talent all of her sisters possessed or would have had their vocal cords remained unaltered. Oh, they could still carry a tune, but they sounded like a boozy jazz singer with a three-pack-a-day habit.

Sirens had to give up their singing voices—and sultry speaking voices for that matter—to prevent one of them from going rogue and tempting humans to do horrible things. Eons ago, sirens would involve themselves in human affairs with abandon. Now, ever since the paranormal world and the many Breed evolved and formed a central organization, The Order of Origin, to keep those inclined to do evil in check, her kind had suffered as a result.

Unfairly, as far as Tarni was concerned.

Having escaped her fate, which is why she is now on the run, Tarni avoided the torture of losing her natural voice, thanks to her mother. Jenny hid both of her daughters for years, trying to prevent the operation. Her crafty mother refused to subject Tarni and her younger sister, Kimberly, to the atrocity of vocal aphonia—cutting and scarring the vocal cords with a magical knife. So one day, Jenny left and didn't return until they were older—past the age one usually had the surgery. No one in her family questioned their disappearance, for her father often went away looking for another nubile female to impregnate for months on end—especially since his witch wife gave him two additional and highly disappointing female offspring. So Jenny going off on her own didn't raise any eyebrows.

Eventually, however, Jenny mistakenly returned to Florida, having run low on funds, yet lived in relative harmony with her estranged spouse and his daughters all throughout Tarni's preteen and teenaged years. It wasn't until her elder half-siblings realized both she and Kimberly were unaltered, and they ordered the procedure, that things became bleak. Tarni never did discover what triggered her sisters to suddenly scrutinize the mother and daughter trio.

Ironically, her half sisters work for the very organization whose sole purpose is to hunt down renegades and eradicate them, one by one. The Biodag, in The Order of Origin—a conglomerate of paranormal Breed police who try and keep order in a world hidden from humans—a paranormal world. Those very humans would panic if they realized the supernatural were among them, should they discover it.

The Biodag reprimanded Jenny and imprisoned her, and Kimberly underwent the magical knife first. Kimberly survived her ordeal. Tarni fought back. She used her dark witch powers to slam magic into anyone and everyone in their attempts to hold her down—and escaped, never looking back.

While all of this occurred, and unbeknownst to Tarni, Jenny lost her life at the hands of a murderous traitor—her own husband. Torrent Danu had already taken another wife, something that was encouraged in the siren world. Tarni lost count of the wives he'd had before her mother. She discovered his treachery upon escaping the hospital ward where Kimberly lay in miserable recovery. It was all anyone was gossiping about.

His betrayal was the catalyst for Tarni choosing a renegade life over conformity.

She did it with Kimberly's blessing, and the pain of separation from her beloved sister left a dry ache in her throat, even as her thoughts turned to Jenny Danu.

Oh, Mom. Suddenly unable to finish her chocolate, Tarni swallowed the last of it along with the sob that threatened to escape when contemplating the death of her unfortunate mother. Jenny did not deserve to die, to be murdered by the man with whom she bore two children.

Tarni couldn't prove it was Torrent that took her mother's life, but she knew. She heard the gossip and rumors. She knew his foul heart, his depraved quest for a son, and his disregard for the female of their species. And someday, Tarni would prove it and see him lose everything.

I will avenge my mother.

It was a promise Tarni made, and the driving force behind her mission to set out on her own, escape the fate that staying would bring about, and begin a life on her terms, even if it meant she became an outlaw.

A small price to pay for being a half-breed, unwanted child of a murderous bastard.

"I need to make a name for myself. I need to be rich and powerful. Only then can I destroy my father. And for that—I need fame. And I will have it." Tarni whispered the words that were carried away by the wind, as the bugs buzzed around her, and frogs sang their song into the night.

Half-breed. It was the reason her father pursued Jenny in the first place, as he assumed a dark witch who held such power could surely give him a male heir especially since she was also part siren. Jenny had escaped the cutting because it was so far back in her lineage as to not be an issue among her people, although she never sang, never used her voice. When Jenny produced two daughters instead of a boy, Tarni's father became disinterested in his wife and his girls.

I wasn't enough for that dirtbag. Tarni thought to herself as she ran off to the side of the highway. *I'm going to put him out of my mind until I am ready to make my triumphant return. He's already a dead man.*

She'd just made it into the safety of the woods as the lights of a vehicle crested the hill behind her. Crouching low, she waited for the car to pass, then crept back out and continued on her way.

The irony was, dark witch power was passed from mother to daughter by chance and had Torrent Danu bothered to notice his young daughter, he might have realized Tarni possessed the dark force. Combined with her siren song, Tarni could be one of the most powerful beings in the paranormal world. Not that she cared. Tarni just wanted to be human. Or live in their world, anyway. *Just like The Little Mermaid*, Tarni snickered to herself in a moment of silliness, then sobered, *and look how well that turned out for her*. As much as she loved that fairytale, the ending never failed to produce countless tears.

Tarni had big plans. She intended to become a famous singer.

She didn't how long it took her to reach this goal. Time was on her side. Sirens lived thousands of years. She was the only female left in her family uncut. If it took her thirty-one years of unsuccessful attempts only to become famous in her thirty-second, what did that matter in the grand scheme of things? Either way her father would still be out there, and she'd still destroy him.

But it was time for Tarni to live her life.

It was too late for Kimberly, and that was her only regret.

Jenny ran away with the girls when they were four and twenty-two months, Kimberly just out of diapers. They grew up witch, with countless human overtones. Tarni was a dark witch and wore that badge proudly, yet knew nothing, really, about being a siren—her mother made sure of it. The only thing the siren world gave her was the inability to sing in an area where she could be overheard, and she mourned her inability to sing aloud.

My voice is stellar, she reflected glumly.

When Tarni was little she discovered just how dangerous her siren power could be. And it made her cautious. How was she supposed to know singing a lullaby to Kimberly would result in her much older witch cousin, Dustin, inviting her to 'snuggle in bed with him a bit?' She was too young to realize she'd enchanted him to the point he'd lost all reason and would have assaulted her given a chance. Thankfully, her Uncle Buddy found her confused and naked in Dustin's bedroom before anything else happened.

Tarni was eight. Dustin was seventeen. He got shipped off to the Army after countless magical spells were performed to alter his memory and remove as much of the glamour as her mother's people could.

It was humiliating.

After that, Tarni promised her mother she'd not sing unless she knew for certain she was alone and out of hearing of others who might overhear and become ensnared. Now, in light of her current situation, the thought of becoming a famous singer made Tarni laugh. The irony of it all. Such a renegade!

So that was what she was doing—embracing a vagabond life at nineteen years of age—running as far away from Florida as she could. Tarni even changed her name in the process, taking the surname Vanderzee, which means *of the sea*—a name she'd discovered far back in her mother's genealogy that had belonged to a distant siren. Choosing her own path left Tarni thrilled to be just another runaway on the streets of America—albeit one who could enchant and influence like nobody's business.

She wasn't afraid.

Jenny didn't raise a fool. Nor would she have. Witch lessons in human weaponry, along with spellcasting and magic control, were part of Tarni's waking life. Siren magic aside, Tarni knew she could handle what the big, bad world would throw at her since she'd decided a long time ago embracing her dark witch powers came with perks.

Which she's welcomed with unbridled pleasure.

Tarni liked having dark spells at her beck and call.

She wasn't evil, however. Tarni decided to tread lightly and cautiously use only the minimal amount of her powers—just enough to keep her from injury and harm. She believed she could avoid the temptation of her strength and all it could bring. Tarni felt every siren should have that choice, and someday she would return—powerful, influential, and wealthy—and prove it. Then change the siren world for the better.

At least that's what Tarni told herself. Right now, she needed to find some new shoes...her feet were killing her!

CHAPTER 2

"How about a burger, kid? You look famished."

The truck driver smiled and pointed to the waitress who was giving Tarni the stink eye. Obviously, she didn't fool the woman one bit, and her *"My parents dropped me off for a few hours while they go out to have dinner,"* story didn't deceive anyone.

Tarni now wished she had just used the gas station bathroom instead of coming in here in the hopes the diner would have cleaner facilities. There was a tiny arcade in the strip mall next door that she hoped would make her story hold salt—plenty of kids got dropped off their while their parents ran errands and such.

Chuckling to herself, Tarni definitely downplayed her appearance and looked way younger than nineteen, so finding the assumption she was young as proof she could pull off the look gave her some satisfaction. Petite in stature, a mere five foot four inches and slim enough people were constantly trying to feed her, she could pass for a pre-teen. Especially minus makeup, with pigtails, jean jacket, Walkman, Keds—and a restrictive reduction bra hiding the fact that she was most certainly *not* a child. Tarni was a few months away from her twentieth birthday and she already felt old, so wandering around in this guise was refreshing.

"At least have something to drink."

"Leave her be, Bert. How would she pay for it?"

"I'll pay. Go get her something to eat." Bert seemed like a nice man, but Tarni wouldn't take any chances that his act of kindness didn't conceal something more sinister. She would have to spell him—once she could figure out how to do it since that nosy waitress kept hanging around. All it would take was a quick scan of his thoughts to see if he could be trusted. She could manage that.

"I'm fine, really. I can go wait outside for my folks if hanging in here is too much trouble." Tarni really wanted to sit for a spell, and the diner seemed like a safe bet. She didn't count on drawing so much attention and couldn't figure out why the waitress wouldn't let up.

Bert shook his head and told her she wasn't a bother.

"You just look a little drawn is all. Like you haven't had much sleep."

"I suffer from insomnia," she said a bit rudely.

"You look like you haven't slept in over a week." The waitress, her nametag showing the name 'Gwen,' said as she plunked down a plate with a burger and fries, then followed it up with a chocolate shake. "Might as well eat up and drink your shake."

Tarni watched as the waitress made her way down the counter then returned to frown once more at her plate. "You aren't a runaway, are you?"

Tarni took a huge bite of her burger and had to stop herself from swooning, then choking a bit when the waitress's words registered. "What? No! Of course not," she said around mouthfuls. "Listen, my parents can pay when they get back. I don't want to get in any kind of trouble here."

Tarni began to make motions like she'd leave her seat at the counter, but Gwen waved her off and told her to remain seated. Tarni continued to eat but stayed watchful.

She felt like zapping that bitch. A little magic would keep her out of Tarni's business.

"Bert will pay if your *parents* don't want to. He doesn't just drive that truck out yonder; he owns the entire company. He can afford it."

Yeah, she *definitely* deserves to be zapped.

Pushing arcane thoughts away when Gwen's words registered, Tarni looked out the front window of the diner with interest at the big 18-wheeler parked off to one side, then turned and gave Bert a calculated look.

"Do you drive across the country with that?" she asked curiously.

"Heading to California on I-40 then turning south, doing my deliveries along the way then looping back east via I-10. Well, I have to go north first through Georgia and up to Tennessee. That's where I pick up the interstate heading west."

Tarni glanced over her shoulder to see how far Gwen was from where they were sitting. Satisfied they'd not be overheard, she leaned toward Bert and turned on her siren voice. In a singsong whisper she said, "You will take me with you."

Tarni could see the confusion as it crossed Bert's face, as he tried to fight her influence.

"I don't know what kind of man you think I am, kid, but I am definitely not into children."

Reaching out, Tarni placed her hand on Bert's arm. "You may not be, but my father is. You *will* take me with you. I need to escape. I have an aunt in California who will take me in. I just need to make it there. Bert, please take me to California."

Tarni finished her melodic plea and watched resigned acceptance transform Bert's face.

Hopping off the stool, Tarni gave Gwen a small wave and rushed out of the diner and around the side of the building, still clutching her burger. Her heart was racing. Either her powers would work, or Bert had enough self-control to withstand her initial magic. Considering this was the first time she ever willingly tried to entice someone, she had no idea how it would turn out.

She tore off into the wooded area beside the diner, and pushed through the bramble, wincing as thorns tore into her, to reach the far end of the parking lot where Bert had his rig parked. Grateful for the new sneakers she'd pilfered from a display at a shoe store near the arcade, Tarni knew she'd still never be able to walk all the way to Hollywood in them, so this might be her chance to hitch a free ride. Waiting to see if her magic took was torture—and so was listening for the police sirens she was certain would herald their approach.

When nothing much happened for the next several minutes, Tarni relaxed, stuffing the last of the burger into her mouth, then sighed in relief when Bert came out of the diner holding a bag and dangling his keys. As he walked her way, she looked past him to see if Gwen would follow. She didn't.

Bert reached his truck, and Tarni made her move. Running over to him, she waited only until his door was ajar, then pushed past him scrambling up inside the cab. Remaining scrunched down low, Tarni gave the startled Bert a look. "You coming, Bert? It's time to leave."

Bert blinked a few times and smiled tentatively. "Sure, sure. Uh, should I tell Gwen you're OK? She wanted to call the cops."

"No, I am OK, Bert. You've got me. You will keep me safe."

"That's right! Don't worry, honey. Ol' Bert will protect you. Let's hit the road, Jack."

"Jack? Oh! That old song." Tarni laughed. "Hit the road, Jack, and don't you come back no more!" She sang softly as she crawled over to the passenger side, noting the dazed look on Bert's face with some satisfaction.

Tarni might not know what she was doing exactly with her siren magic—but obviously she was strong enough—that was too easy!

Bert climbed in his truck, started the engine, and without a backward glance, drove out of the parking lot, taking the road that would lead them to I-75 North. Tarni couldn't believe her luck. California! The land of dreams and magic. Movie magic. And music. Maybe she'd try her hand at acting as well. She always wanted to be one of Charlie's Angels and was still bummed they'd cancelled the television show a few years back when she entered her teen years. She never forgave Farrah for leaving—it killed the series in her opinion.

"You need something to drink for the road, kid? What's your name anyway? You never did say."

"Just call me Jack!" Tarni laughed, and Bert laughed along with her, but she could see the confusion on his face once more. "It's OK, Bert. Really. Call me Jack. And I have an old Perrier bottle in my backpack. I usually just drink water. We can fill it up on your next stop."

"You keep a glass bottle with you? Don't you know they started making plastic bottles you can carry around with water in them?"

"Plastic destroys the environment, Bert. They wind up in waterways, streams, ponds. Then they get out into the ocean and pollute it. I'm happy with my glass bottle."

"You're a funny kid, Jack. Odd. Jack! I can't call a girl that.

Jackie, OK. Just let me know if you get thirsty before I need to stop for diesel."

"I will. But right now, I think I'm going to take a nap if that's fine?"

"Here, grab yourself a pillow from the back. I have like ten of them. I like lots of pillows."

Turning to look, Tarni almost laughed aloud at the sight. Not only did Bert have an appreciation for multiple pillows, but he also had a row of Garfields keeping him company. Garfield in a sombrero, Garfield in a beanie-copter cap, one of him sleeping, drowsy, smiling with no teeth showing, smiling a cheesy smile—all teeth. It was a Garfield-fest!

"I love your collection."

"My granddaughter keeps getting them for me. I love lasagna just about as much as that cat. And that happens to be my last name. Bert Garfield."

"Fitting."

Pushing her backpack with her feet to make a footrest, Tarni snuggled in with a fluffy, soft pillow and one of the Garfields she nabbed and hoped sleep would come quickly. She didn't have to worry. Bert used his signal and turned on the interstate just as Morpheus came, taking Tarni swiftly to her much needed slumber.

She didn't dream.

Tarni's dreams usually led to nightmares.

CHAPTER 3

Tarni, Present Day

I didn't think driving up I-75 would have me recalling the first time I met Bert Garfield. Yes. *Driving.* I've amassed a ridiculous amount of money over my short 47 years, as mentioned, and had a garage of vehicles that I have maintained and babied constantly. I may have spent all my time floating in a pond, but I still had people loyal to me, I still paid salaries, I was still wealthy—and had a magnificent home overlooking the Blue Ridge Mountains in North Carolina with a hidden grotto that led to that little pond on the border of Georgia.

People and Time had forgotten me, however.

Just as I wanted.

I didn't know what my reception would be like when I reached Los Angeles. I didn't know if I'd hit the radar and drag up all the old torrid stories of my life. I'm sure the paparazzi were alive and well-fed with new sordid tales, but I also knew I would cause a minor sensation with my reappearance. Especially since I looked like I was still in my early twenties.

I considered adding a few well-placed white streaks in my

hair at some out of the way podunk Midwestern beautician shop. Maybe I could dress older. Since I have a fondness for small town America, I'm afraid I might decide to stay and continue to hide. No. I wouldn't do something like that. It was time to face the music despite my years of self-exile.

A more ironic statement I could not make. Especially when I considered the heights I achieved. But with that height came the fall. But I didn't want to think about that right now. Especially since I knew I could open my mouth, use my voice, and have all I coveted once again.

Well, not all.

Nothing could bring *him* back.

Not going there.

I can't allow myself to reminiscence, so back to Bert and his Garfield collection. I wondered if he was still alive and well. I certainly hope so. Bert Garfield was one of the good ones. Someone who deserved to play with his grandkids and sit on his dock and fish for decades. I quickly did the math. I supposed he'd be touching ninety today. Not an impossibility, but the law of averages and all made me wonder. How long did human truck drivers live anyway? Even ones who owned the company.

We'd arrived in Chattanooga and dropped off one load, then continued to Knoxville and emptied out his truck. We had to wait a few hours for the next load to get sorted, loaded up, and secured so we could be on our way. Somewhere in that time, Bert got a bit of the tale of woe out of me, knew I had no intention of going back to Florida, and made me promise he'd get to meet my aunt so he could be assured of my safety once we arrived in California. I assured him he could and crossed my fingers I'd come up with something to get out of that sticky situation once we hit Los Angeles.

Because I was traveling with him, and a girl, Bert decided

we'd hit motels along the way so I could shower and do my laundry. It was a bit weird at first, a few of the managers gave him knowing looks, but for the most part no one batted an eye at a young woman traveling with a salt-and-pepper-bearded older dude who was definitely not my father. And wasn't that a sad reality?

For one thing, I had marine-blue eyes, long, silky black hair that cascaded in ringlets just below my shoulders, and honey-gold pale skin that looked like the sun barely kissed it.

Bert was Black.

Yeah.

He'd informed me he was actually more German and English than African, but there was no mistaking his ethnicity if one scrutinized him. That he was the lightest-skinned Black man I'd ever met didn't stop the fact that he was outwardly a Black man. And in the mid-80s, a white girl traveling with a Black man definitely raised some eyebrows. I didn't consider that when I'd sat in that diner and looked into his eyes, into his soul, and read his heart, knowing I found a good and decent man to trust. Thankfully, I didn't get him in trouble.

Much.

"Goddamn it. You stupid freakin' moron! Stop playing games!"

You can thank Bert for my potty mouth. He taught me all of the words on the way to California.

I tapped my horn and moved into the middle lane trying to outmaneuver some idiot in his sports car who was going in and out of traffic like a madman trying to get around me. I was in a brand new inky-black Jeep SRT, loaded to the max and fast as hell, but apparently the dickhead back there didn't like my fumes in his precious face. As he flew past me once more, I opened my tinted window and gave him the one-fingered salute. He did the same.

I watched in incredulity as he roared past me and five other cars, then cut across all the lanes of traffic only to get off at the next exit. It took every fiber of my being not to follow him and read him the riot act. I had to watch my temper. It was legendary and being out and about among the living had woken up more than just these memories. I was coming to life again. Well, as much of a life as I could muster since I felt half dead on a good day.

You couldn't fault me then, when I let a bit of magic out from my fingertips and slammed it into his rear tire. He'd have a flat in about ten minutes or so, and a well-deserved one too.

I hated that I'd sold one of my precious babies, but I didn't feel like driving a convertible across the country, so I sacrificed my 1963 Mercedes 190SL and bought the Jeep—in cash. Now I was glad I did, because I could just see myself tearing up the exit ramp and challenging that idiot to a drag race in my Mercedes.

My temper got me into more trouble with Bert on that six-day trip across the nation more than anything else. That and my penchant for not listening and running headfirst into a new adventure.

Case in point—the rampaging tumbleweed incident.

1986, somewhere in Oklahoma

"What's that? Bert! Up ahead... what is that?" Tarni cried, pointing to a cluster of dark balls of something as they made their way toward the highway. She and Bert were parked on the side of the road having pulled over to access the stop area they'd just left and the all-important bathrooms. Bert had parked on the return road to the highway and away from the usual place trucks parked to avoid more looky-loos from judgmental busybodies.

"What... those? Aw, come on now, girl! You mean to tell me you've ain't never seen a tumbleweed on television?" Bert asked in astonishment.

"Tumbleweeds!" Tarni squealed. "I'm going to take some photos!"

"You can't go out there, girl! Are you crazy?"

Tarni's mood instantly darkened. Her older sisters often chided her as did her father calling her "that crazy witch," and nothing could send her into a tirade quicker than having her sanity questioned.

"Don't call me crazy, Bert! I have a camera and I am going to get a few photos for my scrapbook. You can stay here if you're afraid of rolling weeds!" And before Bert knew what she was doing, Tarni had opened her door and jumped down to the ground where she tore off in the direction of the bouncing balls, camera up and her finger snapping away to record this moment in time.

The wind was wicked, and dust was swirling up ahead creating mini tornados. Bert shouted at her from the truck and ordered her to return. "You are crazy! You are going to get yourself killed! Those tumbleweeds are dangerous!"

Laughing off his threats of doom, Tarni continued toward the tumbleweeds, incredulous that Bert would warn her off them. Hadn't she seen the prickly balls in every western as they gently ambled by in one scene or another? She just wanted to get a photo on her Brownie camera to add to the scrapbook she'd put together once she could develop the film. OK, so it was a harsh wind, and her hair was whipping about something furious, but she'd be perfectly safe.

Right?

The first tumbleweed to slam into Tarni caused her to yelp

as the thorns tore at her legs. That had her stopping short and considering Bert's warning. The next few seconds saw an uptake on the number of tumbleweeds heading in her direction and their sheer volume. A wall of the nasty balls of thistle, easily fifteen feet high and about thirty feet long was bearing down like a locomotive off its rails. Tarni spun, a scream dying in her throat as all the wind was knocked out of her by Bert swooping in and hoisting her over his shoulder as he tore off back to his big rig.

Within the next ten minutes, the highway disappeared in a sea of brown.

Trucks were creeping by slowly as they tried to forge a path through the gnarled bramble, but many motorists chose to stay in the relative safety of the rest area. Bert decided to crawl up the ramp and follow behind the other truckers, but it was slow going and a mess of tangle and wind, with dust that morphed into the mini tornados that danced across the highway or along the ditch adding to the chaos.

"I'm sorry, Bert. I had no idea. They seem so harmless in the movies!" Chastised by her reckless behavior, Tarni hoped Bert wouldn't be too mad at her.

"Well, there's a life lesson for you, Jackie. Never, ever believe everything you see on television or the movies. That's make-believe. This is real life." Bert was bleeding from a cut on his cheek and Tarni felt horrible. "One misplaced cigarette and both sides of the highway would turn into an inferno. Tumbleweeds make great kindling."

What should have taken twenty minutes and a few miles down the highway turned into an hour lost to the bouncing and tumbling balls of death as Tarni chose to call them from that day forward.

Tarni remained contrite and quiet until exhausted and battered, Bert and his semi rolled into Amarillo, Texas, and their next stop. One would think Tarni would keep her temper in check after that unpleasant incident, but she just wasn't wired that way. Instead, after a long, hot shower at their motel and a nap, Tarni was ready for dinner...only Bert had other ideas.

"I'll bring you back a burger, fries, and shake. You need to stay here at the motel...it's better this way."

"Why?"

"Because I say so, is why," argued Bert.

"Well, I'd like to come with you into the truck stop. What if I don't want a burger?" asked Tarni.

"Lord above, girl. You are just being stubborn. Look, this area...it isn't like some places we've been. Just stay here and I'll be back in a jiffy. Plus, who are you fooling? All you've eaten since Florida is burgers and fries!"

Tarni flopped on her bed and gave Bert a sullen look but didn't argue further. Bert took this as a sign of acceptance and went to take his turn in the shower. He'd left his bed a rumpled mess but otherwise kept his things neat and orderly. The motel had a laundry facility attached so Tarni figured she might as well get the wash done while Bert got them dinner.

Gathering up her dirty clothing and adding them to Bert's laundry sack, she grabbed a few quarters from Bert's stash that he kept in an old mason jar and went out in search of the laundry room. She didn't mind doing Bert's personal effects, but the thought of him seeing her dirty undies gave her the willies!

It was four in the afternoon, but the sun was low on the horizon, only a few months left before daylight savings would end. August in Texas wasn't too different from that in Florida, but the nights seemed to cool down quicker. Tarni was surprised when she heard the news guy on the radio state the low would be 64 degrees for Amarillo. Nighttime temperatures in the sixties were unheard of in Florida during the summer. Even the end of summer.

Humming a Psychedelic Furs tune softly to herself and shielding her eyes from the setting sun, Tarni reached the laundry area.

The tiny room where the washers and dryers were kept was empty, but one dryer was making a whirring sound telling Tarni someone was in the process of doing laundry. She dumped all the clothing in one machine and added a bit of powdered detergent followed by her quarters. She didn't have any fabric softener and there wasn't any offered in the vending machine so, shrugging, Tarni closed the lid and took a seat just outside the door on a long, wooden bench made out of logs while she enjoyed the sun's rays. She closed her eyes and let her mind wander.

"Got to keep them pretty legs out of the sun before you burn, missy."

Tarni jerked awake, realizing she must have drifted off, as she squinted up at the man standing in front of her. Right away she didn't like the look of him, nor the way he was eying her body.

Without acknowledging his words, Tarni stood, then walked into the laundry room and began pulling wet clothing out of the wash and dropping it into the dryer. The man, on the short side with a greasy blue shirt half-tucked into worn jeans, stood in the doorway. He kept working a toothpick between his teeth while he watched her every move. Occasionally, he'd scratch his reddish beard while glancing over his shoulder.

"You need some help with that?"

"No."

"Need help with anything else?" he snickered and made to come into the room.

"Why don't you get out of here before you piss me off?" Tarni snarled, whirling around to face him.

Shock registered first, then annoyance. "Don't you be getting fresh with me, little lady.

"No? How should I act then? Grateful that a disgusting old man is hitting on a young girl? Should I swoon because you're so hot, and I'm desperate for a little something? Buzz off, loser!" Tarni sneered then gave the man a knowing smirk. In his lifetime, this goon would never be considered remotely hot.

Tarni wasn't afraid. Not really. Not with the dark magic she possessed and her ability to use it with deadly accuracy. As she made to move past the man, he stepped in her path and reached out to grab her arms. Tarni sidestepped him only to have him grab the front of her shirt and push her back into the laundry room. Backing her up against the running machine, the man placed both arms around her.

"We'll see how fast I can wipe that grin off your face, missy."

The ensuing tussle would have been over in less than thirty seconds had Bert not chosen that moment to come barreling in, arms swinging and their dinner scattering in all directions. Bert slammed into Tarni's harasser, pushing him away as she cried out, afraid the younger man might injure her friend.

"Bert! It's me... Carson!"

"Stay away from Jackie, you filthy cur. What's wrong with you, messin' around a young lady?"

"Aw, I didn't mean nothing by it, Bert. Just having a little fun."

Bert didn't say another word but instead picked up the bags he'd dropped and ushered Tarni out of the laundry room and back toward their motel room.

"You should talk, Bert. Looks like you got yourself a nice little bedmate. You might want to watch your back in these parts, though. Some folks might not be happy with your arrangement, if you know what I mean," Carson called out to their retreating backs.

Bert made to move in Carson's direction once more, but Tarni placed her hand on his arm, stopping him. "Not worth it," she whispered.

After rushing through dinner, Tarni frantically looked through the roadmap she'd found in the room among other touristy items. If what she'd read in Carson's mind would come to pass, she had to do something to prevent it—and save Bert. Carson was evil...pure and simple. Tarni picked up on some things he'd done in the past to other young girls...and his hatred for Blacks didn't escape her as well. What he kept hidden during the day would come out when there were no witnesses to his deeds.

Bert scolded her for not listening to his order to remain in the room, and now she knew why, but it was too late to turn back the clock. He'd gone back to the diner to grab more sodas since the ones he'd gotten wound up all over the floor of the laundry room. Then he'd retrieved their clothing. Now he was just about to drop off which was all Tarni needed before she'd make her move.

Once Bert's breathing became regular, she crept over to his side of the room and leaned close to his ear—and began to sing a powerful lullaby.

Cannon fire wouldn't awaken Bert, giving Tarni all the time she needed.

Pulling off her clothing in a hurry, she pulled her Daisy Duke shorts out of her bag and a bikini top. Quickly applying some eyeliner and lip gloss, Tarni fluffed her hair and slipped out of the room, jogging up the path that led toward the truck stop and diner. Just before she reached the end of the path, she spied two figures coming from the diner, turning in her direction.

Tarni jumped off the path and leaned up against the corner of the motel, hidden in shadow.

And waited.

Without even having to tap into Carson's thoughts deeply, Tarni saw the beating he planned on doling out to Bert...and the man tagging along with Carson looked to be his backup muscle. Heart thumping loudly in her chest, Tarni knew she had to play it cool and keep these two men from ever attacking her sleeping friend.

Once they reached the sidewalk that would take them to the motel room, Tarni stepped out from her hiding place.

"Hey there, Carson. Who's your friend? I'm horny—and both of you have something that can take care of that for me, now don't you?"

And then Tarni began to croon softly.

Two nights later, Bert was still confounded and Tarni could tell he was trying to clear the fog from his brain. She had no choice but to muddle with his memory of that night. They were quickly approaching California, another eight hours or so and they'd arrive in Bakersfield, and she knew it was time to part ways.

Bert had no idea what Tarni had done, and she intended to keep it that way. After all, how could she explain away the murders of two men?

CHAPTER 4

Tarni, Present Day

I wouldn't call it murder. Not today. Justifiable homicide if that. What I read in the minds of those two men and my discovery of what they'd done to countless runaways before me, left no choice but to lure them to their deaths with my voice. Often in my world, those that would harm humans were eradicated, whether they be paranormal or not didn't matter, so I decided to become judge, jury, and executioner. We had entire divisions dedicated to doing just that, although I was hardly one of those sanctioned to perform such tasks.

I wasn't traumatized in the slightest. Should I have been?

Perhaps.

I try not to think about that night. But it creeps in when I least expect it, and once my mind goes there, I let it play out in every gory detail.

I enticed Carson and his friend, allowing them to take me in a car to some lake just north of Amarillo—Lake Meredith—and convinced them skinny-dipping would be the highlight of their night. It was easy. I crooned a soft lullaby and watched in satisfaction as both men's eyes glazed over and they came to me like little lambs heading for slaughter.

The worst part of the night for me was having to sit in between the dip on the bench seat of Carson's beat-up old station wagon while continuing my deathly tune. My impatience was growing with every mile away from Amarillo and I couldn't wait to get the task over with. Once we reached the lake, I led Carson and his friend into the water, then I dragged them to the bottom, one by one and held them there until they were no more.

My only regret was having to place my lips against theirs in a dark embrace.

That wasn't the only dark thing to be found at the bottom of the lake. I discovered the wreckage of a small aircraft wedged into the murky bottom. Finding the crash tragic, yet convenient, I tied Carson and the other man to the rubble of what was once the tail of the small, two-person plane and never looked back.

My first time intentionally using my voice to lure—and the irony that I employed the very thing my family was desperate to eradicate didn't escape me—and it was easier than baking a cake! Did I feel like I did evil that night? Was I upset? Not even remotely.

I enjoyed every minute of it.

I refuse to dwell on obliterating those who bring on the wrath of righteous justice.

I was vengeance that night.

The only thing that mattered to me was that Bert was safe and other young girls would never have to endure the atrocities those brutal beasts committed to countless others. I saw what they did. And I took care they could never terrorize anyone ever again.

I'd recently read an article online about the wreckage being found after years of drought and the lake waters receding. Two canoeists discovered the small plane, but no mention was made of any bodies—certainly not of two extra ones tied to the outside in the debris trail.

I chuckled when I read that I'd inadvertently chosen the perfect spot to get rid of two bodies.

Does that make me a monster, then? Not in my world.

I don't play by human rules.

A judge and jury couldn't convince me otherwise...not when my thoughts return to the vile things I saw in Carson's mind and what he had planned for Bert Garfield.

It hurts to think of Bert now and how I left him. I didn't have much choice because there *was* no aged aunt waiting for me to arrive safe and sound, nor did I have any plans on what I'd do or where I'd go once I reached Los Angeles; therefore, I did the only thing I could—I whispered a suggestion in Bert's mind while he slept that I was a figment of his imagination. Something to be forgotten like remnants of a happy dream, pleasant, amusing, but flotsam that would eventually drift from his mind and occasionally return. Just a dream.

Then I took off like a thief in the night, the only memento of my time with Bert the small, plush grinning Garfield cat I didn't have the heart to part with. Unfortunately, I chose Las Vegas as my breakaway point, and not Los Angeles. So I found myself wandering the streets at two in the morning watching the freak show play out around me.

I choked down a sob as I watched the last of the semi's taillights heading off into the distance when Bert pulled out of the motel parking lot and drove up the ramp that would take him back on I-15 heading west. I sent all my best thoughts and prayers with him that he'd have a grand life and get back home to his grandkids safely. The ache in my chest proved to me that something in my soul was humanlike.

I felt bereft as I turned in the opposite direction from the highway, heading for the strip and meandered down Las Vegas Boulevard.

Las Vegas in 1986 looked nothing like the over-the-top extravaganza of today. Oh, there were still the neon signs in all their glory and people wandering around 24-7, but it was seedier in some ways, yet innocent compared to the corporate-sponsored mega casinos that dominate in the present.

I strolled up and down the strip all night taking in the sights. Suzanne Somers of *Three's Company* fame headlining with the Smothers Brothers at the Desert Inn. Circus, Circus looked like a place pedophiles would hang out offering candy to young girls. Neil Sedaka, Marilyn McCoo, and The Pointer Sisters had performances that week. The Sands, Flamingo, Dunes, Caesars, and Frontier were luring gamblers with their slick promises of easy fortunes to be made while dining on cheap or free eats—the Aladdin even had a sign declaring, "No Way to Lose Here!" And Siegfried and Roy were playing with tigers still. I remember stopping in my tracks and gawking like the naïve young woman I was when faced with a billboard that offered a Boylesque show. I must have stood there blinking a good ten minutes before moving on.

Knowing I needed lodging and a means of transportation, I began to take stock and quickly realized the west was far different from the eastern US. For one thing, the supermarkets and banks were different and even some gas stations. I didn't see a 7-Eleven anywhere although I knew they existed in Las Vegas because Bert had mentioned one. I dared not tap into my stash of money...so I wondered what I should do first. Bert had given me two hundred dollar bills and made me tuck them into my backpack for, as he put it, "a rainy day," so at least I had that burning a hole in my pocket that night. I needed to figure out how to get a fake ID, a vehicle, and a place to stay.

But right now, I needed someplace safe to crash.

If someone jumped me nabbing my backpack, I was done for.

Back then I didn't worry too much about humans and what they might try to do to me. It was the paranormal element that kept me on my toes. I didn't know how to differentiate the Breed from humans, and that was troublesome. Witches were virtually indistinguishable, and I'd never run across any other Breed, so I felt vulnerable. Growing up with my witch cousins didn't offer any opportunities to meet vampires, werewolves, elementals, and other beings that roamed the planet, blending in and keeping a low enough profile that our world remained concealed from the mortals.

That I was so clueless on siren history and lore was on my mother. She kept us away so long I knew everything about being a dark witch, but very little about sirens. Just the basic stuff. I came to regret this as I wandered on my own back then, knowing my stumbling attempts although successful thus far, could easily trip me up—especially if I came upon others of my kind.

I wondered how every other paranormal did it. Detected each other. It's not like we glowed, flashed, or had a special handshake—or did we?

My concern was whether or not that made me a beacon of sorts, a target and susceptible to the more dangerous paranormal beings who would think nothing of attacking or using an unsuspecting young siren for some nefarious purpose.

I didn't know it then, but I had one hell of a guardian angel watching out for me, and the second man to come along and give me aid. And he was lurking just around the corner from where I stood transfixed on that all male revue.

Las Vegas, 1986

"Pretty girl like you should be a dancer."

Startled, Tarni jumped a bit as she turned to face the man speaking to her.

"Pardon?"

"Oh, and polite, too. You should go see my boss about a job."

The man looked to be about mid-thirties, with brown hair and a pockmarked face like acne had played a starring role in his youth. His eyes were haunted and predatory, and Tarni took an involuntary step backward while instantly calling up her magic. He sounded like a gangster from the old forties and fifties black-and-white movie reruns on television, and his accent definitely sounded like someone who'd grown up a stone's throw from New York City.

"Name's Benny. But everyone calls me Dimples. Seeing as how I get three to show up every time I smile. You don't have to worry about me...I'm as harmless as a puppy."

Tarni watched as the telltale indents appeared on the man's face when he grinned at her, yet noted his eyes remained vacant and cold. She felt her fingers tingling with unshed magic and swallowed, moving another inch away from Benny while waiting for him to make a sudden move. It never came.

He'd just reached into his pocket and pulled out a business card when another voice sounded behind him.

"A puppy from hell. Leave her alone Dimples, or I'll tell Gina you were making with another chick while she was working her tail off."

Benny spun around on his heels and growled at the newcomer, a larger-than-life grizzled man with black hair and a beard sporting a hat with skulls on it and a biker jacket. Tarni remained transfixed on the newcomer, mouth agape, as he pushed at Benny to move out of the way. The business card floated harmlessly down onto the pavement and Benny made a move to confront the mystery man, his hands balling into fists and a snarl sounding as he lunged forward. Tarni, distracted by the card's progress, watched where it landed, then quickly turned back to the altercation just as Benny was spun around by his jacket and knocked off the curb into the street.

"Screw off, Jim. I was just offering the kid a job."

"I didn't know you'd moved up from lackey to talent recruiter, Dimples. Or is your boss lowering what little standards he has using losers to find runaways and naïve hopefuls looking for stardom—or a quick fix?"

Benny made to move against the bigger man then thought better of it and spit on the ground instead. Giving Tarni one last look, he mumbled something undecipherable then lumbered down the street, heading toward the action of the strip without another backward glance. Tarni let out the breath she'd been holding then peered up at her benefactor.

"Names Jim. Buffalo Jim Barrier to be exact. And if I'm not mistaken, you are a newcomer to our little cesspool of a city. You running away from something, kid?"

"Something like that. Are you an entertainer or...?"

Throwing his head back and laughing like she'd said something terribly funny, Jim wiped his eyes and grinned. Tarni noted the laughter made it into *his* eyes. "Nah. I used to promote wrestling matches in Chicago—still do on occasion. No. I own a repair shop next door to that goon's boss, and I had a feeling he was asking you to go dance in their club. Stay away from that group, kid. That's a dangerous crowd."

"You mean, like mafia types?" asked Tarni.

"That's the alleged word around town. This is Vegas after all," said Jim. "Hey...do you need a ride somewhere? Do you have a place to be? I can offer you a ride...my car's right over there." Pointing to a big, silver monstrosity, Tarni gulped then gave Jim the once-over.

"Isn't that a Rolls Royce?"

"It is indeed. I have a thing for them," replied Jim.

"Well, I need to find a place to stay for a bit, and I'm looking for a cheap car...among other things. A job, maybe." Why Tarni felt like she could trust this bear of a man, she wasn't certain, but she decided on the spot to take the chance he was a good guy. Her instincts and siren ability already found him lacking in many aspects, but in other ways, Buffalo Jim had a Good Samaritan vibe she just could not ignore—not until her circumstances changed and she didn't need to rely on anyone.

"I think I can help with some of that. What's your name, kid?"

"Tarni. Tarni Vanderzee."

"Well, Tarni Vanderzee. Welcome to Las Vegas. I hope you got a recent tetanus shot. This place can shred you up and spit you onto the street one day and make you a millionaire the next."

Tarni grinned. She couldn't help it, so contagious was Jim's enthusiasm and happy-go-lucky outlook. "That's why I'm here, Jim. I need to make a few million in a hurry."

CHAPTER 5

"What did I tell you about that place? A job! Are you insane, kid? How can you think of stripping in that place?" Buffalo Jim was fuming, and Tarni rolled her eyes at his histrionics.

"Bartender, Jim. I'm working there as a bartender!"

"Who ever heard of a female bartender at a strip club? Those goons are going to eat you alive!"

Sighing, Tarni tucked her legs under her bottom while watching Jim pace back and forth in his office. "The club has another female bartender besides me, Jim. Calm down!"

"Calm down! You are an underage girl working as a bartender in a strip club! And you're asking me to calm down?"

"Shh! Be quiet before someone hears you! You are the one who got me my fake ID and new identity, Jim. A place to live. A car. It's not that I'm not grateful...but I'm making more money than the girls taking their clothes off—and I told you, I need to make a few million." Tarni wished Jim would chill. Las Vegas was not like any place else in this world, and he should know better than to question her business acumen...his rise to fortune was highly suspect after all.

Buffalo Jim Barrier had come through for Tarni in a big way, and she owed him. He was shocked when he discovered a young woman, almost twenty, was hidden under the façade of pre-teen, but he still thought her a child to be protected. If he only knew how strong her witch magic was, not to mention the siren stuff, he might sing a different tune. But Jim pulled out all the stops and she was indebted to him. Not only did he give her a 1968 Mustang convertible, baby blue with a white interior and top, he got her an apartment to share with an old girlfriend of his, and a new identity. Well, her new identity, the name she chose for herself all legalized and legit. How he had done this was beyond her imaginings—and she wisely chose not to ask too many questions. Tarni knew this wasn't a legal transaction despite Jim assuring her she'd have zero trouble going through life with those documents.

She was happy enough working at the strip club. She lied her way through the interview and landed an assistant bartending gig that paid her seven hundred and fifty dollars a week but made triple that in tips. The men seemed transfixed by her looks, so different from the Playboy variety blondes with big hair that dominated the club. With her sleek, long black hair and translucent skin, the men begged her to get up on the stage and give them a show. Tarni wore skimpy outfits that seemed to do more for the guys than the fully naked women gyrating above their seats...and she made out like a bandit as a result. That, and she poured a stellar cocktail.

She had her father to thank for that. It was one way she could keep him from starting in on her mother...keeping him drunk and relatively harmless since he passed out rather quickly once he went on a tear.

She had a little red bartender's guidebook that she'd pilfered from her family compound and knew how to make just about every popular cocktail like a pro...and now she was one.

At least that is what it stated on her fake documents. It also aged her to twenty-two so she could legally pour.

"Are you going to finally allow me pay off that car or do I need to give you the keys back?" Tarni asked Jim, who'd been steadfastly refusing her attempts at payment, insisting he meant to give her the Mustang as a gift.

"Aww, stop hounding me, kid. It's yours!"

Tarni rolled her eyes at Jim's continued use of the "kid" moniker.

"It's not mine until I pay you for it. You know darn well you planned on selling it for six thousand dollars. It said so on the For Sale sign you had in the front window. I feel awful about depriving you of that money, Jim. I can afford it, you know."

Jim started chuckling and shaking his head. "Keep your money, kid. I'm not going to take it. Put it in your Wells Fargo account and start a college fund or something—save it for a rainy day. You never know when..."

Jim's voice trailed off as the figure of a man filled the door to his office and the temperature in the room seemed to drop. Amazing for a place like Las Vegas. Tarni glanced at the newcomer and balked. This man was surely a vampire! Even if she didn't know how to tell Breed apart from humans, everything in her very being was screaming for her to pull out a strand of garlic or find some holy water.

"Are you going to change your mind about working on my car, Barrier?"

The man's voice was gravelly and reminded Tarni of sawdust and sandpaper. It grated on her nerves, and she shuddered involuntarily.

"I've told you time and again I will not work on any of your vehicles. You might as well give up, Romano."

"A pity." Turning to face Tarni, the tall horror of a man

gave her the once-over then smiled thinly. "A bit young for you, no? Hello, little baby doll. Aren't you pretty?"

Jim's face reddened and he made to move against the man who held his hand up, stalling any further action. "Get real, Barrier. You can't do anything to me. Don't make me angry. You won't live long enough to find out why they call me "The Impaler."

Spinning on his heel, the man Jim called Romano took his leave and Tarni jumped up out of her seat and wrapped her arms around her friend.

"Who was that and what did he want from you, Jim?"

"Another mob type trying to get me to work on his fleet...but I'd be nuts to get involved in any way with that guy. He's up to no good and is trying to move up the rungs in the organized crime world. His daddy is a big boss...runs a bunch a schemes in the music world. Rock stars and the mob. What a racket."

Tarni frowned and considered Jim's words.

"The mob runs the music industry? You mean in Hollywood and New York and such?" she asked. And vampires were in the mob?

Jim laughed and rubbed the back of his neck as he regarded Tarni then sighed. "You have no idea, kid. You just have no idea."

Later that night, as Tarni worked the bar at the strip club, a group of brightly-clad men walked in and took the booth closest to the bar area. They seemed out of place, not because of anything outwardly evident, but the fact that they ignored the women on stage and were giggling like schoolgirls tipped Tarni off that they might have caught the Boylesque show and were slumming it at the gentlemen's club for laughs. This was backed up when their ringleader, an over-the-top, made-up guy in an outfit Elton John would drool over, came sauntering up to the bar demanding daiquiris for his group.

"Daiquiris, huh? You men are flirting with the hard stuff there."

"Oh, sugar. You have no idea! We are living dangerously especially with all these mammaries jiggling overhead. A boy could lose an eye in a place like this! Name's Ernie." Ernie held out his hand, and Tarni shook it then got busy putting together their drink order.

"Do you enjoy working in a place like this?" asked Ernie. "My goodness! A girl bartender! Who would have thought?"

"It has its moments. I'm new. I started two weeks ago," replied Tarni. She didn't think it very novel to be a female bartender and shook her head, grinning.

"Where are you from? I can't place that accent."

"Who says I'm not from Las Vegas?"

"Hon, no one's from Vegas. Everyone either came for a visit and got the gambling bug or ran out of money and got stuck here. That or they were heading to California and the lure of quick money was too much for them to pass up," Ernie chortled.

"Is that why you're here? To make money?" asked Tarni.

"Hell, no! My dad is loaded. He's a pharmacist in Queens, NY, and I'm his greatest disappointment. But he gave me my trust fund anyway...so I decided to move to California and become famous."

"Are you famous?"

"Not yet. But I know everyone in the business. I have a sparkling personality and an endless supply of goodies to keep the celebrity set on speed dial, if you know what I mean."

Tarni did not know what Ernie meant but found out she

liked his outgoing personality. So much so, that when her shift was over, instead of heading back to her cramped apartment for stale, cold pizza, and a round of late-night TV, she remained at the club and joined Ernie and his friends for an evening of hilarious anecdotes and gossip.

"Oh, that party was a riot!" One of Ernie's friends, a gaunt, blonde man who looked like he had walked off a runway in Paris, put out his cigarette and leaned toward Tarni. "We crashed Liz's party in Scottsdale, and she was convinced she'd personally invited us...that was a fun night!"

Tarni wrinkled her brow and addressed the young man, TJ, since that's how he was introduced to her, and asked, "Liz? As in Elizabeth Taylor?"

"Why yes! Of course! Who else would it be? It was an auction for the AIDS Foundation, and we even got a photograph with her and George Hamilton! And let me tell you something, that man really *is* tan. I'd hate to see what his skin will look like twenty years from now! His skin will be like an old leather saddle that hasn't been oiled in decades!"

TJ shuddered and fanned himself. Tarni just sat back with a bemused smile on her face. These boys were a hoot.

Another guy, he'd introduced himself as Parker Lovegood, leaned across the table, and in sotto voce informed Tarni he specialized in crashing after-parties and Hollywood events, so much so that all the celebrities were convinced he was a friend of theirs.

"That's how I met Ernie, here. And I'm not looking back! Full speed ahead and take me to where the action is! Why...just last week we partied with Adam Ant. Ernie here has hung with the boys from INXS and Duran Duran. And we were all invited to party with Siobhan Fahey after they dropped their new album. Gosh I love that song...Venus! It's like my anthem!"

"You mean the singer from Bananarama? Wow. I can't

believe all the places you've been and people you've met. I'm jealous!" she exclaimed.

"Well, if you were a party girl, we could get you into any event," said Ernie. Then they all laughed like it was a hilarious joke.

"I am a party girl."

The entire table got quiet as everyone ogled Tarni then glanced at each other. She wasn't quite sure what she'd just admitted to being, but from their reaction, it must hold some weight with this crowd.

"Seriously? You'd party?" Ernie asked.

"Of course! It's one of the reasons they hired me here. If you need a party girl...just come calling, and I'll be there."

The talk returned to people the boys knew and places they'd been, however Ernie remained distracted and taken by this new revelation Tarni handed him. Leaning close, he whispered, "Hon, are you legit? Like...would you like to meet some people and party with us? I have someone in mind for you and... well, let's just say, it could take you places. Big places if you hit it off."

"Of course, I'm serious. Bring it on."

Tarni didn't know if it was the seven daiquiris she downed or the funky cigarette she'd shared which she suspected was laced with some kind of drug, but curiosity and the promise of going places gave her a devil-may-care attitude she hoped she wouldn't live to regret. However, she seemed unable to care about that for the moment and was eager to hear what Ernie was saying.

"OK. Meet me at The Peppermill tomorrow night around midnight. You know where that is, hon?"

"That big diner and lounge near the Riviera and the Dunes casinos?"

"That's the one. I'm meeting some music people and Hollywood types and I'd love for you to mingle. See where it goes, you know?"

Tarni's eyes lit up with excitement and she hit Ernie with a big grin. "I just happen to have tomorrow night off. What should I wear?"

"Doll...you slip on the number you're wearing, and you will be the belle of the ball"

Considering she was practically naked and doubted the proprietors of the restaurant would appreciate her risqué outfit in their establishment—even if it was Vegas, Tarni decided she'd better go shopping for a new outfit after she got some sleep.

Sleep? What was that? This was Vegas, baby!

Little did Tarni know her life was about to take another turn. And this one would take her face-to-face with her destiny.

CHAPTER 6

"How do I look, Marigold?"

Tarni was biting her lower lip and looking at herself in the floor-length mirror that Marigold Tanner had tacked up in between their bathroom and the closet they shared.

"Like you're hunting men and intend to land one. A rich one."

"I can't believe I found these shoes at the thrift store! They're satin and everything!"

"And match the blue of your dress perfectly. You look like a starlet." Marigold, Jim's former fling, a sometime makeup artist, and Tarni's roommate, appraised her outfit and liked what she saw. "All eyes are going to be on you, Tarni. You're a goddess."

Tarni didn't know about that, but she did love the aqua-blue silk dress that was snug in all the right places then flared out a bit at the bottom—perfect for twirling. She slipped on a pair of skintight spandex shorts leaving off her stockings just in case she had the sudden urge to do just that...or handstands. Bare legs were unheard of, but Tarni hated the way stockings felt on her skin.

Adding two perfectly round pearl earring to her lobes, her excitement was palpable and Tarni wasn't sure if it was nerves about meeting Hollywood types or the fact she never did find out what being designated a "party girl" meant. She considered asking Marigold, but when she opened her mouth, she got hit with a barrage of questions regarding her hair and makeup. She had a niggling suspicion she might have cast herself as some kind of hooker, and that wasn't Tarni's intent. Sighing, she decided to worry about it later...I mean, how much trouble could she get in hanging out with a bunch of gay men in Las Vegas?

"I don't need makeup, Marigold."

"Oh, no way! You have to put some on. That squeaky-clean teen look you have going on won't cut it tonight. Here. Take a seat and let me have at."

Tarni nervously did as she was instructed, concerned that Marigold might turn her into something that resembled the lead singer for Twisted Sister, but crossed her fingers and hoped for the best. "Just leave my hair though. I am not into the big hair, Aqua Net and spritzing until it crackles. I will just pin it up with a few tendrils hanging down. That should do."

"With your hair and this face? You could wear it sticking up like a porcupine and the men would throw themselves at your feet. I almost want to come along and chaperone you. Ernie is well known by me...and he is harmless for the most part, but he does have some wild clients."

"Clients?"

"Tarni! Don't you know he's Vegas's very own Doctor Robert or Doctor Max?"

When Tarni looked at Marigold blankly, the woman rolled her eyes and dragged a chair next to the one Tarni was sitting in, grabbing her hands. "Drugs, Tarni. Like the Beatles song reference? Celebrity docs who supply them with goodies.

Doctor Feelgood? Ernie deals in drugs. All kinds. He gets them for everyone from here to Los Angeles and back. He has access...his pop is a druggist after all!"

"Oh! Well...um. Cool."

"Cool? Sweetie, Ernie can get you into any big director or producer's inner circle. Stick with him, and a girl like you, with that face? You can become a star!"

Stardom was secondary to amassing the amount of wealth Tarni needed to take on the powers that be in the world she'd left back in Florida. But it certainly could be the means to getting her closer to that goal. She knew entering a place devoid of anything resembling decency would be part and parcel of her rise...but power came with a price. And she believed she had what it took to ride out that shitstorm and come out on the other side.

"OK, Marigold. Have at it. Turn me into star material."

Marigold worked for quite some time, and Tarni tried not to squirm under her ministrations. Her eyes were starting to water and her nose itched, but she didn't want to do anything that would cause her roommate to mess up her face. Suddenly, Marigold straightened up with a satisfied look and turned Tarni to face the mirror once more.

To say Tarni was shocked would have been an understatement. Who was this creature staring back at her?

"Whoa."

"Whoa, indeed. Totally awesome." Marigold was grinning from ear to ear at her handiwork, and Tarni had to agree she looked beyond beautiful. Her black hair had been piled up in a messy bun with tendrils artfully hanging down and her makeup gave her a feline grace and beauty that she suspected, but never had the time to verify, she possessed. People often commented on her looks, sans makeup. This, however, was something altogether different, and Tarni had to grudgingly admit she was a knockout.

"No wonder you do this for a living!" Tarni enthused.

"There's no one better in the industry, kid."

It was time to head out.

Tarni left her beloved Mustang at the apartment, instead choosing to call a cab in case she became slightly tipsy tonight. Drugs and alcohol didn't seem to affect her the way it did humans, it certainly gave her a buzz, but it didn't act the same way that it would in, say, Marigold. And Tarni would know...she'd spent one too many nights lately holding her roommate's hair back while she upchucked into the toilet after a wild night.

One thing that did affect Tarni was the lack of a vast body of water to dive in and it was doing some weird things to her system... so she wasn't all that certain her faculties wouldn't be compromised because of it. Not being in touch with her siren side resulted in an error in judgment on just how much her body craved swimming. That little dip in Lake Meredith in Texas was the last time she had been in water. She hadn't seen a pond, lake, or large body of water since arriving in Vegas. Living in Florida or Georgia most of her life had spoiled her.

Of course, what she really craved was salt water and lots of it. The idea that the Pacific Ocean was a mere five-hour drive away was making her squirrelly.

The cab ride was uneventful and as it pulled up to The Peppermill with its crazy neon pink, blue, and purple lit up interior beckoning, Tarni felt her excitement hitch.

Climbing from the cab and tipping the driver, Tarni took stock and liked what she saw. Las Vegas was alive with possibilities, and she was fully prepared to dive right in.

Tonight will be totally awesome.

Tarni, Present Day

I was so young. Naïve. Yet had inner strength and spirit. An all-night party and meeting celebrities or production folks was just another fun bit of happenstance, and I didn't consider the company. It never dawned on me to worry about the type of people I might be associating with or if I could trust being around them. Date rape drugs were everywhere but knowing my strengths and weaknesses...and believing I was invincible went hand in hand with being nineteen and running wild in Las Vegas.

Still...how did I not know what was coming? Some warning or signal that my life was about to change forever, with no hope to return to the way it was before that auspicious day. The absolute end of everything I'd ever known about the world, who I was and what I wanted in life... the point I'd look back on and acknowledge if I had chosen not to accept Ernie's invitation, my life's path would have been entirely different. Was my guardian angel on a break? Leaving The Fates: Clotho, Lachesis, and Atropos eagerly watching from the Great Beyond at the meeting that was about to take place—Atropos, scissors paused, hovering over my lifeline should my time be up after stepping in the path of destiny.

I often wondered if he felt the same as me. I never asked him. Not once. But surely he had to have felt something momentous was about to occur in his world. How could he not?

I strolled into the diner, channeling my inner Audrey Hepburn, the *Breakfast at Tiffany's* look on full display as I slithered my way to where I spied Ernie holding court. He had an even more outlandish outfit on, this one silver rhinestone perfection and a decade out of date, all pink, white, and fabulous, but somehow he pulled it off.

"Hello, Ernie. The 1970s called. They want their disco outfit back."

"Tarni! You old dog. Look at you. You fantastic creature! I didn't know you cleaned up this well!"

I laughed off the compliment and made to take the seat near Ernie. And then it happened.

Before I could sit, I glanced up, and my eyes locked with a man sitting in a rounded, plush velvet corner booth two tables from ours, with a ragtag group of people surrounding him.

Now, I wouldn't be able to swear on any Bible that the music immediately began to play in my head or just happened to come on the speakers in the diner and I was imagining things, but "Every Breath You Take" by The Police would forever trigger that moment in time with its iconic opening guitar riff. I will always associate that song with our first meeting and the memories it evokes still bring back every background sound, smell, and taste like nothing else.

I don't remember breathing. As a matter of fact, I think I was incapable of such mundane things like taking in air and letting it back out again. My tongue felt swollen and glued to the roof of my mouth and I was certain if I tried, I wouldn't be able to swallow.

I can't recall how long our eyes remained glued to each other's, but I know my mouth parted and I took in a rush of air and had to force myself to close it lest it remain open and I look the fool. My cheeks felt warm, and my ears were burning, so I knew I must have blushed red. A slight pain in my chest would manifest outward, pulling at my nipples in ways I'd never experienced, causing my eyes to widen as the sensation made its downward journey to my nether regions.

What the holy heck was that?

I remember thinking to myself I must be possessed or perhaps a fever of some kind had set in, and I quickly lowered my eyes and scrambled to take a seat, turning my back so I faced away from the mysterious stranger... that somehow seemed familiar. This alone sent my nerves into the upper stratosphere. And I wanted more. Wanted to know who he was.

What man has hair like that? I remembered thinking. *And those eyes! So dark and brooding with a wicked gleam.*

I'd kissed a few boys and had some mild groping sessions that never led to much more than me laughing and pushing them away while they begged me to "go to second base." I never did. Nor did my body react in any way like it did in that instant.

They say there is no such thing as love at first sight, but what about lust? If my body were any indication, I just rounded third and was preparing to slide into home shouting "wheeeeee!" the entire way in.

I understood I needed to regain some semblance of calm and quickly opened my purse pulling out my Virginia Slims Luxury 120s...my new habit, and one I was grateful for because it gave me something to do with my trembling hands. Ernie lit my cigarette then leaned back with a smirk at the same time he waved over a waitress to take my drink order.

"I'll have an Alabama Slammer, please," I told the girl who came to our table. She didn't even ID me or question whether or not I should be drinking.

The table had various appetizers strewn about and I grabbed an asparagus roll, stuffing it into my mouth in the hopes of settling my stomach which was doing somersaults. "What's this?" I asked Parker, who'd materialized sometime between my drink order and my appetizer consumption.

"Vol au vents. It's a fancy French term for puff pastry with a creamy chicken concoction ladled in it. Eat up...they're fabulous here."

Just then, my drink arrived, and I grabbed it like it was my lifeline, quickly drinking half before settling the glass down in front of me.

"Darling! What's wrong with you? You're buzzing like vibrator set on low!" Parker exclaimed.

"Who's that man sitting in the center of the corner booth behind me, Ernie? The one with the dark curly hair and black eyes?" Oh, you bet I had I'd already taken stock and could probably tell you his measurements, even in that one brief glance. OK, so maybe it was more than a glance.

"You don't recognize him? That's Logan MacDuff...from Somber Sea. That new band from Monterey, California. You know...everyone calls him Duffy though."

"Duffy?" I knew the name of the band and that I liked their music enough I had mixed some of their songs on my cassette tapes but didn't know the names of the members.

"Yeah. Like The Edge. You know, a nickname!"

"The edge of what?"

"Not the edge of anything! THE Edge. From U2. Bono is another nickname! Seriously, woman. Get with it. You are going to mingle with rock stars and actors. You need to know who's who!"

"Oh! Yes...I know them. War. The Unforgettable Fire. Got it. Somber Sea is good too. He's with them?"

"With them? Duffy is the lead singer, honey!"

I remember blanching and swallowing another mouthful of my cocktail which only caused my stomach to lurch. The lead singer of a rock band? Wow. I vaguely recalled their videos playing on MTV and shuddered a bit. The band was good. Like, they would hit the big time real soon if their fast climbing of the charts was any indication.

They weren't quite there yet...but I knew Somber Sea was going places.

"Hey, Ernie, how are you doing, man? And who do we have here? Keeping such a glorious angel all to yourself is an injustice."

Said the Devil by my side.

Why didn't I suspect this would happen?

Seriously, I wanted to have a long talk with my guardian angel or petition for a new one. Why did no premonitions strike when I needed them the most? That I didn't hear him come up behind us or feel a crackling in the very air had me off-balance. I should have sensed his presence, damn it! I quickly had to hide my surprise, barely managing not to jump out of my skin when that incredible voice reached my ears.

I'd like to note, "Every Breath You Take" was continuing to idle on play in my mind.

"Duffy! How are you, man? This is Tarni. Tarni Vanderzee. Tarni...say hello to Duffy."

"Tarni? That sounds like a name you'd give a kitten!"

I glanced up at his words, our eyes crashing together like opposing waves, only this time I refused to lower them like a naïve ingenue.

They say when you die, you are enveloped in darkness and seek the light.

Logan MacDuff was that light.

I felt drawn to him in ways I could not explain, then...and now. Every fiber of my being wanted him to open his hands and allow me to crawl into them, where he'd hold me safe and close to his heart while he whispered sweet nothings in my ear, touching my soul.

I was toast.

A goner.

Completely shattered and incapable of rational thought.

I felt myself shifting and leaning toward him and had to

forcibly stop myself before I wound up wrapped around his body, sniffing his neck.

He was seriously that hot.

"Hello, Logan. How nice to meet you."

Hello...what? How I managed such a calm, cool delivery was beyond me, and it tempered the shrieking going on inside my head. What was wrong with me?

His playful eyes sparkled as he offered up a boyish smile. "No one calls me Logan but my mother."

"No? Well, now there's two of us. I refuse to call a grown man Duffy." I blew my cigarette smoke in his direction and tried to go with the bored look.

Logan raised his brows then barked out a short laugh.

"Feisty. I like that. I wonder if your claws are as sharp, little kitten."

I swallowed again and knew I was treading through dangerous terrain—especially since I knew if he called me kitten one more time I might start purring.

"How about you kids go hang out. Tarni...you should party with Duffy. His group is a lively bunch, and they will show you a good time."

I flicked my eyes over to Logan's "group" frowning then turned back to catch him looking at me in wonder.

What was that all about?

Distracted once more, I watched as Ernie slipped a small case toward Logan who pulled his eyes away from mine to acknowledge the trade—the bag was almost like the ones you'd insert money and checks into then take to a bank. Only I suspected I'd not find any money if I looked inside. Logan reached out and grabbed it then tucked it into his jacket nonchalantly.

"I have a better idea. How about we go for a ride?" Logan winked at Ernie then regarded me once more...a playful twitch to his mouth informing me he expected I'd do anything he suggested.

"She'll go. Tarni is a good girl. I told you she's my protégé!" cried Ernie with some gusto, clapping his hands.

Parker rolled his eyes and jutted his chin out toward Logan. "You usually like them blonde and bubbly. You sure you can handle a little minx?"

Wait. Was this a set up? Did Ernie and Parker promise me along with whatever contraband was in that zippered pouch? I remembered being angry, then rueful in the span of a few seconds. After all, hadn't I insisted I was a party girl? I expected better of Parker...but not Ernie. It was obvious he did this sort of thing all the time. Oh, but who was I kidding?

Grabbing my cigarettes, I stood abruptly and pushed past Logan, marching up the aisle. I knew I insisted I partied with the best of them, but I didn't like the idea of being sold like a box of chocolate to some stoned rocker looking for a quick lay—despite the fact that I'd just been lusting after said rocker!

I made it as far as the front door of Peppermill's before I felt his hand on my arm.

"Hey! Wait up. What's your hurry? We don't have to go anywhere or do anything. We can stay right here and talk for a while. Although, just between you and me, I'd love to be rid of this crowd." Logan's eyes seemed to implore me to reconsider. "My bike is just outside. I know a place where we can go for a spin...and a swim."

I remember searching Logan's eyes and seeing nothing but a friendly offer with no malice. But then his devil's horns popped out as he opened his mouth and ruined it.

"Or are you afraid to go skinny-dipping with me? Thinking I might bite?"

I stood there with my head cocked to one side and regarded this enticing man knowing he'd just thrown down some kind of gauntlet. I watched a river of emotions flow in those dark eyes, from anticipation to worry, anxious need and lust.

I noted with shock I was unable to getting a reading on him and didn't know what that meant.

But then I threw caution to the wind.

Reaching my hand up, I lightly slapped the side of Logan's face. "Oh, sweet thing, if there is any water deep enough to go swimming around here, it's *you* who needs worry about me."

And with those words, life as I knew it was altered forever.

CHAPTER 7

Somewhere in the Nevada desert, 1986

Tarni held on to Logan tightly as he raced off into the southern desert, the city lights fading away with every milepost they passed. The further away from Vegas, the last town of note being Henderson, the more incredible the night sky became, until finally there was nothing but the cosmos and blackness, the only luminosity coming from the headlights of the Harley Davidson motorcycle that rumbled under her bottom.

First time on a motorcycle and it just happens to be with a rock star.

Tarni couldn't believe it. She was still amazed she'd playfully teased this man back at the diner and considered she just may have bitten off a bit more than she could chew. She'd almost balked when he mounted the bike and held his hand out for hers, but then a whiff of his cologne reached her nostrils, and she lost all reason.

Seriously. What kind of scent from Hell, girl-catching, wicked concoction did he have bottled up? she thought to herself even as she gripped tighter and leaned into another curve like Logan instructed. Her cheek was pressed into the leather of his jacket and his hair kept whipping her face, but Tarni didn't mind a bit. Her own hair had since lost the good fight and came cascading down and out like a black banner flapping in the wind. She longed to reach up and touch his curls but kept her hands firmly around his waist, content to sniff the back of his neck for the time being—happy that her brief fantasy back at the diner was coming true. She'd popped a couple of wintergreen Lifesavers in her mouth before she'd mounted the motorcycle and it competed with whatever shampoo Logan used. Seriously, the man smelled amazing.

Tarni felt alive and reckless and found herself smiling. Logan had apologized for having his bike and worried she might not want to climb aboard wearing her short dress. Imagine his surprise when she twirled, and he spied her tight shorts. She'd kicked off her heels and Logan tucked them into one saddlebag, and they raced out of the city as if danger were on their heels. She still didn't know where the moxie had come from, her playful slap and words that were obviously suggestive. What had come over her?

Well, Tarni knew that she wanted to experience life, and this certainly constituted an experience!

After a while, she noticed a subtle change in speed and adjusted her seat when Logan slowed to a gentle cruise then turned off the highway.

"Where are we?" Tarni queried Logan as the motorcycle grumbled along at a sedate pace. The desert landscape had given away to a sprinkling of homes and streetlights, but in no way were they back in Vegas, not with the continued show of stars in the sky.

"We're heading into Boulder City. I want to show you the Hemenway Harbor."

"Harbor? As in water?" Tarni asked curiously.

"Lake Mead is just ahead. Hemenway Harbor is where people put their boats in the lake unless they already have them docked at the marina."

Logan made a left turn and Tarni glanced around the small city...a town really, as they meandered along until they reached Lakeshore Road. One more turn had them heading down a short drive that ended at an expansive parking lot and the marina. The moon shone brightly, a Cheshire cat smile in the sky and the harbor lights gave out just enough illumination that they could see the lake. The night air was warm still, as September weather was in the desert, but Tarni shivered.

Cruising to a stop in the rustic parking lot, Logan killed the engine, plunging them into darkness until their eyes could adjust. Then they walked over to the dock that led to where a bevy of boats were anchored, a few lanterns illuminating their progress. Just the sound of water gently lapping at the shore had Tarni bouncing eagerly in anticipation. When Logan reached his hand out, she immediately clasped his and ran ahead pulling him along behind, chuckling at her enthusiasm.

They followed along the docks until they reached an area with few boats, allowing for a great vantage point and a place where they could sit—Tarni dangling her legs over the edge and toward the water below. She briefly considered she might appear to be the mythical medusa—knowing her hair would be a tangled wonder. Logan's was windswept as well, but he looked delicious.

"This is amazing! I had no idea this was even here!" she exclaimed.

"Hoover Dam ring a bell? You're not from Vegas, are you?" said Logan with an indulgent smile.

"No...I... uh, I moved here a few months ago. I guess I missed the dam when we passed by."

"We?"

Tarni began to squirm and used an incoming fisherman returning from a nighttime fishing expedition to avoid having to respond.

"Oh! Look! A boat. I'd love to go out on the water someday."

Logan didn't look where Tarni had pointed, instead keeping his gaze on her face. He didn't push her to explain either, and for that she was grateful. His intense scrutiny was making her uncomfortable, however. Not in a creepy way, but in a "I still can't get a read on this guy, and please, Lord, don't make him be a paranormal that might eat me!" way.

Tarni giggled.

"What?" Logan asked.

"Nothing. I'm just thinking silly thoughts."

Tarni gazed at the water longingly, knowing she'd probably have her feet in it before long. She wanted to ask Logan why he decided to take her for a ride out in the desert.

"So. Rock star, huh?" she asked instead. *Oh, that wasn't cringe-worthy,* she thought to herself with a mental hand-slap to her temple.

"Hardly. But we're making some noise. This last year we opened for anyone and everyone. But we should be headlining on our next tour," Logan stated with some satisfaction warming his voice.

"That's wonderful. I like your music. I have some of it. "She Cries Softly" is my favorite."

Logan reached out and tucked a strand of her wild hair behind one ear. He smiled briefly and turned away then, watching as the boat reached its slip two docks over. "I wrote that one."

"It's very sad. But I like sad songs." Tarni remained transfixed on his five-o'clock shadow and mouth as he spoke, wondering if his lips would be soft and pleasant to kiss.

"I wrote it for my mother. She always loved tales of the sea and shipwrecks and such. There used to be a small bronze statue of a weeping woman near where she grew up in Eureka. It looked out at the ocean as if the tiny woman wept for her lover lost at sea... or some trivial tale according to Mom. I never could get her to tell me the entire story."

"So, you're from California?"

"Mom is. My dad..." Logan paused, rubbing one hand along the back of his neck as if needing to ease some tension. "That's a complicated story. But yes. I'm from California more or less."

Not feeling comfortable asking him to explain further, especially since she had no intention of talking about her past, Tarni changed the subject, taking it back to the safety of the music business.

"Do you like being a musician?"

"It has its perks. You know, sex, drugs, and rock and roll. Who wouldn't love it? I certainly enjoy the sex."

Logan's words didn't ring true and Tarni wondered at the edge she heard in his voice but chose not to push him to explain further. She instead remained quiet and let her mind wander as she took in the moon's glow on the gentle waves. They remained like that for a good while and it was Logan who finally broke the silence.

"You're easy to be around. Some girls chatter incessantly to fill the void in conversation. You seem content to just be."

Tarni ducked her head, wondering if he preferred the chatter even while commending her for her reserve. Then chided herself for caring...she had no intention of changing for some guy.

"You're not a party girl...are you?"

"I like to party, Logan." Tarni thrust her chin in the air, refusing to give up on this ridiculous game Ernie hoisted on her. Her stubborn streak stopping her from letting go of the ruse.

"Ah. Well... who doesn't?"

"Exactly."

"Call me Duffy."

"I will not."

"Why?"

"Why?! It's a ridiculous nickname and I could not imagine myself calling you that if...um, in any situation."

Tarni could feel Logan's eyes on her face, and she blushed, hoping the cloak of darkness was enough to hide the fact that she was probably as red as a lobster right now.

OK...this has to stop! Seriously! What's wrong with me?

"I'd like it if you'd call me Duffy."

"You'll be sorely disappointed then."

Logan lowered his head and chuckled.

"You're a handful."

"Is that what you call someone who has strong opinions?"

"No. That's what I'm calling you."

Rubbing his chin and rolling his lips in as if to stop from laughing out loud, Logan leaned back and gazed up at the sky instead.

"Do you? Like to party, I mean? I would think being a rock star, you're often out doing whatever it is you rock stars do."

Great. I sound like a dweeb. Tarni scolded herself inwardly as she stifled the groan that wanted to escape her lips.

"Oh, sure. I like to. Girls are plentiful, the drugs are pharmaceutical top-shelf, and nothing beats an after-party when our work is done."

Something in Logan's voice had Tarni turn to him, searching his face to see why he suddenly sounded so bitter. He caught her questioning gaze and grimaced slightly.

"It can get tedious—the after-parties, the hangers-on, the

groupies. Drugs everywhere and everyone wanting to be my best friend. We haven't even reached the top yet. I can't imagine how insane it will be once we do." Logan sighed and stretched then turned to face Tarni once more. "It's a lonely, weird existence. Not that I'm going to complain. It's the life I chose for myself, and I can't deny the perks."

"I would think it fascinating and satisfying to have so many people rapt on every word you utter, every note of music bringing them joy or melancholy with you, the figurehead for them to focus on. What a rush."

"It sounds like you want to be a songbird," teased Logan.

"I wouldn't hate it."

"I don't hate it. I just don't like feeling so alone all the time. Being on the road is a lot lonelier than one thinks."

Tarni didn't understand how Logan could be lonesome surrounded by adoring fans, his bandmates, and friends, but she didn't push him on it, instead choosing to remain silent once more. Logan, however, continued gently prying into her background.

"Do you sing?" he asked.

"Often."

"Are you a singer? I mean, professionally or up-and-coming?"

"No. I'm a bartender."

Logan's eyes widened at that, but he refrained from commenting. *What is it with these men and me being a bartender?* Tarni wondered.

"You could be a singer. You have a nice body. Your face is striking. Of course, you need to be able to carry a tune...or not. I mean, there are ways of making a pretty face sound better than she is. *Can* you sing?"

Tarni felt her nose twitch, feeling slightly affronted by Logan's question, and frowned.

This guys an arrogant jerk, isn't he?

"I'm not sure. Can *you?*" she countered instead.

Logan exploded in laughter at Tarni's response and she became briefly transfixed on the sight of his head back, mouth open wide and the way his face transformed into something boyishly charming.

Wow. A laugh like that could sway an unsuspecting populace and have them eating out of this one's hand. There is power here. In his voice, his mirth. Dangerous!

"What were you thinking just now? You backed away from me a bit."

Tarni jolted back to the present and focused on Logan.

"You must be quite a sight up on stage I would think. I don't suspect you'd *need* much of a singing voice."

That set Logan off once more that only ended when he wrapped his arms around Tarni suddenly and gave her a chaste peck on her cheek.

It was unexpected and Tarni gasped then stilled.

"You're a sweet and feisty kitten but come across as quite an innocent. But I suspect you aren't that virtuous—at least, I hope not."

Tarni knew they were about to kiss, especially since Logan's eyes dropped to her lips and he was feasting on them like a wolf who spied a lonely sheep out in the pasture.

"Now, I think before we do anything further, we should set some ground rules."

"Ground rules?"

"Yes. Seeing as how I feel slightly cheated on my night's entertainment, you should probably pay me back by letting me kiss you. Rule number one: I hate being cheated out of something I paid for."

Tarni blinked rapidly then opened and closed her mouth before getting annoyed and grinding her teeth. All that managed to do was heighten Logan's amusement, setting Tarni's nose further out of joint, and she pushed at his arm.

"You can laugh all you want. One, I never told you to ask me on this ride, taking you away from your 'night's entertainment.' Two, I don't appreciate being part of Ernie's dealings with you—he never informed me I was to be part of the transaction, and three, I don't particularly like kissing so you can forget it."

That sobered Logan up in an instant, and he regarded Tarni with a look of astonishment and skepticism.

"You don't like to kiss?"

"No. When I was younger, every time I ever kissed a boy, they smelled like beer and cigarettes or had bad breath."

Logan pulled Tarni close, forcing her to look at his face. His lips twitched, and his eyes took on a dangerous sparkle that had her insides doing flip-flops again.

"I'd like to point out that you smoke."

"I popped a few Lifesavers in my mouth on the ride over here, thank you."

"Did you now?" Logan's intrigue was evident and Tarni realized too late what he assumed she meant by that.

"Yes, I did. And no, I never did like kissing boys."

"That's the problem right there. You've only ever kissed boys. Perhaps you should try kissing a man."

Damn that stupid song! Tarni let out a frustrated sigh as "Every Breath You Take" taunted the recesses of her mind, and Logan's knowing smirk had her aching to smack his face—hard this time. Instead, she surprised herself by reaching her fingertips out and running them along Logan's lips, then slipped them behind his head and into those glorious curls.

The smoldering look that overcame Logan in an instant and the soft moan that came out of his parted lips was almost drowned out by her heartbeat. She was convinced even the lonely fisherman on the dock could overhear so loud was it thumping in her chest!

"I don't much mind smoke anymore, much," whispered Tarni.

Logan slowly drew his eyes up from her lips exploring every facet of her face and locked his black orbs onto her cobalt blue ones.

"I'm going to kiss you now, Tarni. Would you like that?"

"Yes, I think I would."

Whatever Tarni expected to happen next, it certainly wasn't the crushingly urgent embrace as Logan's lips met hers. What began as a forceful meeting of parted lips, slowly morphed into an enticing exploration of tongue and teeth, breath, and sighs. Sensuous and slow sensations flowed into eager need and a promise of wicked naughtiness and abandon. As she gave in to what had to be the best kiss that ever transpired in her short time flirting with the opposite sex, Tarni knew, in an instant, she was lost.

And yet, strangely at home.

The kind of home she'd longed for her entire life but never truly had until this moment.

She never wanted it to end.

Clinging on as Logan consumed her, had Tarni melting into a languid puddle—molten lava, oozing down a mountainside as everything she ever was gave way into this unbridled passion...and she began sucking on his tongue like it would give her sustenance she'd been missing and desperately needed, lest she expire.

Breaking away from Logan's embrace was like ripping a bandage from a raw wound. Sound came rushing back followed by every other sense, leaving Tarni trembling and unsure of what to do or say next. Even Logan appeared dazed, his perplexed expression and the way his throat moved up and down when he swallowed couldn't remove the buzzing sound now ricocheting around her head. So instead of saying anything, Tarni stood quickly and whipping her dress off in one graceful movement dove into the warm waters of Lake Mead.

Swimming for Tarni was second nature, and she quickly distanced herself from the dock and Logan MacDuff.

Or so she thought.

Speed and grace had her several meters away from the last of the moored boats and out into the lake proper. Kicking effortlessly, she turned to see what reaction Logan had to her sudden departure, only to shriek in shock to find him astride her and smiling. Noting his bare chest and glancing toward the dock brought her to the conclusion that not only had he the time to disrobe, but he also kept pace with her which should have been an impossibility.

"You're fast! Are you a swimmer?"

"High school champion."

The moonlight reflected in Logan's eyes had Tarni mesmerized, and she couldn't help but swim into his arms. Wrapping hers around his neck, she brought her face as close to his as she dared and waited, reveling as his unique scent blended with hers once more. She'd never noticed how desirable a man's breath could be and concluded Logan was correct in his assessment that she'd only been with boys up until this point.

This time Tarni kissed Logan, moaning when he cupped her behind, and lifting her slightly so she was above him, holding onto him, with fingers tangled in his hair. She wanted to devour him. Breaking away once more, Tarni smiled, then nipped at Logan's bottom lip playfully.

She didn't think she'd ever be able to go for long without breathing in his scent ever again. Logan smelled of spices and cedar with a hint of orange, and when her mouth was tantalizingly close to his parted lips, she could taste him just by breathing it all in.

"So, what are we doing out here then?" he asked.

"Um, getting wet and cooling off?"

Logan chuckled and playfully kissed the tip of her nose. "Well, I definitely like getting a girl wet, but perhaps we should head back. The guy on the boat cried out when he saw you dive off the dock. Let's get back before he calls for help."

How naughty. Scandalous man.

Tarni wanted more of this. But perhaps Logan was right in his estimation. The last thing she wanted was a spotlight to hit her with a gaggle of gawking men thinking she needed rescuing.

Tarni and Logan made their way back to shore and climbed up the bank of the lake then hurried down the dock to retrieve their clothing. Self-consciously crossing her arms over her bra, which wasn't doing much to conceal her breasts, Tarni wryly surmised her impromptu swim wasn't the smartest thing she could have done to temper the heat of the moment.

She was shocked when instead of commenting on or ogling her assets, Logan draped his leather jacket around her shoulders and picked up her dress. Then they quickly returned to the motorcycle and pushed it to the other side of the parking area, taking a seat at one of the picnic tables, getting sandy mud on their feet for their efforts. Logan, she noted, seemed perfectly comfortable sitting there in his briefs.

"Will you be here long? In Vegas?" asked Tarni, hating how needy her voice sounded.

"I head back to California tomorrow. The band has one last gig for the year in San Francisco, and we have rehearsals."

"Oh."

"I don't suppose you plan on being in Los Angeles in the near future?" he asked.

"No. I have work, and I just landed this job, so I have zero time off."

"Well then, we should make the most of tonight, no?"

What could have turned into something Tarni wasn't prepared to deal with just yet became a wonderful night gazing up at the night sky and talking about anything and everything. The Cheshire moon kept watch as they embraced, she leaning onto his broad chest as he held her close while the stars twinkled above. Tarni spoke of nonsensical things that made him laugh. He told her more about his family and the outlandish life he and his bandmates lived. She even opened up a bit about her past, obviously concealing her paranormal world but wishing in some strange way she could tell him her plight. It really didn't matter what they discussed, the companionship and laughter felt right, and she didn't want it to end even as the telltale signs of sunrise crested on the horizon to the east.

Slipping Logan's jacket off and scrambling into her dress left Tarni feeling bereft, uncertain, and exposed. It wasn't until Logan put his jacket back around her shoulders that she knew she was utterly lost to this man and didn't know how she would continue on with her life which now seemed somehow mundane. How could a night spent talking with a few stolen kisses here and there cause her to change so intensely?

That Logan opted to be a gentleman and not jump her or even suggest they find a nearby motel left Tarni torn. Would she have said yes, given the opportunity to be with this man? She was a virgin still and those ill-fated attempts by boys who would never come close to comparing to Logan's sexuality and masculine appeal had her understanding she might never get another chance like the one standing before her now with his lopsided smile and gentle eyes.

Oh, they still danced with wicked promise, and he was one nod of agreement away from sweeping Tarni up and taking her to a forbidden and incredible place. But Tarni looked down and the moment passed.

Would she regret it?

Only time would tell.

Logan drove her back to her apartment and a mesmerized Marigold, who looked like she'd eagerly jump the man right there on the landing if he so much as winked at her. Thankfully, he did not. But he did take Tarni's hand, turning it over and stroking her palm with his thumb before leaning down to kiss it, then straightening up and bringing it to his mouth. Pulling her toward him once more, he left her with one more gentle kiss, and she could feel something tugging at her heart when it was over as he trotted down the stairs and mounted his bike.

Tarni noted, dryly, that Logan's kisses tasted of cigarettes, but also acknowledged that somehow, with him, it didn't seem to matter...

...and it left her...

...breathless.

What could that mean?

Would she ever get to taste anything else on those lips—his tongue?

With one last wave, Logan kicked the Harley back to life then drove off into the early morning light never to be seen again.

But the Fates had other thoughts on the matter.

CHAPTER 8

Vegas was dull and boring.

Those words would seem alien to a vast majority of people whether they'd ever been to Las Vegas or not. But that was exactly how Tarni felt after weeks, then months of bartending at the strip club. The holidays had come and gone, New Year's Eve and the insanity of it all in Las Vegas a distant memory. January bled into February and while the cooler temperatures were welcome, the monotony of her life was weighing on Tarni. And she knew who to blame for how she was feeling. While the money was great, the lack of forward progression toward her goal was what she kept telling herself was the reason for her stagnation.

But she knew it was Logan MacDuff. Or the lack of him, anyway.

The irony that she'd suddenly gone from a young woman set on revenge and change for her people to a lovesick teen pining away for a rocker dude she'd only met briefly was not lost on her. Tarni was pissed at herself for being so pathetic. But she could not get Logan out of her mind. Especially since all she kept fretting about was why he'd chosen to *not* take her right then and there in the desert but instead remained a gentleman.

I mean, she liked that he'd shown maturity and restraint.

Right?

"I'm not going to let any man sidetrack me. And let's face it, he's probably forgotten my name and what I look like," she grumbled.

"Who are you talking to, Tarni?" Shelby, the other female bartender, looked askance when Tarni shoved glasses haphazardly onto the shelf behind the bar, as if she'd lost some marbles and needed help picking them up off the floor. "Man trouble?"

"Sorry. I was venting to myself and probably need a pep talk or a distraction."

"Well, if it's a man you are worrying over, the best way to cure that ailment is go get yourself another one to make you forget the one that's making you frown."

"I volunteer!" Jason, a middle-aged father of three, divorced, and nursing his third beer was a regular and was constantly asking Tarni out. He was harmless, and she always left him hoping he might someday get her to go out with him. He always left the best tips.

"Nice try, Jason. But one photograph of you out with me and your ex will drag you back to court and demand more alimony."

"True. But it would be worth it." Jason stood up and saluted with beer in hand and wandered over to the stage where three girls were gyrating in various forms of undress. The music was thumping, and Tarni had the beginnings of a headache.

A string of bad customers, a chewing out from her boss not for anything she did but because his wife caught him making a play at one of the new girls, and too many nights dragging herself home to find Marigold entertaining another loser who was drunk and violent had worn Tarni down to new lows. Especially since last night she had to fight off the drunken boyfriend and added a jolt of magic to get him out of the apartment and away from her girl parts. That he stopped smacking Marigold around was an added bonus and Tarni didn't think either of them would remember the blue flash that bounced around the room when she let loose her magic stream.

Tarni was suddenly overcome with despair and had the urge to run screaming into the Las Vegas night. Instead, Fate seemed to realize she was one bad customer away from a mental breakdown.

"Hey, stranger!"

Looking up at the sound of a familiar voice, Tarni found Ernie standing in front of the bar.

"Ernie! What brings you here?" Tarni was still soured on the man for offering her up as a bonus to Logan's drug deal, but she couldn't stay mad at him for long.

"I've come to see you as a matter of fact."

"Oh?" Tarni wiped the top of the bar then grabbed a shot glass and poured Ernie a whiskey, straight. Jameson's was his favorite and Tarni had grown to like the amber liquid but didn't drink on the job, of course.

"There's a new club opening up in LA, and I thought of you the minute the owner said he'd be interviewing bartenders. He wants hot, young, and hung...or stacked in your case. Interested?"

Tarni stood there with her mouth hanging open as Ernie's words slowly registered. All she could manage was a nod as she placed her palm on her forehead. Was this what she'd been hoping for? A break in the monotony? Change? A new path to wander down? Blinking rapidly, she considered refusing, unsure if the money she was making here could be duplicated or, better yet, expanded in Los Angeles. Didn't it cost a lot of money to live in California?

"I know a great apartment complex within walking distance to the bar, not that you'd need to walk, but at least you won't be stuck in that traffic having to commute anywhere! And it's a stone's throw from UCLA and Hollywood in one direction and Santa Monica and the beach in the other."

"Let me figure out how to leave this place, give two weeks' notice, and get packed, not that I have much of anything yet. And I need to see if Jim is OK with me keeping the car, or if that was just because I work next door. I..."

"Two weeks? Darling...if you want this job, you are leaving tomorrow or the next day and driving that Mustang to Cali, baby. You don't have time to wait."

Needless to say, Tarni worked to the end of her shift, ran home, threw everything she had in her Mustang and hit the road two days later after saying a teary goodbye first to Marigold, then Buffalo Jim—with the title to the Mustang in hand.

Tarni, present day

It seems like yesterday. The years in between a blur, but that time so vivid, so real. Heading down I-15 into Barstow trying to read a Rand McNally map while driving and munching on Chicken McNuggets from McDonald's with a *Dream of the Blue* Turtles cassette sticking out of my retrofit head unit, speakers blasting. Sting wailed about the "Moon Over Bourbon Street" while I tried to figure out the route to my new apartment complex that Ernie set up for me while maneuvering the barbecue sauce-laden chicken morsels into my mouth.

I was excited about reaching California and exploring the city of Los Angeles and thrilled that my apartment was six miles from the Pacific Ocean. The Santa Monica Pier wasn't the tourist destination it has become today—it was in the process of transformation in 1987, but even then, being so close to the pier was a thrill for me.

And the possibility of finding Logan. Hoping he lived in LA or close by sent a thrill down my center.

I finally managed to drive through Barstow and down into Victorville, California before the highway took me through the San Bernardino Mountain pass into Rancho Cucamonga, where I picked up I-10 heading west. I giggled all the way as I recalled Bugs Bunny mentioning the town in the old Looney Tune cartoons.

The traffic became horrific the closer I got to the city, and once I made the harrowing journey through downtown, into Hollywood and over to Santa Monica, I was exhausted and perturbed at Angelenos and their driving habits. Did no one drive the speed limit? And what was with all the traffic? Oh, I had so much to learn!

I drove through my new neighborhood until I found the Westwood Village apartments and parked out front, making sure to lock my doors. One thing Ernie stressed was how often a car was broken into in LA and cautioned not to leave anything of worth in my car. The fact that my Mustang meant the world to me had me frazzled and chewing on my lower lip as I peered around looking for thieves. I was convinced a gang of them would descend on my vehicle once I entered the rental office to get my key and meet my landlord. I glanced back in apprehension at my car even as I entered the building.

Two women seemed to hover at the landing once I entered and climbed the flight of stairs and pounced on me the minute I reached them.

"Oh! You must be Tarni. Aren't you just the sweetest little button! I'm Irma. This here is Clarissa, but don't let that fancy name fool you. She's a tart."

The woman who addressed me was a relic of the 1950s. Bouffant hair, cat-eyed glasses, a drawn-on mole and way too much makeup that was loud and garish. Her hair was henna burgundy, and she was wearing a floral muumuu. Clarissa had on glasses that gave her an owlish mien, a Hawaiian shirt and a miniskirt that did nothing for her considering she looked to be about eighty and her skin was so wrinkled and saggy I thought her stockings were pooling around her ankles. They weren't. She wasn't wearing any stockings!

The room smelled like cigarettes and potpourri.

"Yes, you're correct. I'm Tarni. I have papers to sign? And I need my key, of course."

"That and the key code to get into the parking garage."

"There's a garage?" I was astounded at the news because in Vegas I just parked on the street.

"Hell, yeah. Your car would be stripped in ten minutes if you left it outside overnight. This is Los Angeles, hon. Not...where are you from again?" Irma queried, laughing a bit which turned into a hacking, phlegmy cough. I became alarmed but she waved off my concern.

"Are you far from home?"

"I just moved here from Las Vegas."

"Well, the desert has its own troubles, but here in the big city you need to worry about car theft and wildfires."

"And hoodlums," Clarissa piped up nodding her head and looking even more like a wizened old owl.

"Hoodlums?" I asked.

"Hoodlums. All manner of gangs, thugs, and kids that drive around in souped-up cars that go up and down and up and down with that crazy muchacha music blaring."

"Mariachi," countered Irma.

"Same thing," sniffed Clarissa.

"Now, you must be tuckered out, so just sign these forms and here is your key. You are in the quiet section of the complex, a corner unit, so you'll have to hike a bit to the community pool. The end of each hallway has a garbage chute...make sure you separate your recyclables from the rest of your trash and dump them accordingly down their perspective shafts, and don't overstuff them or they'll clog! No pets allowed and try not to smoke in bed. We almost lost Benny and Sue Ellen Waterford when their apartment caught fire a few years ago. Your mail will come to the office to be sorted into your box." Irma looked at her notes and smiled, handing me the key.

"You're number 300. Third floor, which is where we are right now since you've seen the stairs and climbed two flights. The garage is street level, the second level has apartments and a take and share community library of sorts. This level has the main office, laundry and pool area. If you follow me, I will show you how to get to your apartment from the office. The mailboxes are across the way...and just ahead is the pool i mentioned."

I tried to process the dizzying amount of information overload coming at me and followed behind Irma obediently. The pool was massive and open to the sky with apartments facing it —sliding doors all around in one three sides with the office entry on the fourth. There was a hallway to our immediate right, and I realized that this complex was open-air although covered from the elements, except for the pool. I also noted, dryly, that many of the sliding doors had cats peeking out and the telltale sign of food bowls and cat toys had me quickly realizing the rules in this apartment complex would be lax. At least as far as pets were concerned. I certainly hoped my fellow residents refrained from smoking in bed!

"If we take this hallway to the very end, you will see the elevators and the garbage chute. If we turn left, then follow that hallway to the very end, your apartment is the last one on the right. The last one before the emergency exit. Your key will open that door as well. Your parking space matches your apartment number as does your mailbox in the office. The laundry room is on the other side of the pool area so you will be lugging that as well."

I thanked Irma and noted Clarissa hadn't followed us, then gathered my copy of the lease and ran back down to my car, convinced it would be sitting up on cement blocks while I was distracted by the check-in process. Luckily, it was in pristine condition and unmolested. Following Irma's directions, I noted the side street to my left and made the irksome U-turn on Sepulveda Boulevard, which the building was upon, then turned left onto Sardis Avenue and entered the covered parking garage.

I was home.

I can still recall the tiny thrill of opening my studio apartment door for the first time knowing it was my new apartment—the first one without a roommate. And although it was modest, the living, dining, kitchen combo separated by a thick curtain from the bedroom area and bathroom, it was fully furnished and boasted a huge picture window that looked over the on-ramp from the 405 freeway onto I-10. It had a fireplace and massive walk-in closet, not to mention a balcony big enough for a small table and two chairs that looked down onto the Sardis Ave cul-de-sac I'd just entered near the garage. A tree just outside my window gave me a bit of green—a break from all the concrete, but birds were singing, and the traffic noise didn't bother me at all.

I did a little jig around the room.

I had a few days before I needed to report to work, and I

knew exactly what I wanted to do before I started my daily—or nightly, rather—grind.

"I need to go shopping! This place needs a witchy touch of magic to make it all mine!"

And I was off and running.

CHAPTER 9

West Los Angeles, February 1987

Tarni had a weird and wonderful learning curve for the next two weeks upon arrival in her new city. For one thing, she didn't know any of the store's names—even the department stores were different. Somehow that idea, that different regions would have their own supermarkets, banks, and department stores, and she had to say farewell to Piggly Wiggly, Burdines, and Joran Marsh, and say hello to Vons and Ralphs supermarkets, The Broadway, and the glittering massive malls that dominated the southern California landscape, never crossed her mind. it didn't seem so in Las Vega, but in Los Angeles nothing seemed the same as in Florida. She had spent four hours alone just getting to know the entire Beverly Center Mall on Beverly and San Vicente Boulevards and had never seen anything like it in her lifetime.

A movie theater in the mall? Totally rad. And celebrities everywhere!

Maybe not everywhere, but she'd seen Barry Manilow buying books at Waldenbooks, and Paul Newman was at the same stoplight when she'd exited the mall and took La Cienega down to Pico Boulevard. All the street names to learn and quirky things that made Angelenos the hip, out-there, folks that the rest of the nation shook their heads at—even though most of the trends started right there and made their way across to New York City before bleeding into the collective consciousness of the US.

She'd met several of her neighbors and found that most of her complex had young professionals or Hollywood wannabes looking for their big break. Right across the hall from her lived a trio of lesbian theater majors attending UCLA who invited her to her first Mexican restaurant. Justine, Monique, and Stacey wouldn't take no for an answer. Tarni was surprised she enjoyed the spicy food and most definitely enjoyed the company.

Directly next door was an Asian couple, Mr. and Mrs. Tan, who didn't speak English very well, but they nodded hello and gave her a housewarming gift on her second night in—a tiny jade plant in a terracotta pot. They worked long hours at their Thai restaurant, and she only ever saw them on Sundays when she was doing laundry.

And finally, diagonally across from her apartment was a young actress, a true starving artist named Heather. Tarni found out from the trio that they'd taken to feeding her left-overs and kept an eye out for signs she might not be able to make rent. The poor thing was skeletal and always seemed haunted, so Tarni could see why they fretted so.

The best part of her new life had to be her job. Surprisingly, Ernie came through in a big way, and she owed him one. The owner of the new club, Marco Dimitri, had a speakeasy vibe going in his lounge, but instead of old-time actors haunting the place, it was usually filled with a plethora of wannabes, as well as a few legitimate actors, actresses, and musicians all jockeying for position whenever a big-time director or producer walked in the door.

The club was innocuously called Barney's Down Below, which made little sense. One, you had to climb a flight of steps to get into the place and two, none of the owners was named Barney. There wasn't anything remotely innocent about the goings-on where drugs, sex, and partying was the norm on most nights. Tarni might've been quickly approaching her twentieth birthday, but she wasn't a bit shocked at what being a bartender at Barney's entailed.

"Daydreaming, sexy?" Michael, her coworker and head bartender asked, then winked when Tarni came out of her reverie.

"Just thinking about these last few weeks and calculating how long it will take me to become a burned-out alcoholic with a drug habit—or perhaps it should be a junkie with an alcohol problem."

Michael tossed his head back and laughed, his golden mullet flowing, silky blonde hair going in every direction, and his green eyes filled with merriment.

"Considering I've never seen you inebriated or addled in any way, I'd say you're safe—for now."

"We looking at a busy night tonight, Mike?"

"When are we not?" This was true. Ever since she'd started, the club had been packed, and the intensity of the crowd grew well into the wee hours of the morning until last call. As for drug use, Tarni tried some cocaine and found it didn't make her anxious or keep her particularly alert...it was more a catalyst for her to take long, dangerous swims in the Pacific Ocean for a few hours.

Dangerous, because the first time she'd done so, she'd gone so far out from shore that when she turned to observe how far she'd traveled, the lights and imagery from the beach were barely discernible. That, and Tarni'd felt something bump her from below. Quickly sinking under the depths of the cerulean water, she discovered a Great white shark swimming listlessly. She'd gone from terrified to curious to sympathetic when the beast's thoughts registered. In shock, she realized her ability to comprehend what the magnificent creature was thinking. It sent her conflicting emotions of hunger and sadness, loneliness, and fear.

Tarni tentatively sent back words meant to soothe and was incredulous when the shark seemed to understand her and turned to swim off in search of its next meal.

This incident sparked a renewed interest in her siren abilities...no witch she knew could control a Great white after all—that was pure siren!

"Keep sharp tonight. We are supposed to have a lively crowd coming in," Michael informed her.

"Oh? And when do we not have a lively crowd?"

"True. But we are going to be packed with a few Hollywood brats—more than usual. They tend to liven things up considerably. Make sure to give them a good show."

The movie *Cocktail* with Tom Cruise was in production and hadn't hit theaters yet, but the word was out that it could be a catalyst to transform the industry. One of the assistant producers had come in on a fact-finding mission and informed Tarni and her coworkers of the subject of the film. Bartenders in all the hot spots around the US and world had transitioned from the typical lend an ear, get advice or sympathy kind, to showstoppers who mixed, spun, and poured new and unique concoctions that had people lined up and cheering—at least in the newer hot spots, and Barney's was no exception. Tarni was honing her craft, turning into quite the virtuoso mixer—and had a cult following already.

Tarni had shopped until she dropped trying to transform

her tiny apartment into a cozy home. But in the end she didn't buy much of anything. What little she did add made Tarni happy. Filling an old bookshelf she found on the side of the road then refinished with books gave her some satisfaction. She'd added a few plants, not remotely expecting them to thrive under her ministrations...she'd already drowned them in water and watched worriedly as they drooped from the strain of it all. But they made her happy and she whispered magic into them thinking that might help.

Feeling like Samantha from *Bewitched*, Tarni laughed as she danced around her place using just enough magic to weave protection spells and enchantments she knew would keep her relatively safe and allow her to sleep soundly, knowing if anything "extra" showed up at her door, she'd have fair warning.

Becoming adept at spell weaving and casting protection charms had been part of her growing up life, her mother, Jenny, made sure of it, and Tarni was grateful now that she was on her own in a city known for paranormal activity.

The glamour mixed with hopelessness from those who tried and failed to make it was a tempting feeding ground for all manner of evil paranormal beings, and Tarni knew she should remain diligent.

The last thing Tarni did before her first day of work was register her car, becoming an official resident of the state of California, and she couldn't be happier. Screwing the license plate on her Mustang was the final step to her new life and all the possibilities that awaited her in this land of dreams and movie magic.

By midnight, the club was hopping and Tarni was ready for a break. She'd seen so much of young Hollywood cross the threshold and mix with the enthusiastic crowd, she'd lost count. Musicians, actors, starlets, celebrity brats, rich kids from the valley, all jaded and hopped up on whatever drug was being circulated that evening, thrashing about on the dance floor, or tucked into corners drinking and carousing with no end in sight.

Women dressed in power suits, hair slicked back like Annie Lennox sporting monocles and walking sticks. Men, faces painted, exploring their feminine side—lips red, pink, black eyeliner overused, in bright pastels or androgynous garb, giving Boy George a run for his money. Others going for obvious masculinity: leather, and studs...or jeans and a white tee. Then you had your leftover punk crowd moving into goth. And no crowd would be complete without the ever-present concrete blondes, rockers with bottle-blonde Aqua Net queens in skintight dresses on their arms. Leather and lace, spandex, and blue jeans—Tarni loved it all.

"Brendan, could you bring table six their drinks? Thanks." Tarni handed one of the servers an order and began mixing another cocktail for a woman who looked like she was decades too old to be hanging around this crowd.

"Hurry with that drink, will you, honey? I want to get back to Jack before he goes off with those two tramps over there." The woman had smeared mascara and lipstick. Her dress did nothing to hide her rolls of fat, but Tarni never judged and gave the woman a thumbs-up.

"Go get him, sister. Although you can do better, I'm sure."

"Aw...thanks, hon. You are too sweet."

It wasn't until Tarni followed the woman's progress across the dance floor that she'd noticed who *Jack* was. Well, well...amazing how many big names showed up in their humble establishment!

Another lady walked by with a man on a leash. She was wearing a fishnet stocking body suit and stilettos, and nothing else. He was dressed in business casual. The woman was also carrying a riding crop. Her nudity and confidence stopped Tarni in her tracks. *That's* the kind of confidence she craved! The woman noticed her stare and paused, allowing the man she was leading to kiss her lips then she whispered something in his ear, and he dropped on his knees and kissed her crotch, right on her sweet spot! She winked at Tarni and moved on. Tarni, however, kept an even face, not making a big deal out of it or any of these goings-on, although she did return the wink. This was the protocol Marco expected of all his employees. Live and let live, don't stare, be professional. That's when the man in question showed up at the bar looking harassed and desperate.

"Mike, Tarni...have you guys seen a young Latina girl in here? Probably underage and wearing a green next to nothing dress?"

"No, boss. She important?" Mike asked cutting his eyes to Tarni. She raised one brow noting the plethora of young nubile bodies wandering around, but not many of them fit the description.

"She's the new councilman's daughter, and his people are searching everywhere for her! We need to get her out of here before they find her and cause a scene."

"The dude that wants to run for Congress? That's gnarly, man." Michael looked worried, and Tarni began searching the crowd in earnest.

"Whoa, hang on. You mean that chick in the skimpy, sparkly green dress from earlier?" Brendan had returned to the bar and overheard the conversation.

"Yeah! That's what her keepers said she had on. Where is she?" Marco jumped at Brendan who raised his hands and shook his head.

"No idea, dude. Last I saw her, she had her tongue down Duffy's throat and was trying to lead him away from his table."

Hang on a second...Duffy?

Tarni thought there couldn't possibly be two men with that ridiculous nickname and started to leave the bar area to peruse the room.

"This is a nightmare. She's like sixteen or so. She gets caught with that rocker and there's going to be big trouble...for him and us!" Marco cried. "If it gets out in the press, it will destroy us."

And Logan!

Tarni began rushing around the club looking everywhere for that idiot and the councilman's underaged daughter to no avail. Heading up the six steps to the back area where the restrooms were, Tarni barged right into the men's room taking stock, but only found two glam rockers making out in one stall and a startled guy hovering near one urinal. That left the ladies' room.

Tearing across the short hallway, Tarni pushed open the bathroom door and stopped short. Leaning against the sink with his head thrown back, black leather jacket open, white T-shirt lifted, and jeans riding low on hips that had two hands with blood red, dagger-like fingernails gripping them was Logan MacDuff. The girl on her knees in front of him was so occupied by her loud and sloppy blow job, she didn't bother stopping or turning to see who had entered the ladies' room. Logan, on the other hand, dropped his head forward lazily and smiled.

Until he spied who was standing there watching the festivities, that is.

"Jesus!" he cried.

"I don't think Jesus has anything to do with what's going on here," said Tarni, drolly. "But we don't have time for debate; you need to get out of here...and take the jailbait with you."

"Do you mind, bitch? I'm trying to have a good time here!"

The girl scowled at Tarni, and her frown became even more pronounced when Logan pushed her back, hurriedly zipping up. Tarni was disappointed when he managed to *not* nick himself in the process.

"Tarni? What..."

"Didn't you hear me? Her father's goons are about to storm the club and you need to get her out of here before they find you with her...or the press hears about it."

"I'm not going anywhere until my man gets his rocks off."

Logan blanched and glanced down at the pouting girl like she was an irritating mosquito he wanted to swat.

Sounds of commotion up front caused everyone to turn toward the bathroom door making Tarni peek out to see what was happening. What she saw was two police officers questioning the crowd and a man in dark sunglasses peering around looking like a Doberman on a mission.

"Oh God. You're too late. They are here." Thinking quickly, Tarni reached into her pocket and came up with the keys to her Mustang which she tossed to Logan. "Here. Go up the hallway and out the back door. My Mustang is parked in the alley. Take it and get her out of here before you get arrested. She's like sixteen or something for Heaven's sake!"

"You told me you were nineteen!" Logan scowled down at the girl who finally realized the seriousness of their situation but still had a surly attitude going.

"Sixteen, nineteen. Who cares?" The girl rolled her eyes and stood up teetering on heels way too high for any normal person to want to walk around in and loudly complained when Logan tugged on her arm.

"Let me go. I don't care if they are here. I'm not going anywhere!"

Logan, seeing he was about to be front page news, did the only thing he could think of with such a time constraint. He hoisted the whining girl up, tossing her over his shoulder, and once Tarni gave him the all clear, ran up the hall to the back door.

He only tripped once.

Tarni tried not to feel satisfied when Logan bumped the teenager's head up against the wall when he fumbled at the back door before wrenching it open.

"Tarni, I..."

"Not now. Just go." When Logan hesitated a second longer, Tarni almost screamed with frustration. "Just go, damn it!"

Rushing back to the main room, Tarni stumbled herself, and landed smack into the chest of the goon in the sunglasses. One of the officers was right behind him.

"Oh! I'm sorry. I didn't see you. Can I help you? I'm a bartender here."

"Where were you?" the policeman asked, peering over Tarni's shoulder.

"On a break. I just came out of the bathroom."

"Have you seen this girl anywhere tonight?"

The cop held up a photo of the girl who was with Logan. The photo was of a younger, smirking version, attitude apparent and trouble written all over her face. Yep, one and the same chick.

"Hmm, you know what? I think I may have seen her earlier. I think she came in with a pimple-faced geeky kid, and I knew right away they were too young to be in here. When they came to the bar, I told them to head out, and after a few minutes of posturing, they did just that."

Doberman Guy remained silent but never took his gaze off Tarni—well, she assumed so, because she couldn't see his eyes.

How the hell can he see where he's going with those things on?

Tarni didn't flinch under their scrutiny nor back down. She

didn't even fidget but kept an inane smile plastered on her face. She was tempted to use her siren voice on the duo but knew that would be more trouble than it was worth to attempt.

"We need to check the back," Doberman Guy stated in a gravelly voice.

Whoa! This dude screamed paranormal, Tarni thought. If she had to guess, she'd say he was a witch, like her, not that she was an expert on paranormal detection, but she would swear she saw him flash a bit of magic in her direction and it gave her chills.

"Um...well, sure. Go right ahead."

Crossing her fingers Logan had managed to leave the premises by now, and hoping Doberman Guy wasn't a mind reader, Tarni stepped out of the security detachment's way and scampered back to her station behind the bar.

"Where have you been? What did you say to those guys?" Michael looked worried and kept flicking his eyes toward the hallway.

"Where is Marco? We need to let him know I found that kid and she was with Logan MacDuff alright. I let them out the back way."

Michael whistled his surprise before glancing over Tarni's shoulder. Materializing right behind her, Marco was suddenly and nervously at her shoulder. He gripped her arm and bent close.

"What happened? Was he back there with Gloria?"

"That's her name? Gloria?"

"Yeah. So... was he back there?"

"They were occupied in the ladies' room, but luckily I managed to get them out the back way. I tossed Logan my car keys, and I believe they escaped."

"Oh! Thank God. Kid, I'm giving you a raise. Your quick thinking and actions saved me a ton of grief. Duffy too!" Marco clapped Tarni on the shoulder then his face became animated when the goons reappeared in the doorway. Simpering and scraping over to them, Marco tried to give the impression he was more than happy to help should Gloria show back up, promising quick action and contact the second she did.

"Not that I expect her to, gentlemen. After all, we always discourage underaged drinking, you know."

They didn't know. Moreover, they didn't seem to believe Marco, but with no quarry in sight, the men had no choice but to leave the club. Doberman Guy gave Tarni one last, long look as he pushed out the main door.

He knows what I am!

Tarni hoped that meant he knew she was a witch and did nothing to reveal her half-breed status.

The night was long and Tarni's nerves were all over the place, but ten minutes before closing time she sensed his presence even before looking up and locking eyes with Logan. She was on the stairs about to head down into the main room. Her slight frown, and her jutted out bottom lip left no question as to the mood she was in. Tarni decided to ignore him.

"Tarni. What are you doing here?" Logan asked, ignoring her demeanor.

"Give me my keys."

"Hey. Look...about that..."

"Logan. I don't give a damn about that. I do, however, want my car keys back and hope you haven't done any damage to my Mustang."

Holding her hand out and tapping her foot, Tarni waited, refusing to meet Logan's eyes—she was equal to his height still standing on the steps.

Sighing, he dropped the keys into her palm and stepped back when she stomped down the last two steps, pushed past him, and headed toward the door.

"I'm out of here, Michael. Remind Marco I have the day off tomorrow, will you? Thanks."

And with that, Tarni breezed out of the nightclub and ran down the flight of stairs to the street below where she found her car waiting.

She didn't bother checking to see if Logan had followed.

Nor did she care.

CHAPTER 10

Tarni, present day

Of course, I cared. It's not like I was a jaded adult, full of ennui, who'd been around the block a time or two. I'd never seen anyone give or get a blow job. I'd never done the deed myself having only touched one boy that way in a fumbled attempt to make him happy and keep me from having to go "all the way." I was embarrassed, shocked, and pissed off at myself for being slightly titillated by the sight, my tummy doing butterfly flip-flops and my body reacting in some primitive way to the sight of the man getting pleasured, if I was being honest with myself. And, unfortunately, I was being honest. Logan looked hot with those lazy eyes flush with heat. But damn it all, I was mad that...what?

That he had a life? That he had sex with women...or in Gloria's case, a girl?

It's not like I expected him to be a virgin. I mean, he did proclaim he adored all the sex, drugs, and rock and roll. So, I couldn't claim I hadn't a clue what that entailed. I certainly wanted to go all slut at one point—modesty and expectations of what women should behave like be damned. It was my world, and I would play by my rules, thank you!

I think what was even more disturbing was my reaction to how proprietary I felt. He was mine! Or so my nineteen-year-old-self tried to rationalize. As if Logan belonged to me and he didn't have the right to cavort with nubile young things.

I *was* a nubile young thing at the time, damn it!

I was furious at myself for being jealous. But accepted that I was human, well...you know what I mean...and had to ride out these emotions.

I recalled making it to my car and yanking the door open, tossing my bag on the passenger seat, and preparing to climb in when Logan grabbed my arm, jerking me back into his chest. I pushed him, incensed that he'd put his hands on me and may have let a bit of my magic out because his eyes went wide.

I quickly tempered my anger and just shook my head no, before getting in the Mustang and peeling down Sunset into the early morning air...the trail of exhaust remaining behind with one dejected-looking Logan MacDuff.

When I reached my apartment, I barely made it up the elevator and down the hallway before the tears began to fall. I didn't know what was wrong with me, nor why I was letting this guy and his sexual escapade get to me. So... OK...he was getting pleasured in a bathroom in a club in Hollyweird. He was a rocker...a musician. They all lived that lifestyle. It was part of the deal. I'm sure somewhere, in some manual called Rock & Roll 101, one of the rules of living the lifestyle had, *they have copious amount of wild sex,* as a bylaw. There had to be!

It didn't make it any easier on me at the time.

I sniffled my way into my apartment just as my phone began to ring. Seeing as I didn't have many friends yet or gave out my new number, I peered at the ringing phone with suspicion. Who would be calling me at 4 o'clock in the morning?

Dropping everything on the kitchen table and locking the door behind me, I ran to my nightstand and picked the phone off the cradle.

"Hello?"

"Tarni...we need to talk."

I hung up the phone with force, then removed it from the cradle, placing it on the top of my nightstand. Crawling into bed, I cried myself to sleep and didn't have the energy to wonder how Logan MacDuff wound up with my telephone number.

Tarni, 1987

Twisting and turning all night, Tarni slept in fitful agony, never quite dropping off deep enough to make a difference. She woke grumpy and bleary-eyed, makeup smeared on her face and eyes crusty with dried tears. Somehow in the middle of the night, probably during an erotic dream involving Logan MacDuff, Tarni decided she needed to grow up and take what she wanted, and stop being such a pathetic wretch.

I'm a siren, damn it.

Rubbing the offending crust from her eyes, Tarni tried to focus in the dimly lit room, wondering why it was so dark outside. But the sound of droplets on her patio doors gave an answer to that question and she frowned.

I thought it never rained in Southern California?

Reaching down and feeling around blindly, Tarni lifted the phone receiver and replaced it on the cradle after three fumbled attempts.

Sighing, Tarni stretched, turned over in bed, then screamed.

"What the hell are you doing here?"

Sitting up and all but falling off the end of the mattress, Tarni looked in incredulity at the prone figure of Logan MacDuff stretched out on the bed beside her.

"I believe I am watching you sleep. Well, I was, anyway."

"I don't mean that! You know what I mean, blast it all. How did you get here? In my room. Did you follow me home? You did, didn't you! Pervert!"

And how did you get past my wards? she wondered.

Logan chuckled and sat up shifting on the bed, so he faced her.

"I did not follow you home. But yes, I'm quite the pervert."

Tarni stared at Logan with several emotions coiling around her mind, one of which had murderous intent...but quite a few of her emotions leaned towards the happy side of the spectrum. Traitors!

She went to lay into him with a scathing response, but just then a loud bang shattered the quiet of the room. Startled, Tarni looked at the patio doors and saw that a small bird had crashed into them.

"Oh, no! Poor thing." Before she could move toward it, Logan was already up and outside on the balcony, softly crooning to the dazed creature. He crept quietly over to where the bird was sprawled and gently scooped it up into his hands, murmuring softly to it.

"Is that a finch of some kind?"

"No. It's a black phoebe. Quite common in California. It likes to make mud nets up against structures. This one must have been startled and the reflection from your patio doors tricked it into thinking it was the open sky. Here, let me set her down on the bed and I can examine her wings and beak and make sure she's just rattled and nothing is broken."

Tarni moved over slightly, allowing Logan to place the startled bird on the bedcover. He carefully began to examine her wings, slowly stretching them out and flexing them back and forth. Then he stared for a time at her beak and eyes before kissing the top of her head and releasing her back outside...this time placing her on a branch of the bushy tree growing right beside her balcony. The little bird hopped a few steps away, then made a chirping sound before flying off in the opposite direction of the building.

Logan came back inside and stared down at Tarni. "Do you have masking tape?"

Before she could open her mouth to respond to that comment, her phone rang. This time she was well and truly puzzled because all of the people who possessed her number knew never to ring in the mornings unless someone was dead—her late hours meant she was reversed for social niceties.

Scrambling over to the phone made Tarni relieved that she'd not undressed as she noted her rumpled state, although she cringed inwardly knowing her face must be a sight.

"Hello?"

"Tarni! Oh, thank goodness...I didn't know if you'd pick up."

"Kimberly! Baby...are you OK? You received my letter then."

Tarni watched as Logan wandered into her bathroom coming back out with a towel to dry off. He moved into the living area she assumed to give her some privacy, but in an apartment so tiny, there wasn't much to be had. She'd used a P.O. Box her mother opened years ago that no one knew about, and that was her line of communication to her baby sister. "Is everything OK? Did you forget about the time change? It's only 7 AM here, sweetie."

"Oh, Tarni. Father is on a tirade. He found out you ran away. The sisters are on a full hunt for you. They think you are in Miami."

"Why would they think I'm in Miami? And, Kimberly, you don't have to worry. They won't find me and even should they, I have no intention of going back there. Not without a fight."

"It was me. I may have put out a few false trails. They think you have a boyfriend in Miami, and you plan on eloping then taking a honeymoon out of the country...and have no intention of coming back."

"Elope, huh? That's a good one, sis. But does that put you in any danger? I don't want you to bring any more attention to yourself then you need."

"I'm fine. I pretended to write you and used the south Florida address you have as a decoy, just like you instructed me should the need arise. I did good, right, Tarni?" Tarni's heart ached as the scratchy broken voice of her baby sister continued to speak. "They all ran off to hunt for you down there and Doris is convinced you are already out of the country. I played Panama over and over again, sobbing for you, so now she's convinced that's where you are!"

Laughing a little even as her heart broke in a million pieces for the dear sister she'd left behind, Tarni reassured Kimberly she'd done more than "good."

"You are the best, dear heart. I couldn't ask for a better sister. Now please tell me you are calling from a safe location?"

"I'm on a payphone at the mall. They pay no attention to me anymore now that I've been cut. And Tarni? They've nullified my witch magic. I'm useless to you."

"Baby, you are not useless. How dare they! I'm so sorry, Kimmy. I promise, once I make a name for myself and get powerful, all this will change. Just believe in me, OK? I need to run, but you call me any time...even in the mornings. I love you, Kimberly."

"I love you too, Tarni. Be careful."

When Tarni hung up the phone she remained sitting on the edge of the bed staring out the slats of the blinds on her patio doors as the rain continued to come down in buckets. Kimberly was hardly useless, and it pained Tarni to know she doubted how important she was. Even if Kimberly could do nothing more than send her thoughts and prayers, it was enough. Plus, that girl was the smartest person Tarni had ever known...not only in book smarts, but common sense and street sense. Her intuition was legendary and her ability to solve the most complex problems gave Tarni hope that whatever machinations she'd set to waylay her family from finding where she'd run to would work.

"Family troubles?" Logan had materialized beside the bed, looking concerned and a bit contrite for having overheard the obviously private conversation.

Rather than shrieking in alarm since Tarni'd all but forgotten she had unexpected company, she reached for her pillow instead, slamming it into Logan's crotch.

"How did you find me? How did you know my phone number and where I live? And how did you get in here, damn it?"

Only showing mild alarm when Logan dropped to the ground grabbing his privates in obvious pain, Tarni shot to her feet, hands on hips, glaring down at him. Then she did something she'd been dreaming about for the last few months, she followed him down there, straddled his body, grabbed his face, and kissed him like coming up for air was the last thing on her mind.

After a few moments satisfying that urge, Tarni stood,

albeit awkwardly, kicked Logan once more for good measure, and stormed into her bathroom to make herself presentable while he remained prostrate and groaning on the floor in a mixture of misery and ecstasy.

Serves him right.

CHAPTER 11

Face scrubbed and devoid of makeup, Tarni left the bathroom and stopped short. Looking at her patio doors, she saw tiny strips of masking tape stuck hither and yon in a haphazard way all over the glass. Curious to see where Logan had found tape, Tarni entered her kitchenette, surprised to find him making breakfast. He glanced up then back down to his ministrations which turned out to be scrambled eggs, bagels with cream cheese, and coffee.

"Tape was under your sink. Breakfast is almost ready."

Tarni ignored everything else but went straight to the black stuff which she immediately sweetened, adding a healthy dollop of half-and-half which she knew she didn't have, nor did she have cream cheese in her refrigerator—so Logan must have brought it.

What an odd duck. Who stalks his victims bringing along a container of half-and-half and cream cheese? And who administers aid to a bird then hunts around to find tape to prevent another disaster after getting pillow-smacked in his crotch?

"That bagel is useless to me unless it's slathered in butter. And I prefer poppyseed, so you can have the onion."

And really? Onion? Did he expect me to continue kissing him with onion breath?

"The onion is for me. I got sesame seed, so that will have to do." Logan sliced open another bagel, dropping it into Tarni's toaster while taking a bite out of his bagel. "All that sugar isn't healthy."

"I'm not worried about it."

"You will when you turn into a fat cow."

"I think big women are luscious and sexy. There is nothing hotter than a big woman who is confident about those curves...so bugger off."

"Such language." Logan grabbed her bagel as it popped up out of the toaster and scraped a bit of butter that he'd pulled from her refrigerator on one side. Sighing loudly, Tarni nabbed the butter knife out of Logan's hand and used half the stick to doctor the bagel to her liking.

"Yep. You're going to get fat."

"You'll live."

"I'll live, but you might not with those eating habits."

"I think I will be just fine."

Logan stopped munching, swallowed, and stared at Tarni's face. "Oh, you are definitely *fine*."

Logan grabbed the breakfast fixings and took them into the living room where he placed the items on the coffee table and sat on the sofa.

"Table, please. I don't allow eating in the living room."

Logan looked around noting the "living" area was three steps from the "kitchen." He cocked an eyebrow and plopped down on the sofa, taking another bite out of his bagel. "I can't tell which is which," he said with a smile.

Tarni stood there with her arms crossed knowing they were

playing some kind of dominance game and she just lost a point. She was going to stand there and argue her point, however just then her stomach rumbled loudly, and she caved. Not because she was weak, but...bagel...butter...yeah.

Picking up her plate, she looked around for a fork. There was none. Before she could stand to get one, Logan plucked the plate from her hand and motioned with his index finger for her to come closer, so she scooched over another inch. Taking the fork from his plate, he stabbed a bit of scrambled egg and offered it to her.

"I can feed myself you know."

Logan didn't argue, he just waited patiently for Tarni to open her mouth.

Tarni was discombobulated and became suddenly self-conscious. She'd never had a man *feed* her before! She opened her mouth and Logan fed her the egg then went back to his eggs. When Tarni reached out for her bagel, Logan stopped her and broke off a piece which he held near her lips. She glanced down and observed the butter had melted all over his fingers. When she ate the piece of bagel, Logan licked the butter from his fingertips but never took his eyes off hers.

Whoa baby!

Then he held them out for Tarni to lick. And right then and there she knew she wanted to more than anything. Totally beyond any rational thought except the need to savor the taste of butter on Logan's fingers, she acquiesced. Ten minutes later, she found herself draped across Logan who lay back on the sofa as he proceeded to feed her with his hands. Who knew kanoodling over bagels could be so satisfying? She could feel his erection pressing on her belly and groaned inwardly knowing she wasn't so far gone that she'd have sex with him. After all, he was with Gloria...right?

Logan took a bite from his bagel and a bit of cream cheese

remained smeared on his face, and Tarni became mesmerized by it. Done with her meal, she watched as he chewed then swallowed, liking the way his throat moved and the way his lips twitched with amusement at her close scrutiny.

Then she wiped that smirk off his face by hoisting herself up a bit and licking the cream cheese off his face.

Logan sucked in air and wrapped his arms around Tarni, crushing his lips to hers. The kiss started off intense and hard then became sensuous and slow as he tasted her while running his hands through her long, unruly hair. They remained this way for quite some time until, dizzy in wonder and half wild with desire, Logan broke away laughing.

"Don't you ever come up for air, woman? A man could drown kissing you!"

"Thank you for breakfast." Noting briefly that onion breath tasted good on Logan, Tarni was distracted enough by this revelation that she couldn't think of anything else to say. First cigarettes, now onions. Great...pheromones, gotta love it.

"Heh. You are something else. Do you know that?" Logan sat up and shifted Tarni so she was settled in his lap. He ran his fingertips over her lips then caressed her cheek. "So very different."

"Different from what? Older? I assume you like them right out of braces if Gloria is any indication."

"And here we go."

Tarni tried to get up, but Logan was having none of that and held her tightly until she stopped struggling.

"Yes, here we go. Am I supposed to forget what I saw last night?"

"I should hope not. But there is no reason for you to be so upset about it, now is there?" Logan gave her a puzzled look like bathroom blow jobs were de rigueur in his world, and who knows? *In* his world, maybe they *were!*

"I'm not upset. I was taken aback and shocked that you'd do something so...so...unsanitary."

That set Logan off laughing so hard that Tarni became momentarily diverted by the sight of the man losing himself to gaiety so utterly and with abandon. His entire face transformed into boyish charm again and his perfect white teeth looked good against his California tan. Then she scowled and shook off the enchantment and smacked him...hard.

"Stop it. It *is* unsanitary having your thing out in a public restroom."

"My thing. Oh, but you are cute. And not for anything, um...how else would one use the facilities if it isn't out? I think the only one who need worry is, uh...the girl."

"Oh my God. You don't even remember her name! And I just said it a minute ago!"

"Tarni! It's not like she mattered to me or anything. It was a hookup. She wanted me, and I let her have it. No strings. All in good fun. Of course, it's on me for not verifying her age."

Tarni sat back and regarded Logan in amazement. She'd never met someone so lackadaisical about being intimate and didn't know how to respond. Well, if she wanted an education, she was definitely getting one. Seeing her confusion, Logan sighed and shifted Tarni back onto the sofa then stood up and began to pace.

"We need to lay down some ground rules."

"Here we go again with the ground rules. Do you make them up as you go along, or is this some long-held thing of yours?"

Logan stopped and pointed a finger at Tarni's nose. "Manifesto. This is my manifesto for how I live my life, and you either agree or we part and there are no hard feelings."

Tarni didn't know what to make of that, so she remained

quiet, waiting for an explanation—plus, she wasn't quite sure what a manifesto was.

"You will never meet a more honest man than I am. Seriously. I don't play games. I don't lie. I don't make promises I have no intention of keeping. I am up front—brutally so, some might say. If you want to be in my world, then you have to acknowledge this about me because it's who I am."

"Honest. Got it." It was Tarni's turn to smirk.

Logan leveled a droll look in Tarni's direction but continued.

"Now. I have a lifestyle some would consider hedonistic. I see nothing wrong in this as I am upfront about my intentions with someone I date, so if you choose to be with me, you understand this is how I plan on living my life. I have had many women and will continue to have many women. I enjoy them. I'm intrigued by them. I love to experience sex in every shape or form with them, and I have no intention of getting tied down to one. But this doesn't mean I am not loyal, true, and honest. If you are my long-term partner, we can enjoy a fantastic time, each other's company, and the company of others, without any ridiculous notions of propriety, piousness, monogamy, or other trappings of society that looks to restrict you and put a collar on you."

"By you, we are speaking, quite literally of you, right? And I assume this means should I somehow find myself your "long-term partner," Tarni made air quotes as she said this with quite a bit of sarcasm escaping her mouth, "I would be sharing a bed with not only you, but whatever underage playmate you decide to show up with that night? I mean, somehow I don't suppose you expect me to have many male friends I entertain, and they are then invited back to romp wildly with us in the sack."

"Precisely...well, other than the underage thing. I'm not into children, thanks."

Tarni blinked then set her jaw.

"You're a chauvinistic pig."

"Yes."

"Misogynistic, even."

"No. Not really. Misogynists secretly loathe women. I adore them. And I'd put a caveat to chauvinism, as well. You see...I don't think men are superior to women. I think you definitely hold that title in every way. However, I feel I am entitled to live my life with as many experiences as I can gather, and that includes copious amounts of sex with the opposite gender."

"I see. All gorgeous and incredibly simple, I expect."

Logan cocked his head and considered Tarni's words.

"Of course not! Young, old, fat, skinny, hot, slutty, Black, white, purple, green, kinky, or uptight—I want them all."

"You're incorrigible."

"Such lofty words from one so young," Logan scoffed.

"I'm not that young. Certainly not as young as Gloria."

"Who?"

Tarni opened her mouth to lash into Logan but then realized he was teasing her, so she clamped it shut and growled.

"Is there anything else I should know?"

"Much, but we can just skim over a few and go over the basics. I consider myself the master in this little dance and the women are the willing submissives. And don't let that idea fool you. The subs truly have all the power! In this respect, we don't have to fight over the mundane. I pick out your clothing, I decide where we will eat, vacation, live, and who we hang out with. I take your desires into consideration, I'm not a jerk, but if they don't gel with what my plans are for the day, week, or even year, it's not going to happen."

"You have got to be kidding me!"

"Not at all. Love...this is the best time of your life, this moment, these years. You will never again be so young and ready for exploration—so open to new experiences and an education in all the world has to offer you. All that you are capable of becoming. You will grow to be a strong, independent women who can run circles around the whining, dependent housewives who expect their spouses to break their backs providing, only to shut the doors to paradise every time they get in a snit, leaving their husbands confused, angry, and little in the way of companionship."

Logan paused to reflect on his words, then shuddered in distaste.

"In a few years...closer than you realize, it will all be over, and life will get in the way of adventure. Why not share it with someone like me who can give you everything you desire?"

"Share it with you until you become bored and drop me for the next great lay."

"People always grow apart, love. But think of how wonderful it will be until that happens. And it is mutual...you might become bored with me. Then we part friends with no ill will toward each other, and a fond memory to look back on in our old age."

"And I can have this wonderful life just as long as I obey you."

"Yes."

Tarni's mouth dropped open. "You sound like my father."

"And this is bad?"

"Who do you think I ran away from?"

Logan suddenly became solemn, and a flash of anger passed across his eyes before he got control of his emotions.

"Did he hurt you?"

Confused by the switch in character, Tarni didn't know how to explain her situation entirely...she certainly couldn't let Logan in on her paranormal life and didn't know what to say to assuage his worries.

"It's not like that. He's an important man, powerful, full of himself, dangerous, lives by his rules, is a tyrant and uses his daughters for his own purposes and ignores them as lesser beings who he has to put up with but without having any real love for. He wanted sons. He has eleven daughters that I know of. He keeps us on a leash. He expects us to serve him and uses us to reach his goals. He goes through women like underwear. He wants us to be chaste, obedient slaves he can barter off for power positions and business deals."

"What is he then? A politician? Mafia? Power broker...what?"

Tarni thought it prudent to use something Logan could wrap his head around. "You could say something along the lines of the mob...but different."

"But you can't tell me." It was a statement, not a question, but Tarni shook her head no, anyway.

"I'm nothing like him, Tarni. I want you to experience life and enjoy it to the fullest. I want you to break free from the shackles of society...live how *you* want. Be who you were born to be. Become strong and self-assured."

"While catering to your every whim, I suppose."

"But of course! I'm the teacher...you are the pupil."

CHAPTER 12

Tarni, present day

You wouldn't be surprised to hear I handed the big jerk his walking papers soon after that comment. I even threw the half-and-half and cream cheese out the door where they splattered on his jacket and all over the rug.

It wasn't that I was upset by his proposal. He did say we needed to establish ground rules, and I was letting him know being with me came with certain expectations of intense outbursts and playful banter—sometimes in equal measure. You might have me call you 'Master,' big boy, but I still had teeth. Plus, I wanted him to fight harder for me—and to see if he would.

We didn't see each other for a week. I'd changed my locks, still not sure how he managed to nab a key, changed my phone number, which caused me no amount of stress because it meant quickly getting my new number to my sister so we could continue our contact. I even considered asking for another apartment in the complex, but didn't have the energy or inclination to leave mine.

I liked the corner unit. I enjoyed watching the car headlights as they left the 405 and took the ramp onto I-10. I even liked that funky-looking tree outside my balcony and didn't want to let a puffed up peacock of a man dictate where I should or should not live.

The nerve of him!

Oh, he was honest all right. He set down his ground rules and made it perfectly clear that he thought he should be in control of properly teaching me about life. The damnedest thing was, I was intrigued enough that I found myself thinking about what he offered for days...and nights. It was all I could think of. That, and my sudden and irrational attraction to onion bagels.

I didn't forget who I was and what my end goal entailed. But part of me wondered if I needed Logan's type of education to harden me, create a woman who couldn't be broken by anything, who experienced so much in such a short amount of time that when I was prepared to take on my father's empire and bring it crashing down around him, I'd be a force to be reckoned with—as Logan promised.

After all...this was 1987...very much a man's world still, and I had a lot to learn.

Oh, I wasn't naïve or stupid enough to believe his narrative. This man might be honest in his intentions, but there was more to him than he was prepared to share with any one person, and I suddenly decided I needed to know what made him the way he was. He and his onion bagel be damned! How many layers all tightly held up to protect him from exposure would I need to go through to find out what made the man tick? I wanted to find out. Even if it killed me. Which it wouldn't. Not much anyway.

Oh sure. I can see what you are thinking. I fell for the bad boy, the ne'er-do-well, a cad—charismatic and narcissistic and any and all labels today's world would assign to such a man acting as he did back then. But there were also multiple, fundamentally intriguing layers to Logan MacDuff, and I wanted to peel them away, one by one and discover the truth. What made him the man, and what had happened to the boy to create this unbelievable pomposity of character.

That, and how many men could switch from caring, gentle, fixer of all things broken and damaged like that little bird...how many could be so carefree and open, impulsive, impossible, arrogant, and impervious to everything going on around him, living so in his world as to believe I'd fall in line without question and agree to his terms?

I wanted to throttle him and bed him in equal measure.

What I chose instead was to push him to his limits and see just how far he'd dance with me before I gave in.

Because let's face it. I was heading for capitulation and we both knew it. But I had some ground rules myself—and Logan MacDuff would either be up to the challenge or leave in exasperation, showing I wasn't worth the wait...or the chase.

And I intended to go for the long haul.

"Monique, I'm serious. I've never had sex and I don't want to come across as a stiff, insecure and what's worse, boring lover."

I don't know why I'd confided to my neighbors who were fast becoming friends, but I had this irrational fear of failure when the time came for me to have sex with Logan. "Justine, what about you? If I'm a virgin still, will I be boring in bed?"

"Honey...not that I have much experience with guys, but I think it's not the same for them as it is for us. You could lay there asleep and as long as your hoo-ha is open for business it will be fine."

"Well, *I've* had experience shagging men...why do you think I'm a lesbian?" This from Stacey who rolled her eyes at my discomfort. "I fell asleep once while Chad and I were doing it. Remember Chad, Monique? That idiot kept going at it like a jackrabbit and came all over me. That's when I woke up only to find it was all over and he was now the snoring one. Seriously...you are worrying about nothing!"

"Chad is gay," said Monique with a sniff.

"I know that. *He* didn't know it at the time...nor wanted to admit it to himself. That's why I was facedown, ass to the air, so he could get it up and keep it there. I guess from behind I look like a boy," said Stacey.

"You look like a boy from the front as well," remarked Monique with a deep chuckle.

I'd spent my time working at the club and investigating my father's holdings to the best of my ability, being so far from Florida and in the age right before technology took hold. It wasn't as easy back then as it is today to open Google and do a search. Some finesse and luck and plenty of time and *money* went in to investigating someone—the money I was making. How to go about hiring someone to delve into my father's affairs was another matter.

In the meantime, I began investing in stocks, thanks to Parker who just happened to be a broker, and a great one at that. I watched as my bank account totals climbed, and I diversified and invested with abandon.

With my end goal on the back burner for a time, all my focus was on the issue of Logan and my lack of carnal knowledge for all the big talk I gave. My 20th birthday was two weeks away, and I found myself sulking and thinking I needed a trial run with someone else, so I didn't make a fool of myself with the man I intended to romance.

Call me what you will, but I wanted Logan MacDuff to

take my virginity, and not some random guy. I mistakenly confided this to the lesbian trio, much to their amusement, and found myself paying for it in droves.

"You are such a prude. It's adorable really! I mean, it's 1987 Tarni...women have been liberated—or are getting close to pushing back against the patriarchy and getting what they deserve. If you want sex...go for it." This from Justine who was a bit more militant than her roommates. Justine was a no-nonsense, buzz cut, military brat. That she was one of the most incredibly beautiful women I'd ever laid my eyes on, despite her being a twin to the likes of Sinead O'Connor with peach fuzz and sad eyes to boot had me gobsmacked.

She even had her tongue pierced, something that was only seen in the punk or underground scene in the 80s, and not as widespread as it is today. And tattoos dominated her petite form, wrapping up her neck and causing heads to turn wherever she went. None of it phased this firecracker, and I admired her resolve and self-possession. Justine was the real rock star back then.

I remember waffling in indecision and embarrassment, agonizing over letting the women into my thoughts and deepest fears. "It's just that...part of me wants to save myself for Logan and only Logan. The other part of me doesn't see this as a big deal...but I want to be good at it. How can I be good at it when I've never done it?"

"Oh my God, you are too cute for words." Stacey cried.

"Yeah, she's a real peach," drawled Justine.

"So, sex with men is out then. But I have the answer," said Monique with a wicked grin.

Turning to face Monique once more, I felt a tingle of premonition on what she was about to impart and sat there pensive, waiting for her to continue.

"We can teach you all you need to know about sex. After

all, if you have sex with us, it's different from having sex with a man. So, you'd still be a man sex virgin for Logan but won't be a stiff board in bed. And honey? Not for anything, but if you are doing this for the first time, you might as well be with someone who has the same equipment and knows what *they're* doing!"

That's how I found myself considering the intriguing world of lesbian sex—under the very capable ministrations of Justine, Monique, and Stacey, my own personal Fates—of the sexual kind.

I didn't know what to do and decided making any rash decisions so soon after revealing my vulnerabilities to the trio might not be a good idea. So I thanked my friends but put them off for the time being and made a hard pass turning left...

Directly into my next problem.

CHAPTER 13

Tarni, March 1987

"We should go out, have a drink or something sometime."

The man speaking to Tarni was a new hire and someone she found attractive enough to consider his words, then gently reject.

"I'm too busy right now, Todd. I'm flattered but..."

"You are taking this too seriously. It's just drinks. It's not a lifetime commitment. Plus, you told me you had a thing for musicians, and I'm a musician."

"I thought you were a waiter."

Todd laughed and wagged his finger under Tarni's nose. "You know I'm in a band. I'm a drummer. Hey! You should come see us play this weekend. We are going to be at The Whiskey tomorrow."

The Whiskey-A-Go-Go was a big deal, and Tarni was impressed. So many bands started at the legendary establishment and went on to great things.

"Maybe I will. But right now, my car is at the repair shop. I got a flat this morning and they found a few more issues with it.

Mike had to come rescue me. I'm not sure if I will have it back in time. But if it is, I just might."

"Great! Now, about that drink. If you aren't a drinking girl, how about we go to Canter's Deli tonight after work, just friends getting to know one another and share a meal?"

Tarni was charmed by Todd's dimples and shaggy dark mullet, brooding, chocolate eyes that seemed to have a sparkle beneath the surface, and broad shoulders. What could it hurt? It wasn't like she had to commit to anything, and dinner sounded fun. She was off her game because not only had her car wound up with a flat tire, but she'd also found a note on it that sent chills down her spine and made her distracted and fearful.

Upon opening the note, Tarni discovered it was written in all capital letters and read, "I know what you did. I'm watching."

Who or what sent it? And did it mean someone knew about what happened in Amarillo? Or was it something else? She must have been well and truly rattled for even giving Todd an inch.

"OK. Dinner and that's it, right?"

"Right!"

Todd was beaming at her then glanced up and frowned, his demeanor going from pleasant to perturbed in a matter of seconds. Tarni didn't have to turn around to know what had distracted Todd, making him surly and agitated. She could feel Logan behind her even before he opened his mouth to speak.

"No, it's not alright. Tarni is having dinner with me."

Groaning inside, Tarni turned slightly, tilting her head up toward Logan while peering at him through her bangs.

"I'm sorry, but I don't think you have any say in with whom I choose to have dinner."

"Oh, but I think I do. And it's supper. He's offering you

informal deli food. I'm taking you to Spago. That is a proper dinner."

Tarni gulped. Spago was very exclusive. Chef Wolfgang Puck's bistro that catered to the celebrity set was a hot spot and anyone and everyone of importance wanted to dine there. She'd driven past the 1920's style home in West Hollywood that housed the restaurant and longed to be able to eat there. Not that Canter's was anything to sniff at...she adored the deli.

"Um..."

"I'm sorry, but the lady is with me, and we're going on a date tonight."

Todd stood and squared his shoulders at Logan in a display of some kind of male dominance Tarni knew meant a fight was brewing. Not wanting to cause a commotion in her workplace, she quickly jumped up, placing herself between the men.

"Logan, I'm sorry, but I promised Todd we'd have dinner tonight. Why are you even here?"

"I told you why I'm here. We are going to dinner tonight."

"Listen, you jerk. Tarni is with me. You can just turn around and leave before I toss you out on your ass." Todd did have those broad shoulders while Logan had a slimmer build, but Tarni knew looks could be deceiving.

Logan smirked but that was the only acknowledgment he imparted on Todd, turning instead to address Tarni. "I spoke with Marcus. You have the rest of the night off...let's go."

"I... what? You can't just make decisions for me and go behind my back!"

"Yet, I did."

"Hey! Did you hear me? Tarni is..."

"Not going anywhere with you. So, buzz off like a good little worker bee."

He did not just say that!

Tarni flinched and knew she was in over her head when she saw Todd tighten his knuckles.

"Stop it. Now, Logan. Todd and I are an item. We're going out. Dating. So, you can just scram."

Logan became deathly still. Seriously. He looked like a statue carved of marble or wood. A full minute went by before he flicked his gaze over to Tarni. Then he turned on a dime and walked out of the club, taking all the air with him. Or so it seemed to Tarni, who was trembling.

Great. Now Todd is beaming at me like he won the prize...and in a way he did!

Tarni lamented her brash words and wondered if it were too late to retract them. "Look, about what I said. I was just trying to get rid of that guy. We are strictly going out as friends, Todd. OK?"

"Oh, sure! Sure! I get it. I still liked hearing the words, however. And who knows? We just might be dating before long...so...tonight? Since you are free and I get off in an hour, let's meet up out back and we'll go in my car since yours is out of commission. I can even drive you home later."

Tarni nodded yes, distracted but accepting of her commitment but not without regret.

How do you like this guy? He disappears for over a week, no communication after feeding me breakfast, and now he shows up expecting me to go to Spago!

If she was being honest with herself, Tarni had been the one to toss him out of her apartment, chucking food items at his head, and informing Logan he was never to show up at her place again. So...

Yeah.

Sometimes playing games had a downside. What did she expect Logan to do, pine outside her door so she'd let him back into her apartment? She didn't want that! So she can't be too upset he'd disappeared for a while.

An hour and a half later, Tarni was sitting in the passenger seat of a pink 1955 Cadillac Eldorado Biarritz. She spent fifteen of them singing the song in her head, but decided it looked a bit garish in that color and she would have chosen another. Still, a fun, classic ride for the evening. Apparently, it was Todd's pride and joy, and he went on and on about it.

Halfway through their highly animated dinner—animated in the way Todd talked nonstop about himself and his life plans —Tarni's thoughts began to wander toward Logan and what he might be thinking about now. Was he at Spago having dinner alone? Did he ask someone else to go with him? And the idea he might be with someone else certainly pissed her off. While she kept a bland yet interested smile on her face for Todd's benefit, her inner turmoil was dialed to frenetic.

Why should I care what Logan thinks or does? Because you do...that's why!

A soft sigh relaxed her shoulders, and she made a concerted effort to listen to Todd's unwavering dedication to all things Todd, pushing thoughts of Logan aside.

Until her mind wandered back to Spago and what she might have feasted on instead of the matzo ball soup and a Monte Cristo sandwich—both divine, but her curiosity was piqued. She was on her third old fashioned cocktail and suspected Todd of trying to get her tipsy. It took an ungodly amount of alcohol to make Tarni get plastered...she seriously debated her ability to drink most grown men under the table knowing she'd win every time. She also wracked her brains trying to figure out who might have left her that note. It was unsettling and yet made her determined to confront whoever was threatening her and take him out—or her.

"So that's the plan for the next ten years or so. I think we will hit big next year...or even later this year since we are working on a new album. Plus, with the exposure at The Whiskey? Yeah...big things are coming for my band."

Tarni murmured some innocuous agreement and continued to smile.

"Here. Let me order you another drink."

Seven drinks later, Tarni was feeling the aftereffects and with the top down and Todd speeding through the side streets on the way to her apartment, she let her guard down. For any other woman, it wouldn't be an issue, but for Tarni, letting her guard down meant she started singing. Not loudly, but in a fun singsong way about that pink Cadillac. But that was enough to glamour Todd and Tarni didn't realize she'd done it until they arrived at her apartment. But it wasn't a normal glamour, not even a bit.

"You can leave me off out front. Here is fine as a matter of fact."

"No. I insist on walking you to your door. It's the gentlemanly thing to do."

"Um...OK." Tarni felt a twinge of irritation knowing Todd probably wanted to see if she'd let him in for a nightcap...or more. But also knew she could handle herself in that type of situation. "Park there, and we can walk up."

"No way! I leave this baby out on the street and it will be stripped before I come back down. Give me the gate code and I can park in your spot since your car isn't there right now."

Not having a good argument to the contrary, Tarni gave Todd her code and he drove into the underground garage and pulled into number 300. They got out and strolled over to the elevator, but before she could press the button, Todd grabbed her and dragged her to one side in the small, dark hallway that led to the janitor supply closet. He began kissing her, hands roaming as he pressed her up against the wall.

Tarni wasn't alarmed, per se, nor was she interested, but didn't fight him off or push at his chest, figuring that maybe he'd be happy with a quick feel and kiss. She realized too late she'd sung and hoped letting him paw on her for a few minutes would satisfy him—she knew how intense hearing her voice could be on a human male.

Maybe he will leave now.

Todd had no intention of leaving. He ran his hands up under her top and fondled her breasts the entire time he ground his pelvis into her crotch. Did he think it would turn her on? All it was doing was ticking Tarni off. But still, she waited.

Pulling away from her finally, Todd grinned down with a self-assured smirk like he'd already went far past second base and home plate was in sight. "Come on...let's go upstairs."

"No. That's not going to happen. This is fine here, Todd. I can go up and you can leave. Thanks for..."

The slap came out of nowhere and rattled Tarni's brain since she hadn't seen it coming nor had time to prepare for it.

"I said, 'Let's go upstairs.' "

Tarni was calling up her magic, preparing to slam something dark and powerful into Todd.

But then his fangs punched out.

Oh my God! He's a vampire!

For the first time in her life, Tarni well and truly panicked. She knew they existed, and she had cousins who associated with some, but those were the friendly kind. Many were not so, and Todd, showing his fangs, could only mean he either knew she was paranormal, or didn't intend to leave her alive after he had sex with her...or whatever he planned on doing.

"I'm not going to tell you again. Let's go upstairs, witch."

So, he knew. He could tell.

How does he know? How did recognize what I am?

Tarni entered the elevator in front of Todd, hoping something would come to her in the way of self-defense. She knew she had to remain cool and collected—not set Todd off nor appear that she was planning on an attack of some kind. A witch is powerful—a siren, even more so—but a vampire? She'd never tested her powers on one—dark witch *or* siren. She noted he'd not mentioned anything about a siren, so perhaps something about being one meant that part of her makeup would remain undetected.

When they reached her apartment, she hoped someone, anyone, would be out and about, but then scratched that idea. The last thing she wanted was one of her innocent neighbors to fall prey to a vampire whose intent was violence. She could feel it. While she wasn't quite certain of her fate, Tarni knew a battle of survival might be upon her. Todd snatched her purse, taking half her jacket off in the process, then unlocked the door. She could hear the soft "ping" as her wards shattered when Todd crossed her threshold. Well, at least she knew they worked.

Once inside her apartment, he locked them in and glanced around before tossing her purse and jacket on the sofa. Tarni left the curtain partition open that separated the living area from the bedroom and watched as his eyes tracked over to it. No lights were turned on...assuming a vampire didn't need light to see. Tarni's own eyes could penetrate through the darkest of rooms, so she remained motionless.

"Come here."

Tarni came to stand in front of Todd, and he grabbed her face and began to kiss her again, hungrily and painfully, his fangs still extended. Grabbing her hair, he pulled her toward the bed, throwing her down on the rumpled sheets then covered her body with his. Somehow his pants were already unzipped and slipping lower, and he reached his hands to lift her skirt.

"You're not very wet."

Todd backhanded her again even as his other hand pushed her panties to one side.

"Kiss me some more." Tarni tried to sound eager in anticipation which caused Todd no end to his swagger and his self-assurance she would submit. Tarni tried not to panic when she felt his fingers probing and stayed pliant and open. "Let me touch it," she instead asked.

Todd adjusted himself to accommodate her request, and that was all Tarni needed. Once her hand was wrapped firmly around his member, she let loose a stream of dark magic that would have dropped an elephant. Todd should have gone down, but instead he rose straight up in the air like he'd been launched by a rocket and slammed into her dresser, shattering the mirror. She didn't have enough time to indulge in the satisfaction of having disabled a vampire.

Another figure moved like lightning, and Tarni had to smother a scream as Logan came into view. Where did he come from?! "No, Logan. Watch out. He's...he..."

Not knowing what to say, Tarni paused only to watch in astonishment as Logan lifted the vampire with one hand, dragging him over to the patio doors which he slid open violently, and to the balcony where he flipped him over the railing and left him dangling.

Todd, dazed and barely coherent, the pain probably dulling his wits, finally focused and gurgled in alarm, as the cool night air brought him up and out of the fog. His pants threatened to drop to the pavement below since they were pooled down by his ankles.

"Argh! Put me down!"

"My pleasure. But before I do, don't ever let me see you

within one hundred feet of Tarni ever again. Do I make myself clear?"

Logan didn't wait for an answer and released his hold on Todd who plunged thirty or so feet to the pavement below. It wasn't enough to kill a vampire, but it had to sting.

"My car. It's in the parking garage," he murmured, pain evident in his voice as he hitched his pants back into place.

"It will be returned to the club. I suggest you walk home...or turn yourself into a bat and fly away. Scram. Now."

Todd looked like he would argue, but only for a moment before reconsidering his options. "What are you anyway?" he asked instead.

"You're worst nightmare."

CHAPTER 14

"How long were you in here watching?" asked Tarni.

Logan didn't respond right away. Instead, he walked to the front door and made sure it was locked, not that a normal lock could keep out a vampire. Then he approached the bed and sat staring at Tarni with unreadable eyes.

"The entire time."

"Why didn't you make yourself known right away?"

"I didn't know if you invited him up and wanted it. But then I saw you struggle to push him away."

Tarni knew then that Logan had no idea she'd zapped magic into Todd, and surmised Logan had hit him with whatever power he has at exactly the same moment, causing him to think he'd done the entire attack on Todd by himself. Did he know she was a witch? A siren? She was afraid to ask, so instead she deflected to him.

"What are you?"

Logan didn't respond. He didn't even look like he was conflicted and wanted to. Instead, he repeated the question that was weighing on his mind.

"Did you want him?"

Despite her toughness, despite her inner strength and tenacity and all the weeks then months of being on her own and surviving, Logan's words struck her at her most vulnerable...and Tarni began to sob. Deep, heart-wrenching, guttural sobs that prompted Logan into action.

Lifting her into his arms, Logan carried Tarni into the bathroom and stripped her of all clothing while turning on the shower. He then stripped himself and after adjusting the temperature to slightly less than scalding, he placed Tarni directly under the spray and began to wash her body.

Gently, oh so gently, did he wash her breasts where Todd had so roughly run his hands, all the way down to her privates where he took extra care not to invade her in any way, yet still making her understand he intended to wash every possible trace of her assailant down the drain and out of her life.

Then Logan washed her hair until it squeaked.

Turning off the water, Logan stepped out of the shower and quickly toweled himself off, wrapping the towel around his hips when done. Opening the linen closet, he grabbed a fresh towel for Tarni and wrapped her up then carried her back into the bedroom. Flicking the switch that would turn on the fireplace, Logan sat in front of it with Tarni nestled in his lap, still sniffling.

"I've got you, Baby. I won't let him ever touch you again."

"But he's...there was something wrong with him..."

Not wanting to come out and give voice to her knowledge that Todd was a vampire, not knowing if Logan had superhuman strength but was just that—human—Tarni did not want to reveal the paranormal. If Logan wouldn't tell her what he was, she would keep her cards close as well.

"Don't worry about that asshole. He's history."

"Until I have to show up to work and he's there," sighed Tarni.

"Baby. I promise you; he won't be there. I'm going to take care of everything."

Looking down at Tarni, Logan brushed her wet hair from her upturned face, and when she parted her mouth slightly he gently kissed her. Barely touching his lips to hers.

"Stay with me tonight, Logan? Please?"

Leaving the fireplace on low, Logan scooped Tarni up into his arms and carried her to the bed, but instead of placing her on it, he frowned. Then he set her on her feet and went back into the bathroom.

Before she could wonder what he was up to, Logan returned carrying new bedding. She had two sets, the blue one on the bed and a crisp white set she'd picked up on sale. Logan violently ripped the top and fitted sheet off the bed and flung them into the small hall space between her bathroom entry and her walk-in closet. Then he made the bed and placed Tarni on one side as he did the same for the pillowcases. Another short trip into the bathroom revealed he had also discovered her down patchwork quilt which he draped across the bed, then climbed in to join her after dropping his towel onto the floor.

Tarni couldn't help but stare at his nude state until he slipped under the sheet, tucking it and the quilt around them. Tarni, shy now, but cold despite the fire, snuggled up to Logan, placing her head in the crook of his arm near his heart. He held her close and for what had to have been a few minutes all was silent.

But then Logan began to sing. Croon, really, a soft, sad refrain that Tarni instantly recognized as "She Cries Softly," Logan's hit song.

Of the men in her life
None compared to him
Now he's gone to the sea
Will he come back home again?

Silent tears how she cries
Soft is her lament
Will the stars show her lies?
Is this the beginning of the end?

She cries softly...
To the sea
She cries softly...
Will he return to me?

She cries softly
As the ocean replies
And offers her no lies
"It's not to be..."

"Forget your love, he belongs to the sea"
"Forget your love...he's gone...he remains with me."
"He belongs, forever to the sea."

Logan stopped singing and Tarni remained quiet with a sob lodged in her throat. The lyrics affected her mood but at the same time, his voice soothed her in ways she didn't know could happen. His voice! It was incredible. On MTV she'd heard it, of course, but here in person, the impact of it was truly amazing. No wonder they were climbing the charts!

"You didn't save me, you know," Tarni mumbled into

Logan's shoulder. She decided she couldn't lie to Logan and wanted him to know she had strength.

"I know. I saw your flash of magic."

"It's just that...he's...what? You saw me?"

"Yes, Baby."

Tarni waited to see if Logan would say anything further. When he didn't, she continued.

"Todd is strong because...I mean, I'm strong too, it's just that I don't know if I can take on a..."

Tarni trailed off not wanting to say "vampire."

"There are some strange beings that walk this Earth, Tarni Vanderzee. You can't fight them all by yourself. Perhaps you can allow me to help you from time to time."

Pushing herself up to gaze at his downturned face, Tarni reached out her hand and placed it on his face...then kissed Logan as softly as he had kissed her moments before. Then, exhausted, she curled back up against him and drifted off to sleep even as it registered with her brain that as Logan sang, she could feel magic swirling around the room.

Something to ponder in the morning.

For now? Oblivion.

Tarni awoke to the smell of bacon. Truly one of the only things that could get her up early in the morning besides a hot cup of java. She sat up sniffing, eyes closed, and grinned. Flinging the bedding to one side, Tarni was halfway up and out of bed before she remembered she was utterly naked.

Shrieking a little at the cold as the air slammed into her shivering form, she sidestepped the living area and dashed into her closet even as she heard the telltale sign of Logan chuckling at her from the kitchen.

Pulling on a bra and panties from her new stash, Tarni then slipped an Aerosmith sweatshirt over her head and pulled on some leggings. Heading to the bathroom next, Tarni sighed when she spied the mess of tangles her hair had become due to sleeping with it wet. She knew running a brush through it would do nothing, so she dampened her bangs and blew them out with her hairdryer then swept the rest up in a high ponytail using a scrunchie to secure it.

I look like a total dork.

A bit of eyeliner, a touch of blush, mascara, and barely there shadow was all Tarni could manage before her stomach began to protest since all her senses were on high bacon alert. It would have to do, because just then Logan called out to her.

"Either get in here now, or I'm eating it all."

"You wouldn't dare!" Tarni strutted into the room ready for some playful banter, but instead stopped short in shock and dismay. Logan remained completely and totally naked, and what's more, he was holding the plate of bacon in one hand and her mug of coffee in the other.

Mouth open and eyes looking anywhere but at his nether region, Tarni began to sputter, so Logan did what any logical person would do, he popped a crisp piece of bacon into her mouth and told her to chew. Once she did, he set her mug down on the table with the bacon, grabbed another piece and fed it to her. Once Tarni was done chewing that one, Logan pulled her into his arms and thoroughly kissed her senseless.

The man did not play fair!

"Good morning."

"Yeah."

"No?"

"Uh, no, yeah...it's good."

"You are such a conversationalist first thing, aren't you?"

Tarni scowled and grabbed another piece of bacon, side-stepping Logan and taking a seat. This was a big mistake because it put her at more of an eye level to his, *ahem*.

"Do you plan on staying like that?"

"What? You mean like this? Naked?"

"Well, yeah. I mean...perhaps you should put some clothing on."

"You don't like me naked? Damn. You're making him upset."

Tarni peered up at a grinning Logan and cocked an eyebrow.

"Him?"

Logan pointed at his penis and made a sad face.

"Oh. Well, I'm sure he'll get over it."

"You've hurt his feelings. Of course, you *can* make it all better by kissing him to make up for your callousness."

"What?!"

"Kiss and make up."

"I'm not...how can you? What is wrong with you? Are you always...so...gah!"

Laughing outright now, Logan turned and headed to the bedroom area to don his clothing, Tarni averting her eyes refusing to track his naked progression. Logan then returned to the kitchenette and took his seat.

"Well, I know one thing. You are definitely not a party girl."

Tarni slammed her hands down onto the table and leaned toward a snickering Logan MacDuff.

"I've already told you I like to party. You can just stop your stupid, dumb, goading ways. I party. I party all the time!"

Throwing his head back, Logan laughed until tears formed in the corners of his eyes, and he began wiping them away.

"Oh sure. Yes. Party girl. Right. Uh, Eddie Murphy called...he wants his song back!"

"Very funny. You're a laugh riot."

"Ha!" Logan barked another chortle out of his mouth and proceeded to eat his breakfast, shoulders quivering with glee.

"I mean it."

Logan just nodded and stuffed a forkful of pancakes—the man made a giant plate of them—into his mouth and shook his head, obviously not believing her.

"Goddamnit, Logan. I mean it."

"Then prove it." Slamming *his* hand down on the table with enough force to rattle the table settings, Logan became deathly serious and contemplated Tarni for a long minute.

"I can't. I don't know what a party girl means in your world."

"Do you want to be in my world, Tarni Vanderzee?"

"I..." Tarni paused, considering Logan's words and all they probably could mean. She came to Los Angeles with a goal in mind. Nothing could persuade her to alter those plans. But perhaps she could be with Logan, take what he had to offer her, enjoy life for a while, before the noose of responsibility and the looming confrontation with her family came crashing down to ruin what could be one hell of a romance.

"Yes."

"Then forget trying to be a stupid party girl. Hollywood is full of them. Don't even think you'd need to lower yourself to be like the throng of women who constantly debase themselves to be with me. I need a warrior. Can you be strong for me?"

Perplexed by his words, but mesmerized by the tantalizing glint in Logan's eyes, Tarni could only nod yes this time.

"Yeah? My rules? No bullshit parameters from you?"

Again, Tarni nodded. "Can I think on it and give you my answer tomorrow?"

"Yes. Well, before I take you on as a charity case, you are going to have to prove to me you are up to the challenge. Like I said, I need a warrior...and right now? I see a butterfly."

Oh really? Tarni thought, her ire sparking at the smirk Logan just lobbed in her direction.

Picking up her pancake slathered with butter and syrup, Tarni forcefully smushed it into Logan's grinning face, pushing his head back in the process. Then she drank her coffee.

Welp. This was going to get interesting in a hurry.

CHAPTER 15

Tarni, present day

I'd like to say I had agreed and Logan started my tutelage right then and there. But it was not to be. I had to go back to work, and he had three days of contract negotiations with the band. We made plans to meet on Sunday, and he'd informed me there would be a test. He didn't realize yet that I always aced my tests. And his was one I would excel at.

I'd let him think he frazzled me.

A test! I mean, come on!

I had no idea, not a clue, of how wrong I was on the matter.

I didn't understand then the private hell he was going through which would have changed my opinion of him. Nor did I know I had to toughen up in a hurry for what was to come. When you are going through life, one tends to ignore the signs and remain focused on what is *believed* to be important, when in reality, it isn't. Not really.

I had three days to stew and smolder and I found myself counting the seconds until we could be together again.

I'd promised myself I'd hunker down at work—a place

devoid of any trace of Todd which had me wondering—and keep making serious bank. Marcus came through as promised and gave me a raise with shorter hours, so I was only on Wednesdays through Saturday but making triple what I made before. Plus, I made equal pay to Michael. He congratulated me on staying on the boss's good side.

"Marcus Dimitri isn't known for such generosity. You did good kid!"

Indeed.

With so much free time, I found myself returning to something I'd put off for the time being. Despite my protests to the contrary, I did find myself sequestered across the hall from my apartment on Wednesday afternoon before work surrounded by Justine, Monique, and Stacey...and a bevy of sex toys.

"You need a drink. You are so tense!"

"Can you blame me? I never once in my entire life considered having sex with another woman! And you three are staring at me like I'm a juicy hamburger. I'm freaking out."

"This will be educational."

This from Monique who had been sucking on a giant dildo and grinning at me wickedly.

I don't know why I thought the lesbian trio would be a good idea. I mean, why would three women into women want to give me lessons on how to please a man? Again, what was I thinking?

Justine took pity on me. "Look...we asked Heather to join us so you're not the only freshie in the room."

"Freshie?" I gulped.

"Fresh meat," snickered Monique. I swear she sounded like a witch cackling in front of a huge cauldron. "You're the one meeting Logan this Sunday. He's going to dive into those panties, so you need to be ready."

Heather came in then looking as nervous as I felt. She

signed up for this impromptu "class" because she thought it might help her career as an actress. I wanted to point out the only work she'd ever get to use these new talents in was the kind where the director yelled, "action," and everyone began having an orgy.

"OK. Who's first?" Stacey stood up and disrobed, revealing a weird contraption around her waist with a giant black dildo standing at attention, making her look like a slim, hairless man with stellar tits.

"Holy Jehoshaphat!"

Heather backed up in alarm and I followed suit.

"Maybe I'm making a mistake. Logan told me he didn't want a party girl. He wants a warrior. Of course, I'm not sure what he means by that yet."

Sighing loudly, Monique popped open a wine cooler and handed one to me, then did the same for Heather. "Here, drink up. It will calm your nerves."

Knowing alcohol really didn't affect me unless I overindulged, I did what Monique ordered and sat back down and took a sip. That's when the show began.

I don't know what I expected...but I sure didn't think I'd become so aroused watching my three neighbors get it on, sparing Heather and me from having to take part in the decadence. While they were going at it, I nabbed another five wine coolers and downed them waiting to see if they'd have any effect. Within minutes, I began to relax and enjoy myself, and even participate a bit.

I, Tarni Vanderzee, kissed a girl. And I liked it. Way before Madonna did on live TV with a shocked Britney Spears and certainly decades before Katy Perry sang about it.

But that's not all I did. My three lesbian friends cajoled and enticed me, and I decided to go "there" to places I felt belonged firmly in the "not my circus, not my monkey," wheelhouse.

Heather did not feel the same, although she did allow Stacey to go down on her. After watching Heather moan and squirm in pleasure, I allowed Monique to do the same to me...just to understand what to expect from a man, mind you. Monique informed me that if a man couldn't compete with what she laid on me...he wasn't worth keeping.

Let's just say my eyes were opened that day and move on.

Or not.

OK, fine. I was hours into my lesson and fully embracing my newfound moves all the while wide-eyed at how good it felt to have a plastic, rubber dildo thrusting in and out of me while sucking on Monique's tongue.

There. Happy?

Did I mention that at the exact moment I reached my own sublime ecstasy, Logan MacDuff entered the apartment and smiled down at us?

"And what have we here? Girl time? Can I join in?"

To say I shrieked and flew straight up and away from the melee, as if distancing myself would expunge any wrongdoing on my part, was obvious. That it was equally laughable as far as everyone, with the exception of a starstruck Heather was concerned, was just as obvious.

"Get out! Why are you...how did you...why do you keep doing this to me?"

"I'm not doing anything to you...yet. Mmm...you have a great set of tits, love." This, Logan addressed to Justine who giggled. Giggled! A hardened lesbian, man-hating, card-carrying, no real dicks allowed kind of woman—giggled!

I stared at her, mouth agape, palm out and pointing to Logan and made a "mrphf" sound that she blew off.

"What? He's adorable. I might give him a ride just to show him what he's missing."

I don't know if it was the alcohol or my fraught nerves or

the fact that Logan showed up when he did, but I started laughing and couldn't stop for quite some time. Thankfully, that broke up the party and I scampered back to my apartment with Logan who explained why he'd shown up ahead of schedule.

~

Tarni was back at work the next night and decided that while she was no longer pissed off at Logan, she didn't appreciate his meddling in her affairs.

And why was she pissed at Logan?

He was the reason Todd was gone. Logan explained he'd chased him clear across the state but never managed to nab him. The warning worked, obviously, but Logan should have told her he would seek out the vampire and confront him.

What if he were injured because of her? Could Logan even take on a vampire? And if he could, just what kind of paranormal was Logan MacDuff? Oh, come on! He had to be *something* more than human! After explaining he'd spent time hunting Todd, Logan informed her he had supervisors he answered to, and they had reprimanded him for his act of chivalry.

But he wouldn't say more on the subject.

Logan refused to explain further, stating he couldn't, and asked her to try and understand that he wasn't holding things back from her intentionally. She'd tried pressing him further, but nothing she did would entice Logan to open up.

It was getting irksome to say the least.

Who were these handlers? And what did all of this mean? Tarni intended to find out.

Slamming shot glasses down on the counter, Tarni poured Jameson's whiskeys for a group of newcomers to Barney's and

Los Angeles. They were cute, hometown boy types on vacation and planned on seeing the sights and getting up to all manner of hijinks. Trust fund babies, all of them, at least they were polite and kept it to a dull roar. Tarni didn't think she could tolerate jerks this evening.

"I've got table five, why don't you take your break?" Michael swiped a credit card, putting the receipt in the cashbox after the customer signed the slip. "You've been going nonstop since you got here."

"Fine. Hey...Mike. What ever happened to Todd?" Tarni wanted to know what the story was around the bar.

"Don't know. Apparently he gave notice and is working somewhere down near San Diego. At least that's the rumor going around. Why?"

"No reason. Just curious."

Tarni wondered at that. A vampire choosing to leave rather than remove a person standing in the way of something he wanted was bizarre...if her knowledge of vampires, such as it was, could be trusted. Would her glamour wear off?

She'd taken to wearing all manner of weaponry on her person. Her mother had trained her since she was a child in the art of a well-placed knife to the ribs, or a pencil-thin spike to the throat...but she knew she'd feel better if Todd had left the area permanently.

Logan said he couldn't find any trace of Todd in his search. Did that mean the vampire chose to skedaddle when confronted by Logan's...what? Obviously the man was strong. Tarni didn't know of anyone who could dangle a full-blooded vampire from a balcony and live to tell about it.

She knew she'd have to get answers from Logan sooner rather than later.

Tarni also knew asking Logan to reveal what he was meant she'd have to confide in him as well.

Running a hand through her long locks, Tarni let it tumble down as she removed her scrunchie, sighing as it eased the headache that was trying to take hold. Deciding to head outside for a smoke, she pushed open the back door and sat down on the top step, lighting up. That's when she felt a hand on her collar and found herself being hauled up to a standing position and dragged back against the rough stucco of the club's exterior wall.

"Miss me much, bitch?"

OK, so think of the devil and he turns up it seems.

Tarni tried to remain calm but knew she was in trouble. Big trouble. It wasn't because she was female and weaker than a man...magic tended to equal that out in the paranormal world, but she didn't know *any* Breed that could best a vampire.

Except Logan.

Tarni didn't fool herself into thinking she'd be strong enough to fight him off. Especially since the first thing Todd did was tie some kind of rope around her wrists and hook her onto a spike that used to hold a shutter in place, making her effectively powerless, unable to use her dark witch magic on him.

Her siren magic was another matter, and she considered her options. Could she do it? Was a siren stronger than a vampire? She decided to bide her time and see what he intended before she played that card. After all, Todd thought she was a witch only...otherwise he'd have said something that night. Right?

Tarni hoped this was the case...because then she'd have the upper hand.

She needn't have worried, however, because just as before, her hero came flashing in, in the form of one exceedingly agitated Logan MacDuff. Leather jacket oiled and gleaming, now shrugged off and discarded on the ground with hands ready to dole out some more hurt to a shocked Todd. The vampire snarled and turned away from Tarni to face Logan with his fangs already exposed.

Logan picked the lid up off a nearby trash can and tossed it, not at Todd's head like Tarni assumed, but at the hood of his expensive pink Cadillac where it left a big dent.

"You are going to pay for that."

"No, I believe *you* are going to pay for *that*." Nodding to Tarni's tied wrists and prone, dangling state, Logan squared off and prepared to mete out some justice. Only Tarni had no idea what Logan would employ facing off against the highly agitated vampire.

"Stop it, Logan. You don't need to fight for me."

He cocked an eyebrow at her then over to her tethered wrist like, "yeah, right." Then he brought his attention back to Todd who wasn't posturing this time...he meant business. Tarni determined the glamour must have worn off, so vampires, while initially affected by her siren magic, could recover. She briefly wondered whether this would be the case had she given him the full force of it. Perhaps vampires aren't all that.

Logan flexed his hands and regarded his adversary who had moved closer. What happened next left Tarni under no illusions that vampires were an easy target. Where Todd once stood, dressed all in black from head to toe was empty space, and he somehow flashed over to where Tarni was imprisoned. Like quicksilver, Todd moved with incredible speed and agility. Grabbing her throat, he made to bite Tarni's neck, but then flashed away as Logan appeared behind him.

Spinning to see where Todd had moved, Logan reached up to free Tarni from the bolt only to take the full force of Todd's fists as he super quick punched Logan's exposed side.

Logan went down in a heap while pools of blood appeared on his white T-shirt. That's when Tarni noticed the daggers poking out of Todd's closed fist. And she screamed.

This time Todd went down.

Clamping her mouth shut, Tarni realized too late she'd used her siren voice.

It reverberated around the alley and dogs began to howl in the distance. Tarni felt her eyes go black and her dark witch powers click on. Wind kicked up around her as she began to pulse with power and threw her head back once more to scream into the night.

Todd's body twitched on the ground.

So did Logan's.

Michael chose that moment to walk outside with a cigarette dangling and a look of worry on his face having overheard the commotion, but not in the direct path of her vocal output. He didn't see Tarni hanging beside the door, so he slammed it into her.

That brought her out of her dark mood and her magic fizzled out with a pop.

"Ow. Damn it, Mike. That hurt."

"What the? Tarni...what happened? Who are these guys? How did you...*what* did you do? My God! What happened to your eyes?"

Rolling her eyes and gritting her teeth, Tarni barked out an order. "Not now, Mike. Just get me down from here, quick."

But it was too late. Todd had recovered and loomed up behind the unsuspecting man who had just lifted Tarni off the stake and loosened the rope.

Damn these vampires and their ability to heal so quickly!

Todd grasped the bartender from behind, easily bending his back and would have snapped it in half had Tarni not reacted.

Once more she called up her dark witch magic which came flooding out of her hands in an electric blue arc.

Reaching up for the stake, she used her power to easily free it, pulling it from the wall, and in one fluid movement plunged it into Todd's chest, with a determined look on her face...just as Logan reached up and did something with his hands turning Todd into a charred and smoking mess.

Todd's scream was cut off as paralysis set in. Toppling over even as he released Mike, he went down one last time. This time, even Tarni blacked out.

CHAPTER 16

"We have to stop meeting like this."

After watching Logan drag Todd over to a green Jeep Wagoneer with wooden side panels and hoist him up into the back seat, Tarni quickly whispered in Michael's ear with just enough siren magic to have him convinced he came out for a smoke, tripped, fell, and now needed to head back inside and relax in the break room.

"It has its moments though," replied Logan.

"Indeed."

Tarni was only out for a few seconds. She still wasn't used to letting her dark magic out when using her siren voice. When the two opposing forces combined, she often felt herself going down a dark tunnel to oblivion. Blacking out was not something she entertained, and she needed to do some research on how to stop the phenomenon.

Eyeing each other warily, Tarni decided to be the first to ask the obvious question.

"What are you?"

"What are you?" Logan responded.

"OK, we've quickly established we are both stubborn and have some unique qualities, but I did ask first."

Logan turned and went back to his vehicle—at least Tarni assumed it was his. There was barely any bleeding left although Logan's shirt was torn, which made Tarni suspect he had healing capabilities. Plus, he wasn't showing any signs that her siren voice had glamoured him, other than rendering him useless when she'd screamed. He certainly wasn't her dewy-eyed thrall.

"Hey! Wait. Where are you going?"

Turning back to face her, Logan jerked his thumb in the direction of the back seat. "I need to deal with that first, then I'm going home to get some sleep. It's been a long couple of days."

"About that. Do you plan on continuing your hero act? Or have you gotten it out of your system? I keep trying to fight my own battles and there you are—albeit missing a white horse." Tarni crossed her arms over her chest and waited to see what Logan would say. But then the first part of his words registered, and she glanced at the back seat. "Wait. What are you going to do with him?"

"Figure out a way to stop him from hurting you."

Logan's words chilled her to the bone, and Tarni instinctively gripped his arm, stopping him from getting in the Jeep.

"You can't!"

Logan's response was to cock his eyebrow at her once more.

"I mean. What are you? Really. Obviously you know what Todd is...or, *do* you know what Todd is?"

Logan's cheek twitched and he continued his emotionless scan of her face before sighing loudly. "He's a vampire."

Tarni's shoulders relaxed, knowing that, whatever Logan was, he was assuredly of the Breed. A paranormal, like her. Before he could ask again, she blurted out, "I'm a witch."

Smiling slightly, Logan whispered, "Are you now?"

Nodding yes, she raised her eyebrows in expectation of his response telling her what Breed he might be. When Logan didn't offer any further explanation, Tarni frowned.

"How nice for you."

"Logan MacDuff, are you going to tell me what Breed you are? Or do I have to keep asking until you do?"

"No and you can try."

"But...but that's not fair! I just told you what I am! Someone polite would do the same in return!"

"There's your mistake right there. Believing I am polite. Furthermore, you lied." Logan glanced at Tarni and she realized with some shock he appeared angry with her.

Sputtering, Tarni drew back and let loose a barrage of curses.

"I do not lie, you insufferable bastard. I told you my Breed. Did you do the polite thing and return the favor? No! And now I'm being accused of being a liar?! And where is that attitude coming from?"

"Black."

The fire went out of Tarni, and she scratched her head in confusion.

"What?"

"Horse. Black. I'd come riding in on a black horse, not white."

"Well, bully for you!"

"Not a bull. Horse."

"Ha, ha."

"None of this would have happened had you just agreed to let me train you. But no. I get food smashed in my face and attitude."

"Will you tell me what Breed you are if I agree to your terms?" Tarni watched as Logan chewed this over in his mind.

"No."

"And here I was going to inform you I already planned on obeying your every command!"

"Prove it, and I might consider giving you a hint. Now excuse me, please, I have things that need doing."

Logan yanked open the Jeep's door and climbed in. Tarni remained gawping on the pavement, incredulous that he would refuse to let her in on his Breed then start in with his inane drivel. Horses!

Fuming, she ran around to the passenger side and clambered in just as Logan peeled out up the alley and onto the side street heading north—it was all Tarni could do to close the door in time. She didn't know why Logan was in such a foul mood—with her, anyway—and ground her teeth in frustration.

"Care to tell me why you're pissed?"

"I don't like loose ends."

"Pardon? I mean, I'm sorry, but I don't think I follow."

"Your boyfriend back there. He's a loose end, and a dangerous one. I need to put him somewhere."

"Logan, why don't you just kill him?"

Tarni didn't know if it was the lackadaisical way she'd just suggested Logan bump off Todd or that he was mad at her for coming along for the ride, but he quickly pulled over to the curb, cut the engine, and faced her.

"So, just kill a man. Is that what you're saying?"

"He's not a man, Logan. He's a vampire—and a renegade one at that since he tried to attack me, or hadn't you noticed his teeth marks on my neck?"

Logan's quick movement caused Tarni to jerk back, bumping her head against the seat belt assembly. "Ow, watch it."

Logan ignored her protestations and moved the hair from her neck. Staring at the reddish, bruised scrape marks that went from just under her ear to her jugular, Logan growled, then gently ran his hands along the marks. "Now I think I will kill him."

"You can't, but I might be able to."

"Care to make a bet?"

"Well, if I were more informed as to what Breed you are, perhaps, but until you tell me, I'm kind of flying blind here."

Turning the Jeep back on, Logan carefully pulled into traffic and continued to wherever it was he'd decided to take them. He was broody and morose, throwing guarded, dark looks in Tarni's direction so many times she finally just decided her only course of action was to become a pest. A thorn in his side. The proverbial back seat—or in her case—front seat driver.

"So, where are we going?"

"North."

"North, where? To Alaska?"

"Calabasas."

"Bless you."

Tarni watch with some satisfaction as Logan ground his teeth and focused on the road ahead.

"Sorry, but I thought you'd sneezed. What's a Calabasas?"

"It's not a what. It's a where. A town."

"Is it far? Calabasas? You know, I am new to California, so I have no idea if we should be making a pit stop. You know, so I can pee. I might have to pee. Sometimes when I let my magic out, an aftereffect is having to piddle."

Logan did not respond.

Fine.

Her mind began to wander then returned to the paranormal. What could he be? Logan MacDuff. A witch? She would think there would be some way to discover his secret. A werewolf? She'd never met one before, but his longish, curly hair might be an indication of a wolfish interior...although he wasn't a furry man...much. She briefly considered he might be a half-breed, something highly frowned upon in the paranormal world, at least it used to be, although with every year that went by, it seemed things were easing up in that regard. At least among witches.

Then Tarni's heartrate accelerated, and she snuck a few quick glances in Logan's direction. What if, because he knew Todd was a vampire, it meant that he too, was one. Despite the books and movies and all the lore surrounding them in the human world, many misconceptions abound when it came to what vampires looked like and how they acted. How they blended in with society and whether or not they drank blood—they did—could be in the sunlight—the elders definitely could—and a stake to the heart could do them in—not really, it pretty much froze them alive until removed. But that was the extent of her knowledge, and she wouldn't swear on a stack of Bibles she'd gotten the right of it—no pun intended.

Maybe they had a history? Maybe she would be a threat now that she saw what he did to Todd?

Feigning disinterest, Tarni half turned and looked out the window, but carefully and ever so slowly removed one of the tiny silver needle darts she had tucked in its wrist holder. Slowly releasing the tiny dart and positioning it so she had a firm grip, Tarni waited until Logan came to a full stop at a red light. Then much to his surprise and her determination to discover if she'd escaped from one vampire only to be in the company of another, Tarni plunged the dagger-like needle into Logan's upper arm.

"Gah! Damn it all. What the hell is wrong with you, woman?"

Nope. Not a vampire.

"Stop whining. I got the fleshy part of your arm. You'll live."

"But you might not. Why did you stab me?" Pulling the dart out of his arm and glancing in astonishment at it, Logan turned to Tarni and gave her a fierce look. Once again having to pull over and park, this time bleeding and cursing, Logan turned off the engine for a second time and waited for a response.

"I wanted to make sure you weren't a vampire as well."

"Do I look like a vampire?"

"Well. No. But...does Todd? Really?"

"Of course, he does! He is very tall. He is all angular with sunken eyes. He has ridiculously white teeth and his eyes shimmer if you look directly at them, which you'd have noticed if you were a properly-trained witch. I can only assume you are not."

Belatedly, Tarni recalled that deep sparkle in Todd's eyes, and cringed.

"Are *you* a witch?"

"And here we go again." Sighing and running his hand along his neck, Logan glanced down at his blood-soaked shoulder and laughed. Tarni took this as a good sign.

"I'm many things and nothing. And you'd do well to remember that."

Oh, well fine. Be that way.

"Oh, I will remember that. And you will do well to remember I do not appreciate being called a liar."

"Then you probably should have added you are a dark witch...I felt that magic, tasted it. That wasn't coming from any typical witch."

Tarni didn't know how to respond because Logan wasn't wrong.

"Plus, I saw your eyes change, Baby. You are a dark witch."

One of the telltale signs a witch is dark is her eyes turning black when calling up the dark side of the arcane.

Sighing Tarni nodded yes. "I am."

Logan paused long enough to let his eyes wander over Tarni's face and she knew he expected her to say more.

When she wasn't forthcoming, he put the car in drive and continued up the road without another word.

Tarni couldn't just leave it, so she started in again, trying to discover where they were heading.

"So, what's in Calabasas, anyway?" she asked.

"My band."

Wandering in the hills above the Santa Monica Mountains after exiting the 101 Freeway, Tarni and Logan entered the enclave of Hidden Hills, California. Driving down Long Valley Road, Logan slowed down in front of a massive Spanish colonial home with gates keeping just anyone from driving up to the house.

"Whoa. Your bandmates are living large."

"Billy's family is loaded. This is his place, but he lets the other guys crash here."

"Billy?" asked Tarni.

"Our drummer. He started the band."

Tarni watched as Logan entered the gate code and it slid open. Logan pulled up the curving drive past a fountain and came to a stop near an entry portico. Cutting the engine, Logan turned to face her.

"Do me a favor and wait in the car, OK?"

Tarni made her eyes turn into slits and pouted. "You don't want them to see me."

It was a statement, not a question.

"I don't want them to see the vamp back there and hit us

with a ton of questions. I just need a few items, and I will be right back."

Not waiting for a reply, Logan exited the vehicle and rushed into the house, leaving Tarni sulking in the front seat. After twenty or so minutes, and she considering laying on the horn just to cause him more strife, Logan reappeared with a fresh shirt on, and a bundle in his arms which he placed into the cargo area of the Jeep. Then they backtracked out of the driveway and turned onto Long Valley Road again, continuing to what appeared to be open desert, or a high plains area. It was fairly dark, but Tarni could see the emptiness ahead by the headlights' illumination.

"This is Lasky Mesa. It is a preserve in the canyon here. Las Virgenes Canyon."

"Las Virgenes...The Virgins? Seriously? You have quite a sense of humor."

"The road turns to paved gravel then some turnoffs are dirt. Heck, some of them look like stagecoach trails but this vehicle will get us anywhere. I know of a pretty remote area in one of the valleys, and that's where we unload good, old Todd."

The stars seemed brighter up here, which was amazing since they were still, technically, in Los Angeles, but they seemed more vibrant at this elevation. They went on for a bit longer in silence until Logan made a final left turn on what he most accurately described as a wagon trail. It looked to Tarni like no modern vehicle had every gone this way, and she wondered how much further they would continue.

About five minutes later, she had her answer when Logan came to a stop. "This is good, right here."

"What are we going to do with Todd?"

Logan kept his eyes glued to Tarni's and said, "We will bury him alive."

Tarni felt horror for only a split second. To be buried

alive...for eternity. Shuddering, she nodded in agreement but reached out to stop Logan before he could exit the vehicle.

"I only staked him with iron. I need to use silver."

"How many more of those tiny daggers do you have hidden on you, or should I even bother asking?"

"I have enough. I should only need to use two...maybe three."

"I will do it."

Tarni frowned and sat up straight. "Logan MacDuff! That creature tried to rape me. We both know I only dazed him when I, um, grabbed him down there. He would have raped me and then killed me or raped me and drank my blood, making me his thrall. I think I have every right to stake this douchebag and leave the heavy lifting, or in this case, hole-digging duties, to you. Plus, consider this a gift."

"A gift? For what?" Logan asked, looking puzzled.

"For my Birthday. It's my Birthday today and jabbing this evil bastard is all the gift I want."

"It's your..."

"Yes. Only you seem to be getting a present instead of me. I agree to your "terms." Now get out of my way, I have a vampire I need to stab."

Tarni didn't notice the stunned look on Logan's face or the exact moment when her words registered fully, she was too busy with her own thoughts.

What the hell did I just agree to?

CHAPTER 17

A few hours later, a very dusty and dirty Logan and Tarni wound up back at the Hidden Hills mansion of drummer Billy. Dawn hit the horizon just as Logan put the last shovelful of dirt on the makeshift grave and they left Todd behind for good. Tarni was punchy and starving. Here it was, her 20th Birthday morning and she looked like something the cat threw up. She had mud smudged across her face and her knees were sooty and caked with even more mud, her clothes were ruined, and she'd lost an earring.

Logan looked like he'd been out on a picnic in comparison.

How did he do that? Look so good all the time?

Logan promised her a hot shower and mentioned some clean clothing, but Tarni was nervous about meeting the band members, especially in this condition.

"Trust me. You'll feel better after a shower, some food, and then maybe a nap. I know I could use one. The only band member not here right now is Cash. He's getting in from San Fran later this morning."

The first one to see them come in was the homeowner

himself. Billy Reid looked like a drummer. From his well-muscled arms and torso to his constantly twitching and tapping of his hands on anything and everything, he was like a walking timepiece wound tight.

"Yo."

That was the extent of his greeting when Logan introduced her.

Following Billy into the next room, they found the other two members of the band in various stages of undress consuming what had to be the most expansive breakfast Tarni had ever laid her eyes on.

"Yo, Duffy! Made some huevos rancheros and Deanna squeezed fresh orange juice. Laney made muffins too. You know how much I like Laney's muffins." The man speaking leaned over and grabbed the behind of a statuesque blonde wearing panties and a cut off T-shirt which showed off her lack of a bra. She squealed and tried to run, but Logan's bandmate snagged her and laid her across his lap where he proceeded to spank her bottom.

Logan walked over and patted her behind before addressing the man.

"Dave, this is Tarni. Tarni...Dave. He's our lead guitarist."

"Hi."

"You've got dirt on your nose."

Nice guy. Thanks, Captain Obvious.

Laney wrinkled her nose at Tarni but didn't say hello. The girl Dave had called Deanna walked over to Logan and gave him a kiss. Not a peck on the cheek kind of kiss, but a full on mouth with plenty of tongue kiss, then she sat at the table and ate off Dave's plate, also ignoring Tarni. Deanna was another tall blonde, but hers didn't come out of a bottle, unlike Laney.

"Who's the chick?" This was from the final band member, a tall Viking of a man, long platinum hair hanging in waves down his back with a tightly-shaved slice just above either ear. He looked the part of a rocker and even wore leather pants, although his chest was bare.

"Gunther, this is Tarni. She's a friend. Tarni, Gunther is our bass player."

"No, man, you're *my* singer. I'm *the* bass player!"

Oh brother. Tarni thought. The posturing was ridiculous.

"Not another friend. How many are you up to now man? Two hundred? Three?" Billy came over with a pot of coffee in one hand and two mugs in the other. Tarni hoped one of them was for her. She chose to ignore the friend comment and what she suspected it meant.

Grateful to see Billy plunk the two mugs down on the table in front of them, she nonetheless wanted to freshen up a bit, if just to remove the grime from her face, making herself more presentable. "Um, is there a bathroom I can use?"

"Up the hall. First door on the left."

Tarni made her escape and found the bathroom with little trouble. She grimaced upon seeing her reflection and turned on the faucet. Staring at herself in the mirror, it didn't escape her that she had a haunted look in her eyes and knew, despite her bravado, burying Todd alive was doing things to her psyche. She knew they had little choice. He was a renegade vampire and The Order of Origin, the paranormal CIA if you will, would have put him to death had they captured him. But now she had three men as her body count, and it was disconcerting to say the least.

"Happy Birthday," she whispered to herself in the mirror then washed the grime from her face. Her knees were next, then she tried her best to get her clothing dusted off. When she was marginally satisfied, she came back out of the bathroom and almost ran into another blonde.

What is it around here with all the tall blondes?

"Oops, I'm sorry! I didn't know anyone was in there!"

At least this one was friendly and addressed Tarni instead of ignoring her.

"I'm just leaving. I came with Logan, um, we were out on the mesa."

"I'm Stephanie. Well, that explains the dirt anyway. How do you know Logan?"

"We met in Las Vegas a few months ago and met up recently when I moved here to Los Angeles. You know him from the band?" asked Tarni.

"You could say that," replied Stephanie with a little laugh, "I'm his girlfriend."

Breakfast progressed with Tarni the odd one out as the bandmates caught up on news and the women cleared the table and draped themselves over their men. Stephanie was no exception, now siting firmly in Logan's lap looking like she belonged there. Tarni wanted to stake him and bury him right next to Todd.

There was no mention of their strange appearance or why they were on the mesa. No mention of the mud and dust or the fact Logan had been in and out of their lives for a few weeks. No one questioned her role in his life or acted in the least bit awkward, and it set Tarni's teeth on edge. They certainly didn't mention anything about paranormal beings, so she remained quiet and continued to seethe and observe.

"Well, as much as I'm enjoying this fine morning with you assholes, I need a shower and I'd like a massage." Logan tickled Stephanie and stood. She remained firmly attached to his side. Holding his hand out, he called to Tarni. "Come on. Let's go shower."

Tarni froze in place, not daring to look around to see how this news was received by everyone. When no one as much as blinked, other than Gunther belching, Tarni stood and walked over to Logan with daggers in her eyes.

He didn't bother reacting but grabbed her hand and dragged her after him, with his other arm draped around Stephanie. The three of them followed the long hallway to a back bedroom, and Logan walked over to a bank of windows after closing the door. Stephanie followed and began to undress him.

Tarni made to leave, but Logan snapped his fingers at her. "Stop. Stay right there."

Tarni knew she must have blushed but squared her shoulders, arms crossed, and glared at Logan. Watching Stephanie engaged in her task, something she was obviously used to doing, Tarni let her eyes wander over the semi-naked Logan MacDuff.

"Tarni. Come here."

She should have tossed something at his head, but she did agree to his "training," so now Tarni knew she had to bite the bullet and listen to Logan. Walking slowly over to where he stood, she awaited his next instruction, pissed that her acquiescence had Logan accelerating her lessons. He stood there in his underwear and his dusty shirt, yet somehow looked beyond sexy leaving Tarni mildly disappointed he wasn't completely naked yet.

Well, at least I know what I've gotten myself into now.

"Undress Stephanie."

Tarni locked eyes with Logan and he bit his bottom lip to keep from laughing. She saw more than mirth lurking deep within, she saw a challenge in his eyes. He knew he got her goat up, but she wouldn't let him win. No way. Turning toward Stephanie, Tarni began the humiliating task of removing all the clothing from her body then stood back wondering what would happen next.

"We'll be right back. We'll shower first then you can when we're done. I'll leave some clothing in the bathroom for you."

Tarni seethed and remained rooted to her spot, staring daggers into Logan's back as he sauntered over to the bathroom with Stephanie in tow. Tarni was seething and turned toward the bed, and that's when Logan's filthy shirt landed on her head.

Turning back to the now-closed door Logan and Stephanie had entered, Tarni growled. She could hear the water turn on and giggling then shrieking, as Logan did something to obviously cause Stephanie to go off like that. After ten minutes or so, they came out of the bathroom wrapped in robes, the water still running and they allowed her entry.

Tarni didn't wait long to strip and shower, grumbling as she did so.

That man! He's incorrigible. The nerve. I mean...he has a girlfriend?! All this time, and he has a girlfriend! Do I care that he has a girlfriend? No... I do not.

Much!

Liar!

Tarni stepped out of the shower and toweled herself off discovering a pair of terry shorts and an oversized tee folded on the counter. Dressing quickly, then running a brush she'd found sitting nearby through her damp hair, Tarni sighed, knowing whatever came next would serve her right for agreeing to such treatment from this demon spawn of a man.

Accessing her state of mind, Tarni realized she was curious. What would she find on the other side of the bathroom door? And did she want it whatever it turned out to be?

Oh, you better believe I do.

Taking a speculative step into the bedroom, Tarni came up

short when she discovered Logan standing facing her on the opposite side of the bed. He was in a fresh pair of jeans with his shirt hanging open—but that wasn't the only thing exposed. Stephanie was sprawled on top of the bed; legs wide and working her mouth over Logan's erection which was poking out of his unzipped pants. She was moaning and massaging his butt —her head hanging off the edge.

Does he not ever get fully naked? What is he...shy?

Logan grinned evilly and motioned with one finger for Tarni to join them while Stephanie's loud sucking sounds filled the room.

"Get on the bed."

Doing as he asked, Tarni nevertheless remained well away from where Stephanie was laid out, then watched in half stimulated interest as Logan went down on her.

OK...ask and ye shall receive. Tarni thought to herself and decided then and there she enjoyed the sight of Logan getting pleasured by a woman, but seeing him taste Stephanie was another animal entirely. She found herself longing for him to do the same to her.

Stephanie moaned, and Logan was making it quite evident he'd give Justine, Monique, and Stacey a run for their money. The man had technique...Tarni had to give him that.

Wondering if she'd remain the third wheel and not sure what she'd do if Logan encouraged her to join in—like the lesbians failed to instruct on proper threesome etiquette, Tarni held back from making a move. She wondered if scrambling on Stephanie's face to get a little tongue action was considered impolite—her inner dork smacking her on the noggin again—and causing Tarni to become giddy and stifle a laugh. Rolling her eyes, she wanted to inform Logan she'd had enough of the show. But that's when a load roar resounded throughout the house.

"Where is he? Is he in with Stephanie? Duff! Duffy, you better not be in there or I'm going to kill you!"

Logan detached from Stephanie with a loud pop and look askance at Tarni. "Shit. That's Cash."

"What's he upset about?" Tarni cried, even as a loud pounding and knocking sounded at the bedroom door.

Stephanie sat up, looking mildly alarmed but also rather amused.

"Steph is his girlfriend now. She's actually my ex. But every once in a while I miss the taste of her. Cash told me he'd kill me if he found me with her one more time." Logan said this while scrambling to zip his pants. Reaching out to Tarni, he gripped her hand pulling her toward the patio outside. "Come on...grab the keys, we need to make a run for it. Cash is massive...and mean!"

"Is he another drummer or something?" cried Tarni.

"No. Worse. He's the keyboardist."

Keyboardist?

Tearing through the backyard, around the side and over to their parked car, Tarni wondered if she should let loose her magic in case Cash caught up to them. She could hear his continued roaring somewhere off to the left of the house and knew he was coming quick. Her feet were aching from running on the grounds without shoes.

"Where are the keys? Tarni! Didn't you grab the keys? I asked you to get them before we left the room!"

Keys? Tarni was in a panic at this point and found herself on the driver's side, Logan having dove headfirst through the passenger-side window.

"There you are! You putz! I'm going to mash you into pulp!"

This colossal mountain of a man came charging toward the Jeep and Tarni threw herself in the driver's seat not knowing what she'd do next. He looked like an enraged bull, eyes wide and frightening with veins stretching up his neck—a prominent one throbbing at his temple.

Did he bench press the keyboards or something? Do they weigh a ton? We're both paranormal, why are we running?

"You're dead, man! Dead!"

Reaching through the window on Tarni's side, Cash made to grab a laughing Logan who managed to duck just out of reach. Cash launched himself into the window but then cried out and rolled backwards until he suddenly froze in place.

"Don't you dare touch Logan, or I'll gut you like a pig! Not one more move...do you hear me?"

Cash gulped then winced as Tarni's razor-sharp dagger pierced the flesh of his neck, and he remained as motionless as he could. Logan was laughing hysterically at this point, wiping away tears. He remained mouth open with admiration in his eyes while looking back and forth between Cash and Tarni who was quivering in anger and fear. Not for herself, but that Cash would follow through on his promise and strangle Logan. Despite his abysmal behavior and cavalier attitude toward her, she loved him, and would never let another harm him.

Wait. What?

Logan reached out and gently lowered Tarni's knife hand, then addressed Cash in obvious merriment—and a bit of pride.

"Well, how do you like that, man? Kitten's got teeth!"

CHAPTER 18

Tarni, present day

Yes. I said love. No, I wasn't under the influence of anything. My heart knew what it did and despite Logan being a first-rate cad, I knew I loved him. Hey, we each have our cross to bear. Mine was obviously falling in love with a depraved rock star.

It could be worse.

Knowing I myself am a tad depraved and fully embracing it was probably worse—or not.

But I don't have many regrets when it comes to my youthful indiscretions.

I was so on edge and highly put out by that point, I refused to speak or remain a moment longer at that house, so utterly embarrassed was I. It had nothing to do with Stephanie or Cash or the entire farce. I hated being played and I didn't understand why Logan felt the need to fool me like that. Logan had no choice but to drive me back to my apartment or I was walking. That's what I told him, and he saw I meant every word of it.

Stephanie tried to get me to stay and hang out by the pool

and sun ourselves. She was very nice, really, but I'd had enough of the blondes and their naughty boys in the band. I wanted my bed and to spend the rest of my Birthday lying in a heap while contemplating murder.

Things got even worse upon arrival back at my place. I refused to let Logan follow me upstairs and he drove off in a huff with tires screeching. I'm sure my neighbors loved me by now. I could only imagine what they thought was going on around here.

I didn't want to get into it right then. But I knew I couldn't continue with this wild child-man unless I knew something about him. What could his Breed be and what made him tick? And why did he feel the need to test my loyalty in such a way?!

Cash!

It was all a stupid game to see if I'd protect Logan from attack.

Why was that so important? Wasn't he just a rock star?

He wasn't just a rock star and we both knew it.

My fingertips were crackling with unshed magic, and I knew I needed to gain control of my emotions lest I blast a poor unsuspecting human across the hall and into the garbage chute.

Yes, I was that mad.

When I left the elevator and walked down my hall to my front door, I found a disturbingly large letter taped to it and knew instinctively it was from the same person who'd left the first one

Ripping it off my door, I let myself into my apartment and threw my bag on the table, taking a seat to examine whatever was inside the envelope. What I found sent shivers coursing through my body, filling me with terror.

"I know what you did today," the note said. Accompanying it was a single 8 x 10 photograph of Logan and me burying Todd in a hole on the mesa at Las Virgenes Canyon Preserve. It still smelled of the chemicals used to develop it, and I felt my stomach lurch.

My phone rang, and I knew Logan was down at the corner phone booth ready with an apology.

"Just come back here," I said into the receiver and hung up quickly.

The unmistakable sound of Logan's motorcycle returning once more reached my ears even as I tucked the offending envelope on the shelf of my linen closet.

I'd worry about it later.

~

Tarni and Logan, 1987

The next day, Tarni found herself on a sailboat, alone with Logan.

They spent most of the night arguing about the Stephanie and Cash situation until, exhausted, Tarni crawled into bed and pointed at the sofa to an exasperated Logan.

That he'd returned holding a box of cupcakes with a package of Birthday candles did little to thaw Tarni and the snit she was in—one even wound up smushed into Logan's face after a lengthy and heated exchange of words. She might have pulled his hair a time or two for good measure.

They'd gone at it for two whole hours and Tarni didn't let up until she explained in no uncertain terms that Logan was never to pull that kind of stunt on her ever again. She'd called him every name in the book until, depleted, she fizzled out at which time he pulled her close and kissed the tip of her nose.

"You are adorable when angered. I find it terribly exciting."

Tarni answered by stomping on Logan's foot, slamming a spark of magic into his chest, then pointing to said sofa and climbing into bed.

Logan wisely didn't put up a fight.

He couldn't. He was smoking a little with his hair standing on end and smelled like a charred marshmallow.

They'd both awakened at relatively the same time, Logan stiff from sleeping on a lumpy couch and Tarni grumpy from tossing and turning all night.

"Do you want a cupcake now?" he asked, looking ready to duck should she continue her tirade, although there was a hint of a smile on his face.

"The one still on the floor? It's kind of mushy."

"No, I licked that off my face while brooding on your sofa. I'd rather you had nibbled it off."

"I won't be licking anything until you stop playing games, Logan MacDuff."

"Noted."

"Why *did* you?"

"Play that particular game? Let's head to Marina del Rey and I will explain."

So that's how Tarni found herself sailing on the Pacific, with dolphins frolicking in the bow wake of the Rustler 36 sailboat, leaving her enchanted yet subdued. The air smelled of everything she longed for but didn't know she needed—salt, wind, sand, the brininess of subtle decay a tantalizing and heady mixture. It relaxed her even though Logan's words brought disquiet.

Logan had informed her of his secondary life—about which he gave very little detail but confirmed that he was, in fact, a paranormal—like she had any doubts. He also stated he wanted to see what she'd do in a dire situation and how she'd handle herself. Not to see if she'd save *his* bacon, but to observe how she'd get herself out of harm's way in self-preservation.

"You're not very safety conscious," he chided.

"You should talk. And furthermore...you should *talk*—speak to me about what all this secrecy is about."

"I need you to believe in me. Trust me. I can't disclose anything to you, Baby."

"It's a lot to ask of someone you barely know," she replied.

"It is. Someday I might be able to share more with you. No... I *will* share my secrets. Maybe not all of them—after all, what fun would that be? I certainly don't want to know all your mysteries!" Logan teased but then turned serious once more. "I know things. I know *of* things, Baby. And there are those who I answer to that forbid me from disclosing what I know."

Tarni considered Logan's words and realized his rock star life might be a cover for what his true occupation might be.

"And you do this willingly—whatever this secret occupation of yours is? No one is threatening you or coercing you?"

Logan smiled ruefully and met her gaze. "It's what I was born to do. But my supervisors forbid me from disclosing...things. But... let's just say, if I could run away and forget my responsibilities, I would."

"Why is that? And why don't you, then? Leave these handlers of yours?"

"Because I found you. And now I have no choice."

What did he mean by that?

"And you won't tell me what you are nor what this secret life of yours entails?"

"Exactly."

Tarni was about to open her mouth and argue further but then Logan rushed to grasp her hands in his.

"Baby... Tarni, I know I have no right to expect you to understand or believe me, but when I tell you I am incapable of letting you in on who and what I am, I know how impossible a situation it is and what I'm asking of you is unfair. But if you want to continue our relationship," Logan held up a hand to forestall Tarni's protestations to the contrary—what they had was hardly a relationship yet—and continued, "you have to give me some semblance of trust and allow me this. I have no choice."

Tarni cocked her head to one side and began gnawing on her lower lip.

"You know I'm going to make your life miserable trying to find out, right?"

"I would expect nothing less of you."

"And I need to believe you, Logan. But I find it difficult when you won't open up and insist on secrecy. I'm trying, but I don't understand why you can't tell me something...anything."

Logan stood up and removed his jacket, then his shirt, turning so his back was to her. Tarni's eyes widened at this impromptu strip show, not quite knowing what to expect.

Then Logan turned and Tarni gasped in shock. Carved deeply into his left shoulder was a deep, ugly scar that looked too fresh to be something he'd suffered a long time ago. She stood, reaching out and gently ran her hand across the wound, wondering if this was his reason for remaining partially clothed yesterday. She then wondered if it would have looked worse the day he'd cooked her breakfast and she steadfastly refused to watch him walking away from her totally nude.

"I don't understand."

Logan shrugged his shirt back on and faced Tarni once more.

"That's what happens when I go against their wishes—my handlers—as you call them."

"Who are they? Point me in their direction and I will show them what happens to brutish thugs who'd do this to you, Logan!" Tarni eyes were on fire and her hands were balled into fists, and Logan thought he'd never seen anything quite so beautiful. His fierce, beautiful warrior. Her eyes even began to turn black as her dark witch fury accelerated.

He felt his heart liquify. The very structure of its walls—atrium, valves, ventricle, arteries—all expanding and contracting as he was filled with love for this beautiful creature, then shattered knowing what he knew...and was forbidden to share with the one person who deserved the truth.

"Steady, love. I play by very dangerous rules, and I am well aware the consequences of my actions. No one did this to me, exactly, it is a mark I suffer when I break certain tenets I swore to uphold. But thank you for caring so."

Tarni remained confused, but Logan forced her to turn from dark thoughts and questions he remained unable to answer back to the happy contemplation of the dolphins who continued to follow the sailboat. Logan ran his hand up and down Tarni's back and she began to let go of her anger and relax. Tarni even allowed a bit of magic to come out and sent it down into the waves where it tickled the dolphins, making them jump with joy.

She just hoped the passing boats wouldn't notice the trail of stars that sparkled in a stream behind each jumping dolphin.

"Is this your sailboat?"

"I'm considering buying her," replied Logan.

"Does she have a name yet?"

Logan stared at her with mysterious eyes and playful gaze as he contemplated her, his mouth slightly open and tongue running along his teeth.

"Not yet. But I have a few names I'm considering."

They spent the rest of the day enjoying a quiet jaunt up the coast toward Malibu then back down where they'd docked on Catalina Island, then had dinner delivered. Tarni didn't know how Logan had managed it, but when they arrived, two men were waiting on shore with bags laden with all manner of goodies.

When Tarni inquired as to why they couldn't just go dine at the restaurant who'd provided the meal, Logan looked at her like she'd sprouted horns.

"You'd have me accosted by hordes of adoring fans, all screeching at decibels which would shatter my eardrums in an instant? Let alone the wreckage they'd do to my poor body?"

"Somehow I think you'd survive—and soak up all that female attention."

"Not really. I like to pick my conquests. Not have them jump me in a rush of misplaced passion. Fans are scary things."

"Unless they look like Stephanie, I presume."

Logan frowned and tilted Tarni's chin up, so she was forced to look into his eyes.

"One of the things that made it difficult for me to walk away from you—even though I know better than to pull you into my life—is your strength. Don't show weakness now by being petty and jealous. It doesn't become you."

"Because you laid it all out on the line the first day we met, right?" Tarni wrinkled her nose and stole a potato off Logan's plate. "And I'm supposed to be obedient and proper, not making waves lest you tire of my surliness?"

"Because we go into this as equals. If you can't handle my lifestyle, then you need to walk away now and rip off the bandage even though it will leave me a shell of a man."

"You are such an ass. You are so full of it. What? You are incapable of walking away from decadence, so you'd make me be the one to have to choose between you and your life or one bereft of your company? What a joke. I don't need you, Logan MacDuff."

"That's a lie, and we both know it. From the moment we locked eyes there was no turning back—at least not for me.

Now we have to see if you can handle what's coming on these stormy seas."

Tarni considered Logan's words and knew they rang true. She'd never in a million years have believed in love at first sight, or soul mates...but something about this man had her reconsidering. Still, she wouldn't let him have the last word.

"If there's a storm coming, Logan, watch out—because I'm the Tempest."

"You're more than that, Tarni Vanderzee."

"Am I? What more could I be, then?"

Logan plucked the fork from Tarni's hand retrieving his stolen potato which he popped into his mouth. Chewing slowly, he hit Tarni with a Cheshire smile and answered her query, shocking her speechless when he did.

"Why, you're a siren, my love."

And just like that, Logan MacDuff got in the last word.

Conflicting emotions coursed through Logan as he rode his motorcycle through the streets of Hollywood later that night after dropping Tarni back at her apartment. He should stop this now and he knew it, trifling with Tarni. But how could he? She was his Muse. She was his Fate.

There was no way he could let her in, allow her to know things about him that, while illuminating and would certainly explain his character, would make what he needed to do virtually impossible. That's why he should walk away now, before things got to the point where leaving her would be unimaginable, painful, and the beginning of his end. Who was he kidding? He was already lost.

Damn his life and damn his responsibilities. All he wanted to do was run away from the world and take her with him. Find a tiny house by the sea and lose himself in her and she in him and the world could fend for itself. Let someone else pick up the mantle.

But he knew there was no one left. He alone had to continue this path to destruction.

Unless, of course, he won.

Why didn't he tell her he knew her father? That he was embroiled in circumstances that already put him in directly conflict with the man and would someday mean one of them would cease to be? How could he tell Tarni it was foretold she be in his life and that he was charged with guarding her? Being her protector at all costs?

Her strength and determination to fight her own battles Logan found incredibly sexy and refreshing. She didn't blink when they both decided to bury Todd alive. She didn't get flustered when faced with eminent danger—she fought like a wildcat, brave and resolute. She didn't hop into bed with him the minute he flicked his finger in her direction—more's the pity. But he enjoyed the chase...and his lifestyle had him relishing this novel long, slow, tortuous dance to the inevitable.

He would have Tarni Vanderzee...and she him. And oh, would it be mind-blowing.

But in the meantime, he would enjoy torturing himself—and Tarni—by biding his time. He wanted her first time to be phenomenal—her first time with a man, anyway. Chuckling to himself at Tarni's romp with her friendly neighbors across the hall, Logan knew his siren would be the death of him.

Then he sobered. He meant that quite literally. Tarni would more than likely be the death of him.

With INXS playing on the radio, their song "What You Need" blaring on the speakers, Logan pushed his Harley harder, going speeds no vehicle should ever dare to flirt with on the winding streets of the Hollywood Hills. Another stupid party with people who wanted something from him, more groupies, more drugs, more shady deals—all because the powers that be needed information and needed Logan to weave his magic and discover who the top players were. Would it never end? He was playing a dangerous game with multiple potential outcomes and no guarantees.

On the human spectrum, he felt the pressure of celebrity and the reaching hands closing in on him, and he shuddered. This upcoming tour would do it...Somber Sea was poised to take the prize and leave no witnesses. He knew it was coming like a dark force that was unstoppable—and with it came fear. How would he keep her safe? His Tarni? How could he when the impossibility of his situation didn't allow him the luxury of letting her fully into his world? How could he warn her she was a pawn in a game of Breed elites who could crush her despite her strength?

The Top 40 station switched to a commercial, and he reached out to lower the volume. Tarni was probably at home right now, steaming mad that he refused to answer her queries. Home. She didn't realize yet that wherever she was in this world, Logan would feel at home as long as he was beside her. She also didn't know that he intended she leave her apartment and move in with him. He needed to keep her close—it was in his very nature to protect—and she was the nucleus in his world.

As for the paranormal? He couldn't allow his resolve to falter. He didn't dare tell her anything. He also couldn't ease up on her. She needed to toughen up and become a fighter, and this fact alone broke Logan's heart. For he would be the one to break her.

He had to.

Because *they* would do so anyway.

CHAPTER 19

Tarni no longer worked at the bar. She gave notice and started a new life with Logan. Somber Sea was going on tour that summer...and he insisted she go with him...and she heartily agreed. The next few months would be theirs to get to know each other better.

After the shocking revelation that he knew that she was a crossbreed, Logan and Tarni talked about the plight of siren women, and he listened to her plans for retribution. She opened up to him and told him about her father, her mother, and what her life was like in depth. That he didn't laugh at her insistence she become powerful and wealthy in order to challenge the status quo, and her very own father, won him points as far as Tarni was concerned.

After two days of heading off to work and not being able to concentrate on anything, mixing drinks and dropping glassware in distraction, Tarni resigned herself to the fact that she didn't want a daily grind, and suggested to Logan that it might be best if she terminated her job early—and not wait until summer. He was only too happy to have her with him without the distraction of her work.

Did she miss making an income? Well, she certainly missed her coworkers, especially Michael, and liked the money end of it, but didn't mind giving up the long hours of drunken customers and constant partying. Not that hanging out with the band would be any different. She knew it would be party central with those guys, and Tarni traded one for the other. As for making an income, the investments Parker told her to put her funds with were paying off in a big way...and her bank account was growing. Who knew investing in stocks could pay so well?

The band wouldn't start touring until the end of June, but Logan wanted time with Tarni in between rehearsals and all the other things that go into planning a world tour, so her days of nine to five, or in her case, eight to three AM were over.

Logan asked her to move in with him, although she kept her apartment, making payments on it without telling him. Tarni made quite a lot of money and could afford to for now. She thought perhaps her stalker would remain behind, convinced she still lived there, especially since her friends agreed to open and close the blinds and occasionally check for mail...or strange notes on her door. She put the lights on a timer and crossed her fingers the ruse would work.

Still Tarni kept the stalker a secret, all the while knowing she should tell Logan, but something held her tongue. She figured he already had a lot on his plate with whatever his real profession was and didn't want to burden him with something she could deal with. So instead of worrying about it, she focused on packing.

It was an easy move. It's not like she had much in the way of stuff. She'd arrived with one suitcase and a box of possessions and that's what she left with. She gave her long-suffering plants to Heather.

"I can't wait for you to see this place. It's the first time I've rented a home of my own." Logan was obviously excited about her moving in, and she could hear the pride in his voice when he described the house. It was in Malibu, up the coast and away from the more congested areas closer to Pacific Palisades and Santa Monica.

"How long have you had it?" she asked.

"I put a long-term lease on it the day after I discovered you were here in California." Logan glanced at her with hooded eyes, and Tarni felt a slight thrill go down her body making her stomach do flip-flops.

They still hadn't had sex. Logan seemed in no hurry and it frustrated Tarni to no end. Should she jump his bones? She certainly wanted to...but if he wanted to wait, she wouldn't be the first one to whine about it. She decided to play a deadly game of "dick tease" instead.

That will show him.

What they were doing instead was fighting. But not with words. Logan decided she needed to up her combat abilities. He wanted to instruct her on how to be an even deadlier combatant...lessons to start immediately. She still had reservations on where this was all leading, but she had to admit, staying with Logan gave her some sense of security so rattled was she over this new threat of whomever pulled Logan's strings...in addition to her ninja stalker.

How else was she to think of this unknown person who seemed to be able to follow her every move with ease? Tarni began to question her reticence to inform Logan of what she found in that envelope, but instead of telling all, she readily gave in when he asked her to move in. If he thought it odd she didn't put up a fight, he never let on and seemed giddy with the prospect of setting up house together.

"How close to the ocean is it?"

Logan gave her his trademark lopsided smile. "You'll just have to wait and see."

Back to the nonexistent sex, Tarni wondered if she'd have her own room or...or what? She knew the inevitable was coming. After that romantic cupcake moment with Logan the night of her Birthday, to make up for his tomfoolery, she'd confided she always hoped her first time would be something to remember fondly. Not the groping, rushed fumbling of some boy, taking it from her and leaving her wondering why she bothered. Nor some idiotic ritual on her wedding night with a man drunk from the reception and a night partying with his friends where she'd lie awake staring at the ceiling with disappointment. She wanted romance with a capitol R.

At first she thought Logan would laugh at her, scoffing at her Harlequin Romance novel ideas of what it should be like. But he didn't. He just picked up her hand, turning her palm over and kissed it, saying not a word, but let her continue painting the setting. Roses, music...she even wanted it to be raining outside, her preferred weather. And the last thing she'd mentioned was being able to hear the ocean waves crashing from the bedroom, her attachment to the sea so profound she felt it a necessary part of her becoming a woman.

Now Tarni wondered if she were foolish to have voiced such a private thing to this man who had probably bedded hundreds of women, and probably lost his virginity as an afterthought. No big deal—deed done. Let's move on to the next. But somehow she thought he might not be as jaded as he appeared.

The car slowed down and Tarni strained to see where they were. They'd been driving up the PCH, the Pacific Coast

Highway, for a half an hour and she was growing impatient. Logan turned left off the highway and into a little enclave of beach style homes, and Tarni gasped.

The ocean!

Not that they hadn't been following it all this time, and she had gazed at it longingly, but once they entered the gated section of the homes, she realized there were only three streets with rows of houses on them and expected they'd have some sort of view of the Pacific from some of their rooms.

Imagine her delight when Logan pulled into a home situated at the end of the street, a tall, three-story, blue, modern California beach house with balconies and a tile roof...directly on the ocean. The beach was their backyard!

Squealing with glee, Tarni barely waited for the Jeep to come to a stop before she jumped out, shoes flying, and raced around the side and onto the sand beyond. She kept going straight into the surf, and only then did she turn and watch an indulgent Logan MacDuff following behind.

"Logan! This is incredible."

"I found it by accident, my agent wanted me to see a house up in the canyon, but the minute I saw this place I had to have it."

Tarni shook her head and continued cavorting around the surf. The water was cold but exhilarating and she couldn't believe this was where she would be living. "How far does the tide bring the surf in?" she asked.

Logan pointed to a spot under the raised deck and Tarni's eyes opened in wonder. The waterline went well under the deck and almost touched the house! It would be like sleeping on top of the ocean when that tide came in.

"I love it."

"I hoped you would." Logan held out his hand and together

they went back around and into the front door of her new "home." And what a home it was!

The entry opened to a stone wall which had a water element spilling down into a channel of some sort that must allow it to recirculate back up to the top where it started its downward journey once more. You could choose to go to the right or left, both leading into the sunken living room that faced the sea. On one side was a kitchen and dining area and on the other a library alcove with a baby grand piano. The stairs led to a master suite with an expansive bathroom, his and hers, joining to a common bathing area. The closets were massive, and there was another balcony. Back downstairs were two more bedrooms, a full bath, and a half bath, and a locked door.

"What's in there?"

"Just some stuff. Did you see the backyard?"

There's a backyard? "But I thought we faced the ocean?" Realizing the entrance was actually the side of the house, Tarni let Logan walk her to the front, which he called the backyard, and it indeed was—being completely closed in with an inground pool and a tidy lawn with plenty of chaise lounges. There was even a small bar area and a grill.

"This is Heaven."

"It is now with you here. Why don't you go for a swim in the pool, and I will get dinner going?"

Tarni squealed with delight once more then sobered. "I don't have my swimsuit handy."

"We could go through your things and find it," Logan offered.

Tarni got a playful look on her face and mock sighed. "Well, I could always skinny dip."

And with that, Tarni did a slow, tantalizing striptease in the living room, starting with her shorts, then top, popping off her bra, then sliding her panties down, ever so slowly until kicking them away then sashaying out to the pool, a deep, throaty chuckle trailing behind her.

"She's going to kill me," moaned Logan as he turned toward the kitchen. "But I willingly go to my death as long as Tarni is the executioner!"

Dinner that night was grilled fish and a salad. Logan did the honors, and they shared a bottle of chardonnay...his favorite.

Tarni was pleasantly surprised with how well Logan could cook. Her fish was expertly made to flaky perfection—not to mention delicious.

Noting the candles had burned dangerously low and were about to go out, Tarni swirled her hand using her witch magic and they came alive once more.

Logan's mouth twitched, but he failed to comment on her small display of power.

"Do you know there is a hairy man on the hill behind us who can see down to the pool area? He watched me swimming around naked and waved in appreciation when I got out, dried off, and came inside."

"He's Greek."

Like that was an explanation for his behavior.

"You want me to rough him up for you?" Logan put down his fork and smiled at the still damp woman wearing one of his T-shirts like a dress. That she was completely naked underneath did not escape him.

He swallowed, raising his eyes to her face once more.

"No, he seems like your average friendly pervert. I'm not sure if he was wearing any clothes, however, I could only see him from the chest up—and he didn't have a shirt on. The shrubbery concealed his lower half. Maybe he can teach me how to make spanakopita. I love that stuff."

"No man is going to teach you anything but me—especially half naked, hairy ones."

"Is that an order?"

"It's a... request."

"Sounds like a warning to me, mister man. I don't do well with orders."

"So I'm learning."

Later, while sitting by the fire, Tarni thought her life couldn't get more perfect. But then her thoughts went to Kimberly, alone and hoping for the day Tarni would come to free her. And her stalker worries put a damper on any thoughts of peace and tranquility.

"What happened just now, Baby? Your face just got sad."

Logan reached out and brushed a tendril of hair from Tarni's cheek, tucking it behind one ear.

"I was just thinking about my sister Kimberly. About getting so rich and powerful I can take on my father and end his stranglehold on the women in my family. He's a tyrant."

"I promise we will deal with him someday soon. As a matter of fact, I have some people gathering information on him."

Tarni sat up abruptly, eyes wide.

"Logan! My father is not someone to be trifled with. He's dangerous!"

Logan fixed Tarni with an intense look. "So am I, Baby."

His words sent a little thrill down her spine, and she trailed her eyes down to his mouth wanting desperately to kiss him but refusing to be so wanton in light of his indifference. Two can play at this chaste game.

Instead, Tarni stretched, knowing her breasts would look full and perfect under the T-shirt material, and the chill in the air had her nipples straining, hard and taunting.

"I wonder at that. If you are that dangerous."

Going for an over-the-top attempt at coquettish, Tarni glanced ruefully at Logan and whispered. "I also wonder which room is mine. I think I'd like to turn in now."

Logan gave Tarni a long, calculated look then smiled gently. "Your room is with me, Baby. Let's go to bed."

OK then.

Sleep didn't come easy for Tarni. Curled up next to Logan, he was the perfect gentleman. It was like having a hot, gay roommate...and it drove Tarni mad. She was a tingling mess. So she did what any siren in her right mind would do to cool off.

To say the ocean water was frigid would be an understatement. But it didn't bother Tarni. She ran into the surf after leaving her sleepshirt discarded on the shore. Naked, she embraced the sea only as a siren could and made long powerful strokes out as far as she dared, until the shoreline looked like a row of toy houses was placed on it.

The moon was bright and gave off enough light that she could see clear down the coast to Santa Monica and the pier.

The ocean smelled amazing.

Logan informed her before he drifted off that they'd be doing a combination of martial arts and police self-defense. He didn't give it a name, but she predicted her muscles would be sore. In the long run, they'd tone, and she'd be even deadlier than she felt she already was.

Her mind wandered to Logan and what Breed he could possibly be—it was driving her mental. His reticence intrigued her, but she also knew she had no right to query him, not when he'd so informed her of his reasons not to share it and had shown her the results of his disobedience. One of the unspoken rules in their world was live and let live lest you poke into someone's private affairs, and they zap you to kingdom come. Or suck the blood out of you. Or howl at the moon then attack. You get the picture. Whoever they were, these people that controlled Logan, they must be formidable.

After a spell, her thoughts turned to the more basic, and she pictured Logan pulling her into his arms and kissing her passionately.

Yeah, and the chilled Pacific Ocean was doing nothing for how hot she felt. If only Logan was here to put her out of her misery and kiss her already—arms slipping around her, pulling her close, her head tipped back onto his shoulder and lips parted with...

"Argh!"

"Hi."

"What are you doing out here. Aren't you cold?"

Logan arched his eyebrow and didn't say a word. They both were treading water and faced each other.

"I mean. *I'm p*erfectly fine. I wanted to cool off. I didn't *need* to, mind you." she stammered.

Logan smiled. A wicked gleam reflected back at her as the moonlight danced in his eyes.

"Do you still need to cool off?"

Tarni stared at Logan then dropped her eyes to his mouth. "I just said I didn't. I...no, I need this."

Wrapping her arms around Logan's neck, Tarni pressed her lips to his and they sunk below the surface in a passionate kiss, all tongue, and teeth and...

Shocked that she'd dragged him under had her kicking to the surface even as Logan held her crushed to his torso. The salty water that she'd swallowed made her sputter and Logan chuckle.

"I'm sorry! I guess I just went down, and you came with me."

"I'll always come with you, my pet, just say the word...and you can go down on me any time."

CHAPTER 20

The next morning, Tarni crept out of bed and made it to the bathroom without waking Logan. Damn him for expertly teasing and not following up with any suggestions. If this kept up, she'd have to plan a time to go visit Monique, Justine and Stacey.

Tarni entered her bathroom reveling in the luxury of having a his and hers and loving that she needn't share the toilet with Logan. Having never lived with a man before, she found that end of things rather embarrassing and was grateful that she'd not have to worry about it in this house.

After using the facility and freshening up, she did a quick gargle then skipped back into the bedroom and crawled into the warmth of the bed once more, snuggling up against Logan, who remained snoring softly.

Frustrated that he hadn't touched her other than to hold her close or suggest any sexual activity after the double entendre from the previous evening, Tarni wondered at what mischief he was playing. He obviously expected them to get to that point sooner rather than later, so it did cross her mind that he must have given her a pass for her first night in, and tonight would be different. Especially after the kiss they shared under the stars during her impromptu swim.

He had to be planning on romancing her tonight.

Right?

"My God, woman, your feet are like ice cubes. I'm sure that dip last night didn't help any."

"Oh! Hi. Morning. Yeah...they are always cold, even in summer. But I can warm them up by sticking them here."

"Gah! You are going to pay for that!"

They spent the next few minutes tussling and tickling each other until Tarni found herself lying across Logan's chest, her breasts against him, their noses inches from touching. Fluttering her eyelids, she leaned down and kissed his mouth. Then she scrunched her face up.

"You have stinky breath."

"That's not all that's stinky about me."

Tarni giggled some more as Logan continued tickling her, squirming with every touch of his fingertips until he suddenly went motionless.

"Baby, stop."

"What? Do I weight too much or something?"

"Or something. Just...just stop."

"What is it? Tell me?"

"Baby...if you won't stop rubbing yourself all over me like that, I won't be able to control myself. You have no idea what you're doing to me."

"I think I have some idea." And it was quite a big one at that.

The tense yet enticing mood was broken by the telephone which began to ring.

"Saved by the bell."

Logan snorted out a short laugh then groaned. "I'm going to go take a cold shower. Ignore that."

"It didn't seem to help any last night. I think I'll make us breakfast."

"You cook?"

"Oh, I can cook, mister. Just you wait."

Tarni made crunchy eggs, slightly burned toast, and strong coffee, just as she liked it. Logan looked at his plate in dismay. "What did you do to these eggs?" he asked.

"What? They are perfectly cooked over medium, just as I like them. The centers are even gel-like. Not runny but not hard. Just perfect."

"OK, but why are they brown on the edges and crunchy?"

"Crunchy eggs are the only way to have them!"

Logan wrinkled his face in disgust and uncertainty and poked the hapless egg around his plate. "I like them scrambled."

"You'll live."

"Not after eating this mess."

The days and nights went on like this in a semblance of non-wedded bliss. Tarni discovered Logan's love of the morning comics, especially on Sundays, and they both enjoyed watching Looney Tunes on Saturdays. They were both avid readers, only their tastes were vastly different—Tarni preferring the latest Danielle Steele while Logan, scoffing, reread Siddhartha or caught up on some Nietzsche. Tarni just rolled her eyes at his choices.

They ran on the beach at night well after any other residents might be out and about, and Lorcan taught her all the tricks he knew about martial arts. She was an adept pupil, having already had some training under her mother. She showed him her skills with knives, and he showed her how to disarm an opponent.

She wasn't quite sure why they were doing what they were doing, but Tarni went with it without complaint.

They would go shopping in Malibu, Logan's adoring fans nowhere in sight, the exclusive community giving him the privacy he craved and the freedom to do mundane everyday chores, like food shopping. They enjoyed seafood from Neptune's Net or the Reel Inn, wandered around the farmers market and strolled along the beach at night. Occasionally they'd hit Gladstone's for a clambake...or breakfast on the beach at Paradise Cove. They'd usually end their evenings watching the sun sink into the Pacific Ocean, then go snuggle in bed.

Tarni opened up even more to Logan and admitted she might be considered a renegade witch. He took the news in stride, and they spoke of the society they lived in, the paranormal world and the human one, and how they sometimes crossed over.

He told her of the dangers she might face and his reasons for wanting her to become tougher, bolder, deadly—a force to be reckoned with and someone who could turn off her emotions so they couldn't be used against her.

Logan kept her updated on his success finding dirt on her father and how this information could be used as a weapon against him when the time came. She filed it away in the house safe and compared it to information she'd managed to glean in her own investigations.

With the intensity of his instruction so blatantly obvious, Tarni asked Logan if he thought some kind of major rift was coming in their world. Change for the better—or worse. And how, in recent years, old ideals had gone by the wayside, and they'd slowly progressed past certain prejudices and taboos. If Tarni thought this might get Logan to open up about what Breed he was, she remained sorely disappointed.

"Things are changing. The Order of Origin has the Biodag

policing the Breed. The witch world has backed off their dark practices, most vampires are taking willing hosts and not attacking hapless victims, demons are being kept in check and so many various Breed are coming to terms that humans are not fodder in this world to be used and abused."

Logan sighed and glanced at Tarni, even while they continued to spar. "There is a price to pay for our magic usage. There is always a price. It's doubled when our powers are used against humankind. Don't ever forget this. Every single time you use magic, there is a small price to pay. You become slightly tired or irritated without realizing it. Sometimes in battle you can become so weak an opponent can overtake you. This is why you should always use it with caution and only when absolutely necessary—and fight with weapons, instead."

Tarni felt a trickle of worry. Had she not taken out two men —albeit filthy curs who'd deserved the destruction she wrought? Would she pay a price for doing so? She never felt exhaustion—only exhilaration. What did that say about her powers?

Determined to face anything heading her way, Tarni diligently continued her lessons that day and from that day forward.

Yet, for all that unforgiving practice, most of the time they lived like blissful newlyweds getting to know one another as the weeks passed and the tension—of the sexual kind—built. And Tarni was about over Logan keeping his distance.

He is a rock star for Pete's sake! She thought to herself more than once.

Things would have probably gone on in this idyllic way had two things not happened. One, Logan had to deal with two entire days of contract negotiations with his management and bandmates, keeping him out all afternoon into evening. And two, Tarni discovered The Belly Room above the Comedy Club in Hollywood with its open mic night on Thursdays.

Over the last few months, Tarni had practiced using her siren voice, experimenting with her witch magic to no avail. Then one day while floating in the pool and staring at a cerulean blue sky, she wondered what would happen if she used dark magic in combination. Usually, dark magic was reserved for attacks or things best left undone...but what could it hurt? Or so she tried to rationalize. For three days, she practiced singing softly and dialing her siren magic to a level she thought might be less harmful to humans, but each time she could sense the power of her voice was unstable and chaotic and she remained fearful of trying it out on an unsuspecting human. But on the third day, something happened.

Instead of starting with a song then dialing up her dark magic, she did the reverse. Placing her hands on her throat and touching her vocal cords, Tarni allowed a minute amount of dark magic to be absorbed and began to sing. She could feel the power but also sensed the ability to strengthen or lessen its effects. She became bold enough to try it out on Ernie, figuring if something went wrong, she could remain with him until the glamour ended, or she had to turn him completely...after all, she was almost as bad as a vampire, only with sirens she enthralled her victim with her voice, not a bite to the neck.

Did she feel guilty for using Ernie in such a way? Not really. He still owed her one for practically selling her to Logan. At least that's how she'd rationalized it in her brain. Better he than a total innocent.

"That was incredible. You are single-handedly one of the greatest singers I've ever heard!" he exclaimed.

"Buy me a car."

"What? Um...you have a car. How about, 'why thank you

Ernie old boy.' Isn't that enough? I mean a car is expensive. I might be able to get you brand new tires or something."

"You can afford it. Anyway...I was just kidding. You really think I can sing?"

"Are you kidding? With that voice you can make millions."

After the second day of Logan having to be with management, and Tarni not wanting to tag along, she'd had enough of waiting around and decided to go for a drive into Hollywood. Pulling her Mustang out of the drive, she wound down the PCH to Sunset Blvd and followed it into Beverly Hills and then toward Tower Records. She didn't have an agenda other than to drive around looking at movie star homes and do some kitschy touristy stuff near Mann's and maybe do some shopping for records.

She spied the old-time actor James Stewart, walking down Roxbury Drive near his home and watched Liza Minelli whiz by driving a green Rolls Royce while singing along to some tune. Following Liza down Sunset, Tarni wound up craving a hot dog from Pinks, but traffic had her stuck, so she opted for another stellar joint, Carney's. That desire settled, Tarni wandered back down Sunset only to stop short, causing a small fracas from the cars behind her when she spied a sign near the Comedy Store mentioning open mic night in their Belly Room. Pulling into the parking area for the club, Tarni exited and found herself going up a flight of steps then entered a small, intimate setting with a bar on one end, tables in the middle, and a tiny stage on the far side. A young woman was singing while strumming a guitar, and Tarni took a seat along the wall to have a listen, surprised at how packed the room was considering it was late afternoon heading into the evening.

When the girl ended her song to a round of applause, the woman running the show called out for any newcomers to add their names to the talent list before she closed it down for the night. A few people scrambled up to her and began scribbling on the piece of paper, and something propelled Tarni forward until she was standing there staring down at the list of names. Picking up the pencil, she hurriedly jotted down her name before she chickened out.

"Looks like you're the last singer tonight. Haven't seen you around here before, kid. Good luck," the woman showrunner said.

As the night wore on, Tarni chewed her nails, walked out and down the stairs twice and spent ten minutes in the ladies' room trying to convince herself this was a bad idea. But somehow she wound up back in the nightclub and heard her name called as the final singer.

Walking to the stage was surreal to say the least. Tarni stepped onto the platform and stood looking at the person handling the program.

"Do you have a cassette or need accompaniment? Did you bring sheet music?"

"Um, no... you see, I just...I wandered in and didn't think this through. Perhaps I should leave."

She heard a few snickers from the audience and realized the mic was live and they overheard what she'd said. Mortified, all Tarni wanted to do was make a run for it, but the program director took pity on her and gave her an old stack of sheet music to go through.

"I know this one."

It was "The Rose," the song Bette Midler made famous, and the accompanist asked her what key she needed.

"The original one, I guess."

The lights weren't as dim as most stage's setups, and she could see a few eye rolls and quite a few people were making movements like they planned to get up and leave—some of the tables in the back had folks standing and heading for the door.

Tarni swallowed her pride and tried to block it out and give it her all.

Carefully calling up her dark magic so as not to allow the audience to see it, she put her hands on either side of her neck and let it loose.

"She's trying to strangle herself before she sings one note!" Someone rudely shouted out from the back and there were more giggles and murmurs even as the accompanist began to play.

Then Tarni began to sing.

CHAPTER 21

Logan was heading home from another boring evening dealing with the mundane. The radio station played a popular Depeche Mode tune, but something on his radar caused Logan to lower the volume even more, slow the Harley down, and pull to the curb near the Riot Hyatt on Sunset. A voice. It called to him like a beacon on the sea, a light in the unending darkness, a whisper calling out to him... and he had no choice but to follow it until he found the source.

Leaving his bike parked in the relative safety of a hotel's valet parking and tossing his keys to one of the guys who came rushing over recognizing him instantly, Logan nodded and pointed to the Comedy Store next door, certain whatever snared his soul was residing there.

Waiting.

Suddenly the sound of her voice became clear, and he sneaked into the club, climbing the stairway. Even before he slid into the area reserved for celebrities and power movers and shakers, even before his eyes landed on who was at the mic, some part of Logan knew who he'd see standing there.

Moreover, once the full impact of her voice enveloped him, shattering what little resolve he had left, and his eyes beheld the breathtaking image of her in front of that mic, Logan understood utterly who and what he was dealing with in Tarni Vanderzee. A slim, raven-haired angel with cobalt eyes, standing there in torn acid-washed Daisy Dukes and a Nick Cave & The Bad Seeds tee, her hair piled up in a sloppy bun with no makeup to speak of, and she was the most glorious creature for miles.

There was no doubt in his mind she was the one he'd been searching for. The one he was meant to be with.

His siren.

And as dangerous a creature as was foretold. No one would be able to resist her should she choose to allow her siren voice to come out. No one.

And that's why she was a threat to them all.

The room was still. Not a sound from the audience as Tarni neared the song's completion. Just a momentary flickering of light in a sectioned-off area that appeared to be some kind of private observation room. She was still nervous, but not enough to throw her performance—this was what she was born to do after all.

The last few lines and she ended the song.

Utter silence.

Then in an instant, the clamoring of noise as chairs were flung back so people could stand and cheer along with hooting and hollering and whistles, and Tarni knew she'd done it. Just enough to use her siren voice but not enough to create vocal slaves. Her experiment was a resounding success.

"More! More!"

"Can you do a Whitney Houston tune?"

"Sing something old!"

"Over the Rainbow!"

"Do a Broadway tune!"

Tarni turned to the stack of sheet music and rifled through it until her eyes landed on a jazz standard, a timeless piece of music: "It Had to Be You," written by Isham Jones, with lyrics by Gus Kahn—a favorite of Frank Sinatra and Billie Holiday. Handing it over to the accompanist, Tarni quieted the audience with placating hands, as if she'd been performing all her life and took the mic. Turning to the piano, she said quietly, "In the key of C, please."

Tarni did it slow and sultry, longing filling her voice as the sad, sweet song filled the room:

It had to be you
It had to be you
I wandered around, and I finally found
The somebody who

Could make me be true
And could make me be blue
And even be glad
Just to be sad - thinking of you

Some others I've seen
Might never be mean
Might never be cross, or try to be boss
But they wouldn't do

For nobody else gave me a thrill
With all your faults, I love you still

It had to be you
Wonderful you
It had to be you

The piano player didn't stop there when the song was over, but went right into another old number, "But Not for Me," by George and Ira Gershwin made famous by Judy Garland. And that song sealed her fate, even though Tarni hadn't a clue. For in the audience was one of Hollywood and the music industry's top producers in total incognito mode, wearing a slouchy, wrinkled outfit and sporting a ballcap. He stood and walked to the back of the room where the woman running the open mic night was standing mouth agape, and whispered, "She's mine. Get her info," then quietly slipped out of the club.

They're writing songs of love,
But not for me
A lucky stars above,
But not for me.

With love to lead the way
I found more clouds of gray
Then any Russian play
Could guarantee

I was a fool to fall
And get that way
Hi ho! Alas! And al-
So, lack-a-day!

But still, I can't dismiss
The memory of his kiss
I guess he's not for me

Thunderous applause and a rush to the stage from people wanting to be near her, touch her, ask for autographs, and just be in her orbit, and Tarni knew without a doubt, she had her ticket to fame, fortune, and most importantly, the power that it would bring in her grasp. Now all she needed was a way in the door of that very exclusive music industry club.

Tarni Vanderzee had arrived.

CHAPTER 22

Riding the high of her performance, not even the rain pouring down or the wondering of whether or not Logan was back from his meetings could ruin Tarni's mood. Tonight was everything she'd ever dreamed about—and more.

Thankful she had left the top up on the Mustang, Tarni flew down Sunset, heading back toward the ocean and the turn leading her to Malibu. She briefly considered heading to her apartment to check on things and see her neighbors but quite frankly, she wanted a shower then bed—she'd stayed behind after the last of the crowd dispersed and spoke with the woman running the open mic night as well as the man who'd so beautifully played the piano for her, only leaving when the sounds of protest from her stomach made themselves known rather loudly.

But Tarni couldn't think of eating...she was too hyped up.

Invited back in two weeks to do a private show of ten songs, Tarni could think of nothing else. A showcase! Ten songs all chosen by her and performed in a set. And the caveat? Industry people would be invited. She was quivering with excitement.

If they liked her...if a producer was there to give her the career she longed for, nothing would stop her, and she'd be that closer to world domination—and the power and prestige to take on Dear Old Dad. She needed to speak with Kimberly and give her the good news!

Pulling into the drive, Tarni noted Logan had shown back up, and her exhilaration was hitched knowing he'd be pleased by her success.

Or would he?

After all, he was preparing for a world tour and perhaps the timing was wrong for her own ambitions.

Thinking he might be upset she'd disappeared without leaving a note behind, and preparing to eat crow, Tarni was pleasantly surprised to find him sitting by the fire watching the flames intently. He didn't seem upset.

"Hey."

Logan looked up at the sound of her voice.

"Hey."

Something smelled incredible and Tarni's nose twitched.

"I made dinner. Filet mignon, au gratin potatoes, and a salad with red wine vinaigrette."

Tarni's mouth flooded, and she looked over to the table that had been set with finery. Candles set the mood, and she wondered what Logan had up his sleeve... if anything. There was a bottle of red wine open on the table, and the sounds of old jazz standards reach Tarni's ears before she could register it was Frank Sinatra—a very young Sinatra—crooning softly for their pleasure.

"This looks and smells amazing."

"So do you." Logan's eyes smoldered as he took her in and Tarni's eyes went wide. Logan walked across the room and the fact that he moved gracefully, catlike yet dangerous, wasn't lost on her. Instead of kissing her, Logan reached out asking for her hand. She obliged and shivered when Logan brushed his lips against her knuckles.

So formal. So sexy. How does one resist that?

Logan smelled of Ivory soap, spices, steak, and man, and Tarni felt like nibbling on his neck for good measure. Instead, she allowed him to lead her to the table where he served her dinner.

"What's all this for?" she asked.

"I can't make dinner for my girl?"

"Well, sure. But...this seems like a smidgen more than our usual dinners at home."

"It is. I received something tonight, several somethings as a matter of fact, and I felt like celebrating."

"Oh? What are we celebrating?" Tarni took a seat at the table as Logan brought a platter in from the kitchen. Placing it on the table, he smiled at her and responded.

"This, for one." Logan held out a slip of paper that happened to be a check written out to him for earnings from their last tour. It was for a little over two hundred thousand dollars, and Tarni gawked at the number.

"Jeebers!"

"Right? And this upcoming tour, we finally headline, no more opening the show for others. This number is going to multiply."

Tarni leaned over and threw her arms around Logan, planting a kiss on his mouth with a loud smack then opened her mouth as he fed her a piece of tender filet.

"What else are we celebrating?" she asked, curiously.

"The rain."

Tarni looked up confused.

"Come again?" she asked.

"I'm celebrating the fact that it's finally raining again... and we live on the ocean."

At first, Tarni was confused by Logan's comment. But the meaning behind his words came crashing home even as the sound of the waves doing the same finally transmitted. Glancing around, she took in the candlelight, the fire, the rain coming down hard against the windowpane, unable to drown out the waves as they slammed against the rocks below. The music was soft and perfect and Tarni knew. Without a doubt or any reservations, Tarni knew tonight she would willingly become Logan's in every way, and it was all she could do not to ruin the mood by saying something innocuous or trivial.

She'd stopped eating, but Logan was having none of that and proceeded to slow down her racing heart by having her clean off her plate—hand-fed morsel by every hand-fed morsel. The beef tender and buttery, and each tiny bite followed by a slow and sensuous kiss or a nibble on her lips.

Oh, he was pure evil and perfect in every way!

Tarni knew she'd never be able to eat steak again without thinking of this.

The wine went down like tart, slightly bitter silk, and she thought she'd go mad when he pointed to her salad and potatoes. But like an obedient child, she ate every bite of the meal he'd prepared for her.

Tarni inwardly groaned when Logan insisted on cleaning off the table and washing the dishes while she watched, liking the way he looked in a tight pair of jeans and a simple white dress shirt, followed by cappuccino he'd brewed up in his machine and two crème brûlées so perfect he must have acquired them from a high-end café or restaurant.

The meal complete, Logan once again offered Tarni his hand, and they walked over to the stairs leading up to the master suite. That's when she noticed the rose petals, a mixture of white and red, sprinkled on the steps like a trail to be followed.

So she did.

The sight that met her eyes was one for the romance novels or a sappy chick flick. Candles were lit in the hundreds, their glow the only light since the fireplace was burning embers. The balcony doors were open slightly to allow the resonance of the surf to reach their ears. They could still hear the music from below and the sound of Sinatra singing "Time After Time" melted her insides just as the crisp white sheets on the bed and the abundance of white rose petals everywhere she looked had tears forming in her eyes.

She knew that no matter what the future should bring between she and Logan MacDuff, she'd always be grateful for the gift he was now giving her.

Peering into the bathroom, she saw Logan had drawn a hot, steamy bath and was beckoning to her, already fully naked and waiting like an attendant to serve her every need. Standing before him, she discarded her clothing, not trying to be sultry, knowing she might trip or worse, start giggling uncontrollably, and slid into the hot, bubbly water followed by a flushed Logan.

He bathed her body and hair, offering a sensual massage while washing the scent of the day away. He lathered up her hair then rinsed with a cup using the running water from the faucet then began working on her muscles from her neck downward. His hands were gentle but insistent as he carefully administered to her with the bar of soap. Logan then switched to just his hands, sliding them over her body, across her breasts, and down into her soft folds.

Tarni's breathe caught and her mouth parted as a soft moan escaped.

She became supine and relaxed, leaning up against his torso, the sound of Logan's heartbeat reaching her ears. She could feel it pounding even as he appeared unflustered by what he was doing to her—seemingly unfazed when his middle finger probed at her clit and slid expertly inside. Tarni's eyes flew open, and she gasped.

"Shh. Not yet. Slow down, Baby. Let me bring you there slowly," whispered Logan, his lips running up the side of Tarni's neck and into her damp hair. He pulled at her, expertly maneuvering her to face him and when she was straddling him and hanging on to his shoulders, Logan cupped her behind and squeezed, teasing, and nipping at her bottom lip.

"Let's get out of here. I'm getting a crick in my neck."

Tarni giggled at Logan's woebegone face, and her nervousness fell away with her laughter.

Logan rinsed her off and wrapped her in a towel. She began to mewl a bit as he dropped his mouth to one breast then the next, teasing her with his tongue and making her moan.

Logan, a master of lovemaking or a devil out for torture, delayed the moment even longer by insisting he dry her incredibly long hair, lovingly and slowly brushing it through as he used the dryer to make it sleek and slightly curled once more. Only then, once she was fluffed and petted to the point of distraction, did he take her to bed.

"Only the whitest sheets for my raven-haired beauty. I never want you on anything else."

Then Logan placed her on the bed and covered her with his body.

And Tarni finally knew what it was like to make love to a man.

After their lovemaking, Logan seemed melancholy and was extra tender toward Tarni. She, on the other hand, was purring like a kitten and hoping for more of the same. She wanted to sing about this moment. Write songs about it. Tell the world—

or at least give Justine, Monique, Stacey, and Heather the CliffsNotes.

Sighing in contentment, she snuggled up to Logan, giving him a puzzled frown.

"What's wrong? You seem sad. It's not... it isn't me right? No buyer's regrets or anything like that?"

"Remorse."

"What?"

"It's buyer's remorse. Although it means the same thing. And no, Baby. Never. Never would I regret this moment."

"Then what is it?" she asked nervously.

"I'm afraid you've allowed a monster into your bed."

Shifting upward so she was on one elbow and peering at Logan's face, Tarni could tell he was serious.

"And how are you a monster, Logan MacDuff?"

"Because my sweet, I will show you the world, take you to places you've never been, have you experience things impossible to dream up in your mind. I will make love to you in forests and on the beach, in a penthouse high above the city, and in places no woman should ever enter. I will bring you to the edge of it all and take you like a doll to be discarded...and then I will destroy you with the kind of love I have to offer. And when we part, you will understand why I call myself a monster. I'm afraid I'm going to lead you to the gates of Hell."

Shivering a little at Logan's words, Tarni felt a premonition of some kind, some fissure, and became grave.

"You could never hurt me."

"But I can. And I will. And you will leave, or I will. But we will always come back together, and you must promise me, Tarni—in those times between...when you feel nothing for me but hate, you must let me in. I might break you, but I still need you to trust me."

"I promise to always trust in you, Logan."

Logan looked rueful as if he knew she just gave him lip service and no more.

Resting his forehead on Tarni's, Logan whispered, "I will go through Hell and back for you, Baby. Even if it means I spend an eternity there."

Again, a flutter of something...a sense of impending doom.

Shaking it off with a resolve only a young woman flush with love could muster, Tarni returned to snuggling, trailing her hand down Logan's chest, and slipping it under the covers until her hand touched his already half hard erection then said, "Well then, I must be deranged or a psycho chick, Logan. You won't be rid of me that easily. Because I can't think of anyone I'd rather spend an eternity in Hell with than you."

CHAPTER 23

The next five days the world outside didn't exist as far as Tarni and Logan were concerned. After the hundredth time—or what seemed like—that the phone would interrupt them, Logan finally yanked the cord out of the wall, and they continued exploring one another's bodies with abandon.

Five days. Breakfast. Make love. Lunch...reading in bed. Soaking in the tub. Making love. Gentle, sweet, and tender lovemaking until Tarni raked her nails down Logan's back and demanded hot sex with more intensity.

Logan willingly obliged.

They were consumed by need and lust and everything else to the extent no one or nothing could cause them to leave the beach house.

"I can't believe you'd leave me for a bagel."

Logan moaned in response as he shrugged into his leather jacket.

"Hey! I said to get onion as well as poppyseed! Somehow I crave them now. Although I still insist on butter."

"You will give in to cream cheese yet, woman."

"Cream cheese is for babies. I want a copious amount of butter slathered on my bagel—I may even rub some melted butter all over my body."

"You have become a wanton hussy, you wickedly evil child."

"I'm hardly a child...furthermore...oh!" Tarni blushed and looked a bit nervous, and Logan instantly rushed to her side.

"What is it, Baby? What's wrong?"

Tarni looked Logan over, peering intently at his face and hair then letting her eyes wander down before looking away.

"Um...I never asked you... I mean, just how old are you anyway?"

Snorting with amusement and holding tight his sides as if laughter made them ache, Logan flopped on the sofa, letting out his mirth complete with tears streaming down his face, then sat up, wiping them away before he answered.

"I'm twenty-six. What? Did you think I was a creepy old man or something?"

"No, but...well, even that. I had no idea you were so old!"

"Old! Only a flipping child-woman would think someone three years older than she was a doddering, geriatric Methuselah!"

"You're almost thirty!"

"I'm three and a half years away from it for Pete's sake!"

"Still..."

"Still nothing. I am not old, nor will I ever be. You should know better, being a siren and all. Most in the Breed don't even begin to date until they are approaching fifty! We are breaking the mold."

Realizing belatedly that Logan must have seen her fake ID, Tarni bit her lip and knew she had to come clean about her age.

"Six."

"Six what?" asked Logan.

"I'm six years younger than you. Well, after what you said just now, six and a half. That Birthday I just had? I just turned twenty."

Logan contemplated what Tarni'd said for a minute then wagged his eyes at her. "Well, then, it looks like I am a dirty old man and robbed the cradle. And you really are a baby."

Squealing as Logan dove, pinning her to the sofa, Tarni noted sadly that her bagel consumption would have to be delayed an hour...or four.

April quickly turned to May then June arrived. Their time was running out before the tour started. Rehearsals were beginning to get in the way of their free time. Tarni only had a moment of slight regret when Logan informed her she wouldn't be performing at The Belly Room any time soon back in April. She'd confided in him about that night and how the proprietress offered her an hour set in front of industry movers and shakers, but Logan insisted he was too busy with this tour and other commitments to hand-hold her through her fledgling career right now, and that there would be plenty of time for that when they returned.

Tarni reluctantly agreed and knew Logan was right, but couldn't help feeling some disappointment. She had promised Logan she'd follow him and quite frankly the thought of remaining behind to go it alone didn't seem very appealing. She knew the music world would be waiting for her upon her return.

"We should go to Carmel-by-the-Sea."

"What's there, other than the sea, I assume?" asked Tarni.

"You'll see," replied Logan.

"OK, that's just corny, you big dumb idiot."

The next day, they drove up the PCH following the ocean for five hours until they reached Carmel. Logan seemed to be offering Tarni an apology of sorts for asking her to put a hold on her dreams for him. Checking into a seaside hotel, Logan wined and dined Tarni and they shopped and took a boat ride in Monterey, visited a few museums, and danced at a small music festival arranged and thrown by the town.

They drank way too much wine and made love in a secluded spot by the Pacific Ocean with waves crashing around them—a very *From Here to Eternity* moment and Tarni was in Heaven.

Afterward, they sat and spoke of dreams, plans, the future, and their fears...although Tarni was more open than Logan. He seemed distracted.

"Tell me about your family, Logan. Why do you never speak of them?"

"I could say the same about you."

Tarni ducked her head and fussed with the hem of her skirt. "It's OK. Forget it. I was just curious."

"You know what they say, Baby. Curiosity killed the cat." Seeing her discomfort, Logan capitulated and pulled her close, allow her to snuggle in while he rocked her and ran his hand down her hair. Kissing her temple, he spoke.

"There once was a boy with two older sisters...much older. The sisters were mean to him, but that doesn't matter. His parents would throw the most lavish parties and always had important people over, some of them politicians, some wealthy bankers...even a few Hollywood elite. They always fought, his parents, constantly bickering—usually over the father's incessant flirting with the opposite sex."

"One day, the boy's mother came home very drunk after a night out with her friends and found her husband in bed with his secretary. Life after that changed. The boy's mother moved out, the two daughters, the boy's sisters, went with her. But the boy's father would not let his wife take his son. So father and son lived alone, and the boy hardly saw his mother and sisters after that.

"Years passed and the boy celebrated his twelfth Birthday, his father overindulging him with too many gifts to make up for never being around. The party should have been children only, but the father liked having his friends around. As the night wore on and the children fell asleep after having too much cake, only the adults were left to party. Things got out of hand, and the boy found his father in bed with two women, while a few of the other guests had also gone off to partner up. The boy was shocked and confused, for he always assumed his mother would come back someday."

"A few weeks later, the boy was playing in the yard with a gift one of the women had given him. It was a book to draw in and colored pencils. The boy secretly wanted to be an artist someday, so he was thrilled with the gift. He spent hours drawing and was rather talented for his age. He was especially proud of one drawing in particular, an ocean scene with a tiny sailboat off in the distance, waves foamy with white caps and a setting sun sinking into the horizon. He showed it to his father and boasted that someday he would like to be a painter or a poet. His father, incensed that his only son wanted to be "some kind of fairy," took the drawing and ripped it up, then beat his son until the boy's sobs ran dry."

Tarni sat up and looked askance at Logan and went to speak, but he shook his head, settling her back against his chest and rocked her once more.

"A few days later, the father announced the boy would have a nanny to look after him while he was off at work, it being the summertime. The sitter was a flashy young woman who spent most of her time flirting with the father and ignoring the boy.

One night, the boy had a bad dream, and he rushed into the bedroom only to find his sitter in bed with his father. When he went to run away, his father insisted he join them on the bed and gave the boy lessons on how to be a man. Over the next year, the sitter would visit the boy in his bedroom, took his virginity just before his fourteenth birthday, then overdosed one night, leaving the boy in a mental state that was deemed unstable."

"His father shipped him off to live with his mother for a time, but when he asked for the boy's return, his mother refused and took her ex-husband to court. And that, my dear Tarni, about sums up my family. Mother fawned over me only when she had a party or needed to look like a proper parent. Father spent his entire life making sure I didn't turn into a faggot—his word. I haven't seen my sisters in years...although now that I'm famous, they all suddenly want to be a family again. They can forget that. I will make my own family someday."

"That was abuse, Logan. You were abused as a child."

"Ah, Tarni...it's OK. It's different for boys, I guess."

"Bullshit! Logan, I'm so angry for you. For that little boy."

"Baby! Baby, it happened a long time ago. I have you now. Just stay with me forever and none of that will ever matter to me again."

"But Logan. What Breed would do that to their offspring? Can't you just tell me that much?"

Gazing at Tarni with eyes so sad just looking at them made her ache, Logan shook his head no, then dropped his head.

"I can't, Baby. Please." Logan raised his gaze, giving Tarni a pleading look. "I can tell you this. What I was at birth, I am no longer. My Breed has been forever taken from me, and what I am now dictates discretion and concealment. It's not that I don't want to share myself with you, it's that I can't."

~

The next morning, they went shopping in Carmel, and Logan brought Tarni to a jewelry store. "Buy something. Anything you want. I've got it."

Tarni was about to resist, but saw instantly how important this was for Logan, so she looked around. She chose a tiny pendant, two pearls, one white, one black, on a white gold box chain. Logan made the purchase then slipped it around her neck.

"It's perfect. Thank you."

"It would look nice with something like this to go along with it." Logan held out a beautiful pearl band. It almost looked like a wedding ring. Each pearl was delicate and very small and alternated black then white. Logan was correct; it would go perfectly with the pendant he'd just bought her.

"I... it's lovely...but..."

"That's a nice wedding band. I can wrap it up for you two lovebirds if you'd like," the owner of the jewelry shop offered with a smile and a wink toward Tarni.

"No, thanks...I'm not the marrying kind," replied Logan. Killing the moment as his eyes locked with Tarni's, "Unless you want it?"

"No....I..." Not knowing what to say, or what Logan was trying to convey, Tarni let her response trail off.

"It's just a ring. Let's go," said Logan with cold eyes.

Tarni wasn't sure if she should have accepted the ring. She didn't know if this was a game. If Logan was in a strange mood after last night's conversation, or if he wanted to see if she'd pressure him into something he said he'd never wanted nor ever would. She was beyond confused.

"Thank you for the pendant. I love it."

Logan just smiled slightly then said, "Something for you to remember me by."

Tarni and Logan left Carmel the next day and returned to Malibu.

Their vacation was over.

CHAPTER 24

Logan watched Tarni in the light of the bonfire on their last few nights at home before the tour started. The final rehearsal was tomorrow, and there would be a host of Hollywood types invited to watch the show before they kicked it off later that week. But for tonight, Logan and Tarni had been asked by a few residents who shared their exclusive stretch of beach to join them for a cookout, and Logan decided to be neighborly and agreed. Tomorrow, Logan would drop a key off with Monique and Stacey, who would stop by the beach house a few times a week to take in the mail and check on his orchids and other house plants. But for now, he and Tarni were hanging out beside the glowing fire, drinking wine, and nibbling on cheese and fruit, with good company and nary a care in the world.

Or that would be the case if Logan could curb his worrisome thoughts.

How do I continue with this farce? He wondered as his eyes raked down the length of Tarni's body while she slowly began to spin, her head thrown back, a bottle of grenache in one hand and her half-filled glass in the other.

She wasn't supposed to be this beautiful.

Or this vulnerable.

Oh, she played at being tough, so tough nothing and no one could harm her, but Logan knew better. He understood how damaging her father's actions scarred his beautiful mermaid and caused her to put up this wall of impenetrable coarseness, a thickened skin that no one was allowed to breach.

But Logan understood the situation better.

He received information today that chilled him and caused no end of worry. Tarni's father was out for vengeance. He had plans for his renegade daughter whose impulsive actions and blatant disregard for the law of their people caused him no end of embarrassment—and loss of stature. When a siren male could not control the women in his household, the value of that male as a leader diminished.

Torrent Danu was out for blood. Tarni's blood.

Tarni needn't have worried about trying to hide who or what she was from him...Logan comprehended her situation more than she could ever imagine. He suspected she was the one intended for him when they'd first met in Las Vegas, but he didn't act on it—knowing if it were true, their paths would cross once more—and they had.

Once that happened, Logan tried to get confirmation from those he answered to, those that controlled his freedom and kept him on a short leash—on the path for which he was chosen —and they verified Tarni was his destiny.

But Logan already knew.

Fate...it was preordained in his childhood, that this woman and he would be forever entwined.

The air she breathed filled his senses with sweet intoxication and longing he thought no woman capable of doing—and it frightened him.

Tarni caught him watching and quickly turned away in

seeming shyness. How did she *do* that? Even after their constant lovemaking, the next time he took her, it was as if she gave him her virginity anew... and it never ceased to amaze him. How fragile and desperate the love she gave him, how innocent yet at the same time reckless. Fervent. Loving. Wild.

Timeless. Her lovemaking was eons in the making.

And it left him breathless.

It was like making love to an ancient, worldly being who charmed him into believing she was an ingenue instead of a Lilith—taking her pleasure while draining the life from his soul with every kiss.

His siren!

And he knew of Tarni's family, her father, and what his transgressions and tyranny meant to those Logan answered to. And that the man needed his authoritarian rule to be ended at all costs. Despite what Tarni thought she understood, Logan knew more than she could ever imagine possible.

The last of the neighbors bade their farewell and drifted slowly back to their darkened homes, but Logan remained close to the fire, alone. His heart rate accelerated at the sight of Tarni, windswept hair catching the breeze as the moonlight made her appear ethereal—otherworldly.

Standing up and walking to the water's edge where Tarni now stood gazing out at the darkened sea, Logan wrapped his arms around her and whispered, "There's a penny in my pocket."

Tarni spun around but remained in Logan's embrace. Then, glancing down, amused, she took in his rather garishly loud swim trunks.

"Do you often keep spare change on you when you hit the surf?"

Snorting in amusement, Logan rested his forehead on Tarni's. "Do you not know the saying, a penny for your thoughts? I observed your shift from happily dancing free spirit to a contemplative soul seeking answers from an endless sea."

"She's not endless...just vast."

"*She*, is it?"

"Oh, of course. The Pacific is a woman. Sometimes quiet, calm, and forgiving—other times vengeful and filled with such fury. But always beautiful. Always. Even as she brings destruction and rips you from the safety of your vessel, carrying you to her depths where no man should ever venture nor hope to return."

"That's your definition of a woman?" Logan asked, his lips now inches from Tarni's.

"That's my definition of *this* woman."

Logan's nostrils flared, and he breathed in the night air and this woman who drove him mad. "I'll gladly lose myself in you, Tarni."

"But will you give up your life for me? Is that what you're saying?"

"I already have, in more ways than you could ever know."

"Prove it."

Faster than anything Logan had ever witnessed before in his life, Tarni broke from his hold and dove into the ocean, quickly distancing herself from the shore. Logan gave chase and thought he'd catch up to her only to find he'd lost sight of where he thought Tarni was swimming. He searched this way and that in a mild panic.

Did she go under? Have I become confused in the darkness-chasing vagary and the trick of the eye? Is Tarni even now laughing as I bumble along blindly?

Treading the water and pausing to gather his bearings, Logan realized he was far from the beach with no Tarni in sight. No sound other than the lapping waves and wind. No figure of someone swimming in any direction he could ascertain.

"Tarni?"

Logan cried out, not yet in a panic but slightly disturbed by the dread overwhelming his soul, the sense that he was utterly alone, and she had decided to abandon him to his fate. At the same time, she took to the sea, her natural home as if returning to her true love—he was just an insignificant imposter. One she trifled with but never intended to allow the kind of permanency or eternity for which he longed.

Logan remained in the frigid waters—for how long, he couldn't have recalled—and prayed for Tarni's return. Even as his body became numb and his senses dulled, still he held on. While the last remnants of hope began to seep from his mind allowing toxic doubt to weave their way to his core, hoping to break him, he whispered her name, "Tarni."

As he slipped under the surface of the sea, he felt her arms go around his body, and her lips sought his bringing warmth and assistance even as she plunged in a dizzying rush of power and urgency. Logan knew she was dragging him to the bottom of the ocean—and he didn't care if he died.

He wouldn't mind, not as long as it was Tarni ushering him to his eternal slumber.

In a place beyond all imagination, Logan felt the sand beneath him. As he landed on his back far below a depth even the sea creatures dared never to wander, he felt Tarni straddle his body and remove swim trunks that now seemed ridiculous in this alien world. She never broke the kiss—if anything intensifying it until he became so consumed with passion he felt his body react, despite the frigid, forbidding temperature and surreal circumstances.

And Tarni took him.

Sliding onto his rock-hard erection, Tarni pinned Logan's

arms up above his head, holding him by the wrists and in every way imaginable had her way with him. Starting with slow rotations of her hips that languished then teased with the achingly slowness of it all until she progressed to a frenetic bucking that drove Logan to the edge of madness. Still, Tarni did not ease up on the wanton consuming of his flesh as her body tightened then eased only to grip him with such intensity he knew he was lost—and about to explode.

When Logan came, Tarni released the sucking hold she'd had on his mouth as he cried out in pleasure and not a little pain. And the sea filled his lungs quickly, knowing he had lost the fight—until he felt they would burst from the pressure. And then the magic happened, which brought him no end of wonder.

Logan realized he could breathe.

Logan felt the sun caress his body even as the harsh, gritty sand had him realize he was lying on the beach. Blinking away the sleep from his eyes, Logan moved to a sitting position and found he was alone near the smoldering bonfire.

Was it a dream, then? Had he remained here the entire night, and his imagination conjured the incredible experience?

"Hey, neighbor. Nice view, but you might want to cover up before old Mrs. Swanson comes walking by with her dog and gets ideas."

Startled by his neighbor Gordon's playful banter, Logan glanced down and discovered he was sans swim trunks and half hard—not to mention covered in fine sand.

"Rough night?" Gordon was standing over him now, giving Logan an appreciative once-over. Gordon was gay, so Logan knew he'd just made his day.

"I think?"

"Well, if you have to think about it first, hon, it was *definitely* one for the record books."

Standing albeit awkwardly, Logan wrapped his beach towel around his hips—much to the disappointment of Gordon who waved and continued his stroll down the shoreline with his tiny Pekinese dog, Lottie, following at a sedate pace. Logan made his way over to the beach house, the morning sun burning the last of the mist off the ocean which reflected in the windows as he drew near. Climbing the stairs to the deck, he found the sliding glass doors open. Logan smelled bacon...and coffee.

"There you are."

Tarni was naked, wearing only a frilly apron she'd picked up at a small shop in Malibu.

She had a spatula in hand, and Logan knew she was charring the bacon to a crispiness level only she liked—and he tolerated. And in that instant, Logan knew he loved her. He truly and utterly loved her beyond reason.

Walking toward him seductively, she handed Logan a mug of coffee even though she knew he preferred Earl Grey tea.

Tarni held the mug to his lips, and he took a sip which she followed with a light kiss, then twirled and thrust her chin in the direction of his prized orchids.

"You may want to check on them. I bumped into the table and knocked one over. I'm convinced the poor thing will never bloom now."

"Tarni...about last night..."

"Please! The next time we have a bonfire, can it be with people I know? I felt awkward with all that old Malibu money and stuffy women I have nothing in common with!"

"Tarni..."

"And who doesn't like grenache? I mean, really! 'Thank you, dear, but that is beneath my station.' Who talks like that?

Next time, let's have Gordon and Joel over and that young starlet and her boyfriend...I can't remember their names."

"Tarni...what..."

"No arguments. I wanted to scream after about twenty minutes—even though that director, Stephen, was it? Could grill some mean shrimp."

"For feck's sake, Tarni. Shut up a minute."

Tarni clamped her mouth shut and stuck out her bottom lip in a pout, but her eyes remained lively and sparkling like she was in on some kind of joke he was not privy to.

"Did we, or did we not have sex last night while dwelling at the bottom of that infernal sea you love so much?"

"Why are you wrapped in that towel?" was Tarni's playful response.

"I don't know. I seem to recall you whipping my trunks off me somewhere under the ocean, and I fear them lost."

"Well then, I think you have your answer."

"Tarni, I need to know..."

"No. You don't. Just leave it, Logan. Please, I..."

The telephone rang, bringing an abrupt end to their awkward conversation as Logan stomped over to answer it.

"This is Duffy."

Tarni rolled her eyes at his use of the nickname, causing Logan to reluctantly grin.

"Chuck! Yeah, man, we'll be there. Two o'clock. Got it. Tell Billy to grab my Fender. OK...later, man."

"Duty calls?" asked Tarni, taking a bite out of her bacon slice.

"Well, final rehearsal today and schmoozing with the Hollywood elite. The countdown to the tour's kickoff is here. Excited?"

"You know it."

Watching the gamut of emotions play across Tarni's face,

Logan felt momentary guilt knowing he'd asked her to delay her own career interests so he could focus on his—and keep her close to him.

"You know I will be there for you when this tour is over and it's your turn in front of the mic, right? It's just that..."

Her face clearing and quick to assuage any worries, Tarni brushed off his concern. "Logan. Stop it! If I didn't want to wait and start my singing career, I don't need your permission, and you know it. I am freely putting my ambitions on hold to be with you. I want to. I'd be crazy not to!" Tarni closed the distance between them, resting her hands on Logan's shoulders. "Think of everything I will learn on a real rock and roll tour! I can't wait!"

"It's not as glamorous as you might think. A lot of it is tedious boredom and two to three hours of exhilarating work, mixed with an endless sea of interviews and faces, most of whom you will forget five minutes after meeting them. But I love it anyway. And I love standing in front of that crowd giving myself and getting back an endless supply of their love."

"You were born for this."

Logan stilled at Tarni's words, gazing deeply into her eyes.

"No. I was born for *you*."

CHAPTER 25

"Duffy is so freakin' hot. I want him to take me up against the wall."

"As if."

Tarni listened in amusement and slight irritation as two minor female starlets ogled her man as he stalked across the stage doing a soundcheck. She couldn't believe how many people turned up for the free concert, which was not only the first time the band performed their new album to a crowd, but the first they'd had an event catered with the press in attendance as well. It was a mob scene.

"I heard he's back with Stephanie again."

"No way. Joannie saw him sniffing around a statuesque redhead last year—not that that's his type or anything. Duffy likes blondes."

"Duffy likes anything with a vagina."

"Oh, for sure!"

"Well, my vagina is willing and able...and I have a few more places he can have me."

The women giggled and moved off on matching hot pink

stiletto heels and painted on short dresses, leaving Tarni following their progress to the edge of the stage. Logan glanced down and smiled but didn't linger on them unnecessarily long. His indifference caused the women to pout and Tarni to grin.

Stephanie sidled up to Tarni and elbowed her. "You ready for the groupies?"

"I can handle it."

Stephanie smiled in sympathy. "Sweetheart, Duffy might be flying solo with you right now, but once the craziness of the tour takes hold, he is going to sleep with everything that catches his eye. So, talk to me a month in and *then* tell me you're OK."

"I can handle it, Steph. I'm looking forward to the experience. And not for anything; I'm used to males with insatiable appetites and a legendary sexual drive. If I didn't want that, I wouldn't be with Logan."

"Logan, huh? Never Duffy?"

"Nope."

Tarni left Stephanie and made a beeline to the long buffet table setup. She knew she was putting on a brave face for the others and still wrestled with the knowledge that she was dancing with the devil as far as Logan MacDuff was concerned. Not being raised with many constraints where religious dogma and morality were concerned, Tarni had a mother who instilled propriety in her own way. Nevertheless, an inner ethical clock had Tarni realizing this lifestyle was not considered normal by any stretch of the imagination.

Yet what *was* normal?

Who was to say having a monogamous relationship was the only way to go? Or a polyamorous one? Way back in the lore of her kind, wasn't it the siren females who had multiple lovers? OK...so they lured them to their deaths after the act, but still!

Perhaps Tarni should consider this new adventure as a

loose guideline on fast-tracking oneself to a hedonistic life and something to chuckle at fondly in her old age.

If she made it.

Logan was already giving her countless sleepless nights—in one way or another. He didn't hound her after their trip to the bottom of the Pacific, but she understood his wonder at what had transpired. It isn't every day a siren gives you her breath allowing you to breathe for a time under water!

Stopping at the hors d'oeuvres section, Tarni perused the offerings and scored some caviar. Not having ever tasted the expensive delicacy, Tarni was eager to give it a try and picked up the tiny spoonful offering. Placing it on a toast point like she observed a nondescript woman doing, Tarni wondered, briefly, if she'd like the texture. Since this same woman put the entire square in her mouth, not nibbling or taking a small bite, Tarni did the same...and almost spit the concoction out in horror.

"Heh, that's funny, sweetheart. I think I will use that scene in my next movie."

"Oh! I'm sorry. It's just that...what a horrible taste. I didn't mean to be rude." Then, cringing inwardly, Tarni couldn't believe she acted like a dufus in front of someone who was obviously, *someone.*

"Hey, if you don't like it, you don't like it...am I right? Names Penny, you?"

"Tarni."

"Nice to meet you, Tarni. If you don't like the caviar, stay away from that foie gras!" Pointing with her chin to a grayish-red glob of meat and grinning, the pleasant woman walked off into the crowd leaving Tarni to sample the better-known offerings. She'd stick to the tried and true from now on, thank you!

Hearing a commotion behind her, Tarni turned to observe Logan heading slowly in her direction as he addressed the many adoring fans in the celebrity set who were fawning over him. Her bullshit meter was going off the charts, and Tarni was amused to see how well Logan handled the sycophant behavior that was part of the deal in this business.

Everyone wanted a piece of him, to bask in his glow even for a few moments. The men to say they slapped his back and enjoyed the acknowledgment he bestowed upon their girlfriends or wives—as if a nod of appreciation from Logan meant they chose well and could continue with the relationship. Logan knew fully well his powers in this regard and always left the men smiling from ear to ear and the women panting. Thoughts of tonight when their eyes would be closed while their significant other took them to bed—and it wasn't their men with whom they'd be fantasizing!

The women, young and old, acted like a wild pack of feral beasts circling, constantly circling, flashing their wares in the hopes Logan would be dazzled by their sparkle. The older ones were predatory as they sized Logan up and found him more than satisfactory, while the younger ones screamed wet, hot, and ready to be sullied by a rock god in the making. The air was thick with lust, and Logan strode through it all as if he belonged there—which he did. He was in his element.

Reaching her side, Logan beamed at Tarni and pointed to some Swedish meatballs.

"Feed me, Baby. I'm starving."

"Shouldn't you wait until after the show? Spice and all that?"

"Nah. If I belched, this crowd would try to bottle it and keep it locked away on a shelf somewhere."

Tarni laughed in delight and proceeded to pop two tiny balls of meaty yumminess into Logan's mouth.

"Those as well." Pointing to some shrimp-filled deviled eggs, Logan waited for Tarni to take care of his needs, savoring the way she playfully fed him. Neither were aware of the heated and glowering looks most of the women in attendance threw their way.

Tarni continued to circle the table with Logan in tow as he selected items for her to feed him. Each bite became a seductive dance that they knew would lead to something incredible when they finally returned home and spent their last few nights together before boarding the tour bus and starting their strange journey.

"You're a tad hyped," said Tarni with a smirk as Logan grazed from one offering to the other.

"Ernie is here. He brought the good stuff, and that always leaves me hungry!"

Tarni frowned but didn't say anything that would appear she was scolding Logan, although she clenched her jaw and surveyed the room. Now Ernie, on the other hand, she would reprimand. Logan needed to keep focused, not get wasted and make a mess of things.

When Logan was satisfied, he allowed Tarni to wipe either side of his lips and turned toward the stage. "It looks like we are about ready to start the show. I better get in the back and put my eyeliner on."

Tarni thought it amusing that all the guys in the band applied makeup—mainly concealer and eyeliner—so they wouldn't fade into obscurity, blobs of nothingness, while up on stage. They didn't go the glam rock route with lipsticks, eyeshadow, or the heavy punk or goth look. They just kept it honest except for kohl eyeliner and sexy outfits—and she loved it.

"OK, break a leg or something."

"Aren't you going to eat?" he asked, looking at her mouth the entire time he asked.

"I could eat."

"Then here." Pulling her into his embrace, Logan crushed

his lips to hers, and they spent a few moments in a passionate kiss. Then, pulling away, Logan reached down and popped a meatball in Tarni's mouth. "Have some cake. It looks incredible."

"I'll save you a piece."

Logan took three steps toward the stage, then spun and rushed over to the dessert table. Bringing back three delicate miniature cupcakes, he proceeded to feed them one by one to Tarni until she laughingly pushed him away. Tarni made shooing motions for him to head backstage—but not before Logan made her lick the buttercream from his fingertips.

Tarni decided she'd had enough snacks and silliness and moved to take her seat in the front row.

"You know he won't remain with you, right?"

Tarni paused and gazed at the woman from earlier, adorned in her hot pink sluttiness, and feigned disinterest.

"Pardon?"

"A guy like Duffy. He plays the field. He might be with you currently, but before long, he will flitter over to another butterfly. So please don't feel too bad when he does. You don't know how lucky you are—but *only* for now."

Tarni let her eyes wander down the length of this woman who obviously thought she'd get a rise out of her.

"Perhaps Logan is the lucky one for being with me."

And with that, Tarni turned and reached her seat, not giving the woman another glance. She could hear her snort of derision and the laughter that followed as it slammed into her back.

The announcement came that the show was about to begin, and everyone made their way to their seats. Tarni found herself wedged between Stephanie and Laney. Deanna sat to Laney's right.

"Don't let Piper get to you. She's a bitch," said Deanna, leaning forward so she could speak to Tarni.

"Piper?"

"The bottle-blonde bimbo who was just talking to you. She's just pissed off. Logan has never slept with her."

"That's not why she's upset," smirked Stephanie. "She's upset because Logan slept with her mother who held it over her head. Piper has been trying ever since to get into Logan's pants, but he wants no part of her."

"Her *mother*?" squeaked Tarni, giving Stephanie a wide-eyed look.

"Oh, sweetie. The woman was a huge star in France or something and looks like Bridget Bardot. But, of course, she's only thirty-seven, so chill out. It's not like he banged an old lady or anything."

"But...how old is Piper?"

"Your age, I guess. Piper's mother had her when she was like fourteen or something!" Deanna giggled. "I know, right? But don't feel sorry for that skank. She asks for it. Piper's been passed around the rocker brigade. She's done everyone from the underground mosh pit losers to the big boys in this business. Last week, I heard a rumor that everyone in Motley Crüe, from the top down —from band members to the roadies—had her. The girl's a slut!"

"Totally!" said Laney with a derisive sniff. "But Piper isn't wrong. Duffy will move on to another, and you will either hook up with the next rocker or be left in the dust. It is what it is."

"Laney!" Stephanie scolded.

"What? It's the truth, and you know it! How long did you two last?"

"That's beside the point. Us girls need to stick together and not tear each other down. Right, Tarni?"

Tarni just smiled and looked forward as the light began to

dim and the excitement from the crowd took on a will of its own. Even as they quieted down, the anticipation was palpable, and the energy was electric, and Tarni knew the cacophony would be tremendous once the concert began.

Now, if only she could clear her mind of everything she'd heard tonight, perhaps she could enjoy it.

Or not.

The show was everything the band had promised and more. They ended with a standing ovation from their peers, and the night's partying went on long after it was supposed to end. Tarni, knowing Logan would be in no position to drive, did the honors by bringing him tonight in her Mustang. Now that it was time to drag him home, she gathered their things and proceeded him to the parking garage where she'd left her car parked.

Logan called out he'd follow her in a minute as the stragglers and hangers-on still surrounded him, getting the last bit of his glow for themselves to savor over the next few months.

When Tarni reached her vehicle, she felt her blood run cold.

Tucked under her wiper blade on the driver's side was a large manila envelope. Slowing her forward progression, Tarni knew she'd find something disturbing, and she acknowledged her unknown stalker had discovered her whereabouts.

But how?

Quickly ripping the envelope off her windshield, Tarni tore open the seal and peered into the opening. Feeling her mouth go dry, Tarni began to quake and felt the earth tilt. There were several photos inside taken the day before at the bonfire...and even some of her ocean swim. What was even more disturbing, from the positioning of these photographs, one could say with some certainty that the photographer must have been reasonably close and above the party-goers. Almost as if the photographer had taken the photos by standing on a deck and shooting down.

Tarni and Logan's deck.

CHAPTER 26

"I'm hungry."

"Hungry? But you ate and performed, then ate some more! How could you be hungry?"

"After doing what I do up on that stage? I'm famished," complained Logan.

"Do you want me to stop somewhere?"

Tarni spent the entire ride glancing in her rearview mirror as if expecting a huge, black sedan to be tailing them like in the movies. But all that was following behind her car was a Pontiac Grand Am and a Datsun of some sort. Traffic was surprisingly sparse for Hollywood on a Friday night—a rare enough occurrence that it seemed surreal.

"Let's go to Pinks. I want a hot dog."

"Your diet leaves much to be desired."

"Yeah, yeah. Just take me there, woman. Sate my hunger."

"Your wish is my commander, Master."

Logan growled in a proprietary way and leaned over to whisper in her ear. "Keep that up, and I will take you right here in this car."

"With me driving? I'd like to see that!" laughed Tarni.

"Don't tempt me, Baby. I'm hard just thinking of you calling me 'Master' every time you respond to something I ask of you."

Giggling, Tarni tore through the streets of Hollywood until they arrived at Pink's, where Logan hopped out to grab a few of their famous hot dogs. His delight was contagious, and Tarni shoved her worry to the back recesses of her mind. She wouldn't let this stalker get to her. Not right now. Perhaps she'd ask Ernie if he knew of someone who could look into it for her.

Or maybe she'd give Buffalo Jim a call.

He'd already had come through for Tarni and nabbed some solid information on how she might damage her father's assets and cripple him in such a way he might not ever recover. But it involved dealing with some rather shady characters. The name Romano was mentioned and Tarni recalled the nasty-looking brute of a man who'd eyed her at Jim's repair shop back in Vegas. She wondered briefly if her father had dealings with the beefy mafioso vampire.

A disturbing thought.

She'd discuss it with Logan later that night or even the next day, so sure was she that he would drop off the minute they reached home—and a soft bed—but decided he should be in on her nefarious plans to do in her father.

The shrieking of young girls reached her ears even as Logan raced toward her Mustang, top-down, and dove into the car laughing all the way. A trailing group of teenagers tried desperately to follow and were sorely disappointed when she tore off into the night.

"Make tracks, Baby. They spotted me!"

Feeling reckless, Tarni flew through two red lights as they made their way to Sunset Boulevard and the left turn that would take them winding through Beverly Hills into Bel Air, then Brentwood and down to the PCH where they'd make a right and head for home.

"It's only going to get worse after this tour," sighed Logan with a snicker. "The rumors are already starting about us landing a few MTV awards and possibly a Grammy or two."

"They'll be no living with you then!" replied Tarni as she shot ahead of a red BMW and careened around the bend on Sunset. Driving past the Chateau Marmont and the Pink Taco, she continued to race past Carney's when Logan signaled she should pull over up ahead at Tower Records.

"Stop in at Tower. First, I want to get some stuff, then maybe we might stop for some dessert somewhere. I'm still ravenous."

"Two hot dogs wasn't enough? Almost getting mauled by a randy pack of pre-pubescent teenaged girls. And now dessert on top of those hot dogs?"

"Just pull in, woman. I won't be too long. Plus, if you behave, I just might take you to the premier of The Lost Boys. I nabbed two tickets tonight from one of the producers."

Tarni clapped her hands in delight since she'd been bugging Logan about those tickets ever since she found out when the movie's release date would be. She left Logan to peruse the shelves in the iconic record store, noting Somber Sea had earned a spot on the side of the building, their new album, *Breathless*, painted in a kaleidoscope of stormy ocean-inspired colors on its wall. Somber Sea was skyrocketing to the stratosphere of fame—and the album sales backed that presumption as Tarni contemplated the artwork.

Her thoughts turned to her quandary and Tarni briefly wondered if another vampire might be her stalker. Who else could silently come and go and would know about Todd? And what of Todd? Her stalker knew about what they'd done...what did he do about it? What *would* he do? Perhaps going to see

The Lost Boys might not be such a good idea after all. She was already up to her eyeballs in vampires!

When Logan returned, a square-shaped package in hand, Tarni was delighted to see he'd purchased the album, although why she had no idea. It wasn't like he couldn't get it from the bands' personal collection. But leave it to Logan to need to grab his copy from a record store and pay for it out of his own pocket.

"You bought your album?" Watching as Logan ripped the protective cellophane from the cover, Tarni's eyes went wide when he pulled a marker out of the bag and began to sign his name—but not before leaving a personalized inscription on it for Tarni.

To Baby,
My Muse...the inspiration
These songs the result
Your presence in my life leaves me...
Breathless...
Logan

Tarni felt a lump forming in her throat and couldn't utter a word as Logan handed the album to her. Instead, she accepted his gift with a sigh.

"You like?" Logan asked expectantly.

Tarni nodded and pressed her lips together, her eyes misting over as she gripped the album in both hands.

"Here, hop over onto my side and let me drive the rest of the way. You look dazed."

Logan opened the passenger door and walked around to the

driver's side while Tarni scooted over. He slid into the front seat and rested his arm over the back of her seat.

"What?"

"I love it. Thank you."

Logan smiled. "Home?"

"I could have a slice of chocolate cake, perhaps. Maybe."

"Let me turn around," Logan chuckled.

"Turn around?"

"Baby, you want cake. That means Canter's seven-layer cake, right?"

"Oh, God...yes!"

Logan peeled out of Tower Records and cut across oncoming traffic as Tarni screamed in mock horror, then tore down Sunset to Fairfax. Visions of Canter's famous seven-layer cake and a cozy booth had Tarni drooling as she leaned against Logan while he concentrated on driving. She loved the way he smelled after performing—not that she had much experience with concerts. Not yet. But they'd been rehearsing for weeks. The smell of the stage and sweat and his unmistakable man scent had her snuggling up against him and sniffing.

Tarni refused to discuss what she'd done to him in the ocean. But she knew he'd remained behind in the water waiting for her, never losing faith that she'd return. And when she felt him slipping into the abyss, she'd taken him to a place hidden from the world and joined him in a dance as old as time...and she knew her heart was lost to this man.

Hurriedly parking in Canter's lot then running around to the front of the building, Tarni and Logan entered the storied deli and took a booth tucked away from the hustle and bustle—for even at midnight, Canter's had a crowd. Those that were looking for a late-night meal, others hoping to satisfy their sweet tooth, and even a few starving actors and actresses that never got turned away if they didn't quite have enough money to cover a bowl of matzo ball soup or mish-mosh.

Tarni grabbed a menu and perused it. "I am hungry."

"When are you not?"

"You should talk! You just ate two hot dogs."

"What do you want, then?" Logan indulged Tarni and pointed to her favorite menu item. "Let me guess, the Monte Cristo?"

Tarni nodded and clapped her hands again, and when the waitress came to take their order, Logan added carrot cake to Tarni's order along with two coffees.

"I can't believe you are going to stuff that sandwich down then polish it off with seven-layer cake."

"And a bite of yours. No? You won't let me have any?" Tarni widened her eyes and hit Logan with a soulful look that she couldn't quite pull off due to the mischief lurking in her round cobalt orbs.

“Evil child.”

When the waitress returned with their order, Logan took a bite of cake and watched Tarni as she continued to pout.

“Open your mouth.”

Placing a forkful of carrot cake in Tarni's mouth, Logan appreciated the way she savored the tart, sweet cream cheese-laden spiciness, licking her lips then demanding more with those captivating eyes. He couldn't get enough.

“Are you excited about going on tour with me?”

“Yes.”

Logan frowned.

“But?”

“But nothing. I'm excited. I can't wait to see what it's like. It's just... I heard from Kimberly, and I'm worried about her. She insists she is fine, but I hear something in her voice that has me worried. I tried to get it out of her, but Kim has a mind of her own. You can't persuade her to do or say anything she's not ready to divulge. Stubborn brat."

Logan could hear the fondness and love Tarni had for her sibling.

"And the others? Your older sisters?"

"I never considered them my sisters. It's funny. I mean... we are related but only by half. They are my father's daughters... not my mother's. Kimberly and me? We are sisters. The others? They're the enemy," replied Tarni darkly.

"You don't get along with any of them?" Logan asked, intrigued that Tarni was so forthright. Usually, she avoided his questions or pretended she hadn't heard him ask.

"Oh, I guess they're OK. I mean, Doris is a pain in the ass. She's the oldest. Pearl, Skye, Nerida, and Merra are the youngest of that bunch and don't give me much trouble. They were rather friendly toward Kim and me. Riva and Aulani are twins and total bitches, but in a self-centered, 'we only think of ourselves' kind of way. Celestine and Cordelia are the next oldest behind Doris and they are her henchmen. Those three just won't let up on...um...familial matters, and I'm always in trouble when it comes to them."

"What of your mother? You said she only had you and Kimberly?"

"Mom is dead. My father killed her." Tarni mumbled this out between sips of coffee, and the news stunned Logan. He'd heard plenty about Tarni's despicable father, but he had no idea Tarni's mother had lost her life at his hands. She failed to mention that little tidbit when speaking about her past.

"Are you sure it was he who did this?" he asked gently.

Tarni looked up, her eyes fierce, her jaw set.

"I'm sure. I didn't even get to see Mom. He had her cremated and tossed into the Atlantic somewhere off the coast of Florida. So, I never got to tell her goodbye."

"I'm sorry, Baby. So sorry."

Tarni gazed up at Logan, eyes blazing.

"Someday, I am going to return and kill him myself to avenge my mother, and when I do, I want to make sure the last thing he sees is my face before he closes his eyes for the last time."

Tarni's words sent a chill down Logan's spine, and the look in her eyes caused him to swallow several times, then censor any comments he knew would be empty words in light of her fury.

Did he believe her? Absolutely.

She had the look of an ice queen—or a sociopath. Her fingertips crackled with unshed magic. Yet, despite her anger, Tarni had a cold detachment Logan had only witnessed in those who worked as assassins or spies. Ruthless killers who didn't associate with those in a proper society but lived on the fringe. Would his Tarni go through with this promise to kill her father? Was she so unstable that her mild indifference and seemingly blasé attitude when discussing what came down to patricide had her as vulnerable as a newborn child?

What did it say about his mental state that he found Tarni's decree a turn-on? Her lust for vengeance. Her thirst for justice served the darkness within.

Logan knew he was a lost cause when it came to Tarni Vanderzee, because despite all this, he wanted her. And quite frankly, who was he to judge?

Did he hope to sway her from this path? He knew he wouldn't be able to, and it worried him beyond all reason. Logan knew what was waiting for Tarni should she succeed and put an end to her father's life—and Logan intended that she never have to suffer those details nor face that task she put on herself. So if it came down to it, Logan decided he'd be the one to kill the bastard.

Even though those he answered to forbid him from getting so involved, little did they know he was already too invested in Tarni's future to accept their archaic rules.

Tarni was his Fate...his destiny.

And he'd go to his grave to protect her.

"I've ruined your night with my tale of woe." Tarni sulked, tilting her head so her hair cascaded down around her shoulders in such a way Logan found himself momentarily dazzled by it.

"No! I'm happy you trust me enough to open up a bit more. That's all I was thinking."

"You aren't upset that I'm a witch? A *dark* witch?" she murmured, glancing around the deli to make sure no one had overheard.

"On the contrary, it excites me. I like having my fiery, little witch trying to fight my battles for me." Logan scraped his fork across his plate and licked the cream cheese from it as he ate another piece of cake.

"And what battles would those be?" asked Tarni, watching the way Logan's mouth moved as he polished the icing off his fork then swallowed. Tarni was forever fascinated by Logan's throat and how it moved when he did the mundane like swallowing or running a razor across it.

"Oh, I don't know. Fending off the multitude of women who would have their way with me. Only allowing those through that I've shown some modicum of interest. You know. To while away an hour or so with."

Logan's words broke Tarni's reverie, and she bared her teeth at him then growled.

"You're a dog."

"Woof, woof."

"Seriously, Logan. You are a pig of such epic proportions I

have a mind to let you go off on tour and remain behind to find myself a proper boyfriend."

"You can't leave me and remain behind. I'd get lonely. When I'm lonely, I do all manner of naughty things to make up for my boredom. And boyfriend? Tarni, love, I'm not your boyfriend," scoffed Logan with a snort.

Tarni stilled. Her demeanor changed as she became grim, barely breathing before asking, "What are you then?"

Tarni observed Logan as he pondered her words and reached deep inside for just the proper response. But when he gazed into her eyes, his wicked and gleaming with ungodly mirth, he allowed only the slightest movement of lips to show just how difficult a time he was having controlling his laughter before responding.

"Why, I'm your Master, of course."

Logan gave Tarni such a look of smug cockiness, and she did the only thing she could think of to garner the result which would give her satisfaction. She picked up the last bit of Logan's carrot cake and smashed it into his face with as much force as she dared to employ. Then she stood up, straightened her skirt, and sashayed out of the restaurant to await Logan in her Mustang—and she would drive, thank you!

Bubby, one of the men who worked the counter, walked over to where Logan was wiping the cake from his face and gathering up the mess, placing the soiled napkin on his plate.

"That one is a real firecracker, Duffy. I think you need to hang onto her, you know?"

"Oh? And why would I possibly want to do something like that, man?"

Bubby watched as Tarni strolled out the front door, head held high and shoulders back, and smiled. "Because, if you ever need to go to war or want someone to watch your back? That one there is who I'd choose to fight your battles for you. She'd take care to make sure you'd come out on the other side of any skirmish then would spend the rest of her days nursing you back to health—if you know what I mean."

"Oh, she'd nurse me back to health alright, Bubby. But then she'd kill me for good measure."

Bubby smiled down at Logan and slipped him the bill. His shirt was rumpled, and his apron wasn't pristine since he spent most of his time working in the kitchen preparing the food. Picking up the bill and standing, Logan slapped Bubby on the shoulder affectionately and continued, "After all, Bubby, Tarni might have my back, but what good will it do me if I wind up dead? She's a man-eater."

"Yeah, Duff...but what a way to go, man. What a way to go."

Logan nodded in agreement.

"The only way to go, Bubby. The *only* way."

CHAPTER 27

The night before they'd start touring was upon them and Logan had one thing on his mind. Making sure Tarni got in one last lesson before they left.

"Seriously? Now? Why don't we make an early night of it? Or better yet, let's create some heat between the sheets, mister!"

Tarni was furious at Logan's insistence they train.

"Where are your daggers, woman? You need to be able to whip them out faster than you've been doing."

"I'm going to use them on you if you don't let up on me."

They continued sparring on their private beach well into the night. No one bore witness to the two paranormal beings flashing and fighting and even allowing a bit of magic to surround them—at least as far as Tarni was concerned.

Logan didn't comment when she let loose a stream of dark magic and watched with some interest as it danced around the shoreline then dissolved in a spark and puff of smoke.

"Was that supposed to scare me or something?"

"Or something. But this should give you a thrill."

And with that, Tarni placed both hands on either side of

Logan's face and kissed him...but at the same time, shot a jolt of witchy magic into him that caused his knees to buckle.

Falling to the ground and landing on his bottom, Logan looked up at the evil sorceress, noting her shoulders were rocking with unbridled merriment.

"Evil child. Was that to prove your strength? Or do you have more in your arsenal?"

"Silly man. That took barely any effort on my part."

Logan's eyes widened in wonder. His siren was strong—even more so than anyone had suspected, and he was suddenly overcome with a sense that he might have bitten off more than he could chew with this one.

"Do I scare you, Logan MacDuff?"

"No, you excite me, you incredibly strong woman."

Before he could reach out and pull her into an embrace, movement from the shoreline drew his attention, and before Logan knew what had happened, a large looming figure appeared before them.

"I've been looking for you, baby doll. Remember me?"

The man Buffalo Jim called Romano was suddenly upon them and belatedly Tarni remembered he was a vampire.

"Logan, watch out! He's a... oomph!"

Before Tarni could finish her words, the vampire had his hand around her throat and began to squeeze the life out of her. Logan was already on him but before he could react, Romano flashed away then doubled back and slammed his fists into Logan's back. When Logan buckled to his knees, the man wrapped his arms around Logan's torso and sunk his teeth into the artery on Logan's neck.

Tarni, dazed and slightly winded, looked on in horror then sprang into action.

Like a demon from Hell, she threw herself at the vampire, but not like some unskilled buffoon trying her best to be a mouse who would charge at an elephant. Instead, Tarni let loose her siren voice and hit decibels no mortal or immortal should ever have to live through. Much to her amazement, as well as Romano's, her voice shattered his eardrums causing him to lurch back and drop to the ground.

Logan was in a semi-prone position, woozy from the bite, but with it enough to have blocked Tarni's voice with his own magic. And not a moment too soon. Seagulls dropped out of the sky and Logan was certain dolphins and a few whales responded to Tarni's utterances, and he blinked in amazement.

But what took him even further in his incredulity was the change that overcame his siren.

Gone was the beautiful girl who'd been teasing him moments earlier, and in her place stood a woman frightening in her fury. Eyes black like obsidian. Wrath and vengeance transformed her face into something terrifying yet magnificent at the same time, and Logan was in awe.

"My God. She's incredible."

His veneration was short lived, however, especially when Tarni chose that very moment to crush her lips to Romano's open mouth, her teeth becoming as sharp and dagger-like as the vampires. Dragging him into the surf, Tarni proceeded to plunge to depths Logan was sure no vampire had ever been before.

And Logan didn't think Tarni planned on making love to the man on the bottom of the sea when she reached it.

"He looks kind of lumpy."

"Bloated. I think the word you are looking for is bloated."

"Bloated then. I've never seen a dead vampire before, and didn't think water would affect them so...so..."

"Squishily?" Tarni offered.

"Is squishily even a word?" Logan asked, taking his eyes from the mangled corpse of the vampire Tarni informed him was named Romano.

"It is now. So... about this."

"Yeah."

"I'm not sure what came over me. When I saw Romano bite you, I flipped my switch."

"You could say that again."

"You have no idea, then, why he came after you?" asked Logan.

"None at all. I only met him briefly back at Buffalo Jim's."

Tarni bit her lower lips contemplating the dead vampire.

"What do we do with him?"

"We could burn him. No body, no evidence."

"Do vampires even burn?"

"They used to in sunlight before they discovered ways of defending themselves from it." Logan noted how nonchalantly they were coping with this new situation, and he wondered if the two of them were damned beings or slightly insane.

"You couldn't leave him down there? Maybe feed him to a passing shark or something?"

Tarni snorted. It was the only response she could muster.

"Perhaps we should just throw him back into the ocean and hope he becomes a shark biscuit?" Logan offered.

"I think we need to burn him...scatter his bones and ashes and pretend like we are none the wiser if anyone comes looking for him," replied Tarni, shrugging when Logan raised his eyebrows.

Yep. Definitely damned, thought Logan.

"What? It's either burn him out in the desert somewhere or I will have to swim around all night looking for Jaws. And not for anything, I need some sleep before we depart tomorrow, or

I'll probably murder Billy in his sleep. Did you notice he never seems to stop drumming on whatever is nearby? It makes me nuts."

Logan shook his head and laughed.

"What?" asked Tarni, her brow wrinkling in confusion.

"My dear, you are dripping with sea water, your hair is caked with sand and God knows what else, this man's vile blood is soaked into what's left of your clothing and you are worried about Billy's drumming keeping you awake and cranky."

"Yeah...so?"

"So, all I can think about is how incredibly hot you are, and that despite being weakened and in a state of sheer exhaustion, I want to bed you right now, and I fear the two of us are deranged and beyond all hope."

"I think it's terribly sweet the way we lust after each other with a corpse a mere two feet from where we're standing."

"Yep. We're mental. I fear the two of us will wind up in over our heads and floundering out at sea."

"Why Logan. You know I wouldn't have it any other way!"

CHAPTER 28

Somewhere in the USA, early August 1987

Riding on a tour bus going from gig to gig had its moments, but also became trying, especially with five man-boys up to juvenile hijinks and their girlfriends allowing it.

Kimberly had called informing her she'd found a stable boyfriend whom the sisters had approved, and when they were otherwise occupied with their mundane chore of ridding the world of renegade witches, werewolves, and sirens that went bump in the night, Kim had run off to move in with the lad and his parents. Tarni was thrilled to find out they were witches—and knew her mother's family.

Tarni also knew the time was drawing near that she'd have to move ahead with her plans to damage her father's dynasty—even on a small scale. Knowing Kimberly was out of harm's way gave her great comfort and she wanted to open up to Logan and make him aware of what she'd cooked up. That, and perhaps in light of the vampire attack, it might be time to inform Logan she had a stalker. Tarni almost convinced herself it must have been Romano who was behind the notes because they stopped showing up.

Tarni wasn't deluding herself that she'd wouldn't have to confront whoever was stalking her someday if Romano wasn't the culprit, but right now she was deliriously happy just living in the moment of all this craziness.

Alive, in love, taunted by her wanton lust for a man she now needed beyond reason, thrilled to see the workings of how a tour went down, and amazed at being at each concert, either front and center or backstage where she'd wait, towel in hand, for Logan to make his triumphant exit from the stage—a sea of screaming adoration in his wake.

She would wipe the sweat from his face even as he laughingly grabbed her and threw himself into a passionate kiss, Tarni screaming a little at having his sweat-soaked body enveloping her.

Somber Sea was breaking records, making the news, and climbing the charts. The new album debuted in May to stellar reviews and a spread in Rolling Stone magazine, and ever since, life as Logan knew it had changed. He could no longer go out and about without some kind of disguise. But since he embraced the lifestyle and accepted the accolades reveling in the sound of his adoring fans slamming into him every night, and the *ka-ching!* of his bank account soaring with every successful stop, he had little to complain about.

"Where the hell are we anyway?" Cash complained loudly. The first night riding the bus to their next location, Cash had surprised Tarni by lifting her top and pulling it over her head then running his hands up and under her bra. "Give me a kiss."

Tarni looked at Logan who shrugged. "Fair play. We're almost to Sparks, Nevada."

Tarni acquiesced and wriggled a little with a gasp while

Cash slid his hand between her legs. "Nice and wet. She's a keeper, Duffy."

Knowing most people wouldn't understand her acceptance of everything Logan asked of her, Tarni was secure and confident in what she wanted, what she deemed OK, and how she wanted to go about experiencing everything. Logan laid everything out from day one, just as he told her he would, and Tarni readily signed on the dotted line.

"Never show anyone you are intimidated. You keep that head high and take whatever you get and own it, Baby."

And she did.

Those were Logan's words to live by and Tarni obeyed.

Pushing Cash off with a giggle, she waited to see what he'd do or say next.

"Tonight, let's swap Duff...I want in this one."

"Oh!" screamed Laney, "Let's have a big orgy by the Washoe Lake. We haven't done that in ages, and we will be there in a few hours."

"Bonfire!" cried Deanna with a wink toward Tarni. "Wait until you experience one of those! I call dibs on Logan."

"You always call dibs on Logan," cried Gunther.

And so it went...all the way to the lake.

That night the bonfire did rage, but as the flames grew high into the air, Tarni's anxiety grew right along with it...and Logan could tell. He slid down on the ground next to where she was sitting and prodded her with his shoulder.

"What?"

"What do you mean, 'what?' I didn't say anything."

"You didn't have to. Your forehead is creased, and you keep biting your lower lip."

"I don't want to be shared with Cash. I'm yours. I understand you play around and have causal sex with other women.

OK. Fine. I don't have to like it, but I accepted your terms. But no. I can't do something like that."

"OK."

Tarni blinked and let her air out in a whoosh.

"That's it? OK? You aren't going to scold me or belittle me."

Logan's face became animated in anger and frustration. "I would never belittle you, Tarni. If you don't want the men to touch you, I respect that and they better, or they will have to answer to me. Just remember, someday something might happen where a man gets to you and uses you for his pleasure. I might not be there to save you. If that should ever happen, don't let it break you."

"You insufferable bore. I can save myself."

"I have every confidence that you can." Logan leaned in and whispered, "Dark witches are badass. Sirens even more extraordinary. But even so...don't assume you can get out of every situation that comes your way. If something horrid happens to you...you need to keep your fighting spirit. Don't let it break you, Baby. Ever. Sometimes those that are the sweetest are made into something horrible. Not because they were weak, but because they cared too much. If something evil should come calling, play along, bide your time, then fight with everything you've got. You can only do that if you refuse to let whatever is done to you break you. I might not be around to back you up in a fight for your life."

Tarni's heart thumped loudly in her chest, and she felt that fissure again, a premonition that something in Logan's words rang true, and she wondered if the upcoming fight to take down her father's dynasty and extend it to the other leading males in the siren world might bring her ruin. Did Logan feel it too? That she would see horrific battle before the victory was won?

If this were the case, something like Cash wanting to bed her was the least of her worries—and the lessor of evils. She knew what the males in the siren society would mete out to her if they ever captured her and she couldn't fight back.

Surprisingly, the band sat around the fire that night, got stoned, laughed, danced around, and each went off with their prospective girlfriends, leaving Logan and Tarni alone by the edge of the lake.

"I made a mountain out of a molehill, didn't I?" she asked him sheepishly.

Logan smiled while staring at the lake.

"Baby, despite my shortcomings, I would never let another man touch you. Not unless it was something you wanted. Someone you wanted more than me."

Like that would ever happen, Tarni thought to herself.

"Why do you do what you do with other women? Is it because of...?"

Logan squeezed her hand, stopping her question midsentence, and didn't answer. He just looked down then sighed.

"Don't ever hate me for who I am, Tarni. I know it's not right to ask you to accept me as I am, but that's what I'm doing."

Tarni placed a hand on Logan's cheek. "Tell me."

"Baby, it's something I'm forced to do despite any decision I may have to the contrary. I'm a slave to this need. It fuels what I am. I can't control what's inside me."

Logan stretched out on the ground and looked up at the stars for a while then closed his eyes. Tarni traced her finger down his face and across his lips then looked at the water, deep in thought.

What on Earth could Logan mean? What kind of Breed was a slave to sexual desire? A demon? Could Logan be a fae...or succubae of some kind? The thought was disquieting and Tarni swallowed loudly even as she gently pet the unruly curls that framed Logan's face.

How could someone who looks like an angel have such demons?

Just then, a flicker of light reached them from across the lake, not far from where they were camped, yet in an area that didn't have any trail nearby leading to it. Tarni suddenly had inner alarm bells going haywire and kicked off her sandals.

"Wait here."

"Mnnhmm." Logan was drifting away half asleep, so Tarni didn't hesitate.

Plunging into the lake, Tarni swam strongly, efficiently, and silently just under the surface, coming up in the general area of where she'd seen the movement. At first her eyes, needing adjustment to the darkness, didn't see anything out of the ordinary, but slowly, as shapes began to take form, Tarni spied something that appeared out of order in the desert vista, and she crept out of the lake to examine it.

Feeling ill and breaking out in a sweat, Tarni found a large white envelope imbedded into the bark of a tree with a knife. Not caring if she were damaging any prints in the process of removing the envelope, Tarni pulled the contents out and used the moonlight to examine the photograph inside.

It was a photo of the makeshift "grave" she and Logan had dug and placed Todd in.

And it was empty.

CHAPTER 29

"I didn't much like Portland or Seattle, but Canada was fun." Tarni was trying to read on the tour bus while the boys—she refused to call them men—were having a Silly String fight. The place was a war zone.

"Hmm? Oh, I liked every place we've been," replied Tarni.

Stephanie sighed, stretched, then sighed again. "I'm bored."

Exasperated, Tarni slid her bookmark in place to save the page she was on then turned to Stephanie. "Why don't you find something to read?"

"Read? Are you serious? No. I want some attention. They've been goofing off for days and none of them have paid any attention to us in the slightest."

"We could always make out in front of them."

Tarni didn't know why she said it other than it was the quickest way she could think of to stop the band from tearing up the bus and get them horny and in focus. Once they had sex they'd all fall asleep, and she could get back to reading.

What? I'm at a really good part and don't want any distractions! She'd scolded her inner voice.

"Let's go for it." Stephanie whipped off her top and French kissed Tarni. It only took ten seconds for the bus to quiet down, especially when Tarni stood up so Stephanie could begin to undress her.

It was amazing how well-balanced one became when you spent most of your time in a moving bus wearing stiletto heels while French-kissing someone.

It certainly got the boys attention.

Tarni gave it thirty minutes, certain she'd be back reading her book by then.

~

"I gotta pee," Deanna complained loudly.

"So? Go use the john then, and shut up about it," replied Gunther.

"Have you been in there lately? It stinks and the toilet's backed up. Hey, Phil! Find us some place to stop so I can go pee!" Deanna shouted at their hapless driver.

Billy sat up straight and had an evil grin on his face.

"We should get you girls some litter boxes to use on the bus."

"Ew, you're sick, Billy. But I'm not kidding...I gotta go."

The other girls on the bus began to make similar noises and Tarni had to admit she'd been holding it in for quite some time now.

"Phil... stop the bus." Logan called out.

"What? We're in the middle of Nebraska! There isn't anything for a few miles yet."

"Phil, I said stop the bus," Logan repeated. "We're in Whitney aren't we? Isn't that the campground up ahead?

Phil confirmed that it was and upon Logan's instruction, slowly maneuvered the tour bus into the old, now-empty campground and left it idling. The two semis following with the gear and lighting and wardrobe changes did the same and the roadies spilled out to see why they were stopping.

"Ladies...take your clothing off and use that sand over there like a litter box," Logan ordered. He was met with a wall of resistance.

Smirking like he'd already won some kind of prize, he climbed back into the bus then came out with a goodie bag of drugs and a wad of cash.

"Five thousand dollars apiece and all the finest prime middle cocaine old Ernie just delivered in Utah for any girl who does what I say. Now...take off your clothing and go use your litter box, ladies. Oh...and make sure you meow for us. Loudly."

A few hours later and after a lengthy swim in the lake, all the girls who partied were exhausted and sleeping quietly on the tour bus—only Tarni remained awake.

"You don't obey me much, do you?"

"There were plenty of women willing to jump through your demented hoops tonight."

"That Melissa chick...she is going to be sore for weeks. I've never seen one woman do an entire band, all the roadies, and even Phil in one night."

Tarni didn't comment. She just continued looking out the window as the road markers went by, counting the miles.

"You're mad at me."

"No. Maybe a bit disappointed, but not mad."

"If I could just be the man you want, you'd be happy...is that it?"

"I am happy, Logan."

"And why is that?"

"Because I love you."

It was the first time she uttered those words to Logan and

his face looked stricken instead of joyous, and Tarni didn't understand why. He pulled her close, giving her a gentle kiss then got up and went to the back of the bus and crawled into the bunk he shared with Tarni.

He didn't tell her he loved her back.

A few minutes later, Tarni followed him into the bunk, curled up against him and fell asleep.

He remained flat on his back, staring at the bunk above his as the bus drove on into the night.

CHAPTER 30

"Duffy! Duffy! Oh, my God, there he is!"

"Marry me, Duffy!"

The screaming girls, the cacophony of being part of a large tour was incredible, frightening, and exhilarating and exhausting all rolled into one—and Tarni loved every minute of it. Well, maybe not the screaming groupies constantly trying to get backstage and into Logan's pants.

"This is nuts."

Logan smiled as Tarni commented, peering out of the tour bus and surveyed the fans holding all manner of signage and other oddities, waiting for the band to exit.

"Look at that girl...she has pom-poms and is covered in glitter!"

"Forget her, look at that one in the bikini top with roller skates on. Every time she rolls by, she flashed her tits in our direction!" Logan laughed and glanced at Gunther. "She's your type."

"What? Blonde and hot?" replied Gunther.

"No. Willing to show her tits with little or no motivation."

"True. That is my type."

"I think that's all our type," said Cash as he lit a cigarette and leaned back in his seat, looking bored. "Right?"

"Perhaps." Logan raked his gaze over Tarni and gave her a soft smile that made her shiver from the top of her head down to her shimmery, purple-painted toes. She wet her lips unconsciously and turned back to contemplate the throng of females clamoring for attention outside the bus. She didn't notice Logan's nostrils flare and the way his black eyes went from playful to molten with hunger and longing.

"I can smell the Aqua Net from here," sniffed Laney.

"Oh, please! You went through a bottle in a week. You're just jealous because they have better hair than yours," cried Deanna who was snuggled up against Billy, filing her nails.

"Well, at least I bother doing my hair. Some people don't seem to care what they look like," replied Laney, cutting her eyes toward Tarni.

Tarni ground her teeth but didn't take the bait. Over the last several weeks, Laney had been making such remarks and then feigning innocence whenever one of the other girls commented on it. Tarni hadn't bothered engaging her and chalked it up to the fact Logan had refused her advances and called her a slut when she kept hinting they should all swap partners or have an orgy.

It wasn't that Logan suddenly morphed into a monogamous saint, but he refused to let Laney and her sudden jealousy of Tarni give her the upper hand by giving in to her games. At least that's how he explained to Tarni his abrupt, barely concealed, animosity toward Laney was all about.

Dave brought another girl, April, into their group and had been all but ignoring Laney for the better part of two weeks. That was probably another reason for her sour disposition and attempt to use Logan to make Dave jealous. When her plans went awry, her attitude soured and plummeted to mild nastiness.

Tarni noted, however, Laney's willingness to jump into bed with Dave and April whenever he snapped his fingers at her, so she had very little sympathy to give. Not that she was any better. The after-parties had involved so many different faces, all willing to spend a few moments with Logan then be forgotten, sweet memories, as he moved on to another town and the next group of fans.

She asked Logan in a moment of exasperation why he kept taking different groupies to bed when he'd all but told her he'd rather not. "I mean, can't you tell your superiors you'd rather not?"

"Aw, sweetheart. But so many times I do want. And I get turned on even more when you watch me...or join me. What does that make us?"

In times of doubt, she'd reflect on her own situation, her upbringing and animosity toward her father and his treatment of women and wonder if her acceptance of Logan's "manifesto" had something to do with her relationship with her loathed parent.

But then she realized part of who she was didn't want or expect the person she chose to be with to change who *he* was to please her—nor did she expect Logan to stop her from being who she intended to be and where her plans would take her. Logan told her from the start what he was like, and she willingly went into his arms and into his crazy life.

It was certainly the education she'd asked for, and she couldn't deny how incredible Logan looked surrounded by all those women in his bed and how hot it got her watching him have sex.

"I'm a deviant."

"What?" Logan chuckled and brushed the hair from Tarni's face.

"Nothing. Just making an observation."

Logan leaned close and whispered in Tarni's ear. "Maybe when this tour is over we can make a run for it, and I won't ever have to be this way again. Maybe your magic can heal me when the punishment appears on my body."

Oh my God! thought Tarni, *Logan can't escape this situation without those wounds appearing on his back. What kind of sick game are they playing with him? Who are they anyway...and why Logan?*

The concert that night was extraordinary. It was being filmed, and the crew was getting every angle imaginable to capture every crazy moment. Tarni watched from just offstage as Logan strutted across the expanse of the stage then out on the bridge that brought him into the center of the audience where he'd taunt them just out of reach—the security guards ready to toss an overenthusiastic fan back into the mass of humanity, lest they dare try to rush him.

The band gave the fans two extra songs during the encore despite the playlist being set, as a reward for the intense stomping of feet and sheer loudness in their cheering—and that they'd continued an entire fifteen minutes after the final song.

"You are going to get billed extra for going over time," Chuck, their tour manager, complained.

"Who gives a shit about the money?" said Logan. "Listen to them! They deserve it."

When the lights came up once more, the sound of the crowd slammed into Tarni and was unlike anything she'd ever experienced before. She knew, without a doubt, she'd need this for herself. This adoration and love flowing into her by adoring fans. And she'd get it. She promised this to herself.

Once Logan is done with this tour, it will be my turn. And he will be there holding the towel for me like he promised. And I can't wait. Then watch out Daddy-O, because once I make it, once I'm powerful enough, I will come calling and vengeance will be mine.

She watched Logan take the stage again and was gobsmacked when the crescendo of sound from the audience grew even louder.

How is that possible? It's already earsplitting!

Logan chose that moment to seek her out, his eyes peering into the darkened area of the place she remained hidden from sight by the audience but in the spot Logan knew she'd be. His face was triumphant and full of exhilaration even as he gave her a "Can you believe this?" grin.

As the fans chanted, "Somber Sea, Somber Sea!" over and over in a frantic homage to their band, Logan prowled the length of the stage like a panther stalking its prey to the delight of everyone present.

Just before the end of the final song, Logan maneuvered himself to Tarni's side of the stage and winked in her direction before running and launching himself into the crowd to their delight, and the utter horror of management and security. The band didn't miss a beat and kept playing like this was par for the course when it came to one Logan MacDuff.

Tarni's heart, lodged fully into her throat, didn't calm down until two of the security guards managed to wrestle Logan out of the frenetic clutches of his worshipping fans and back to the safety of the stage...shirt gone, hair tousled, and with a swagger that left her laughing and shaking her head at the insanity of it all.

Tarni waited, towel at the ready, as Logan made his way to

her, seeking her out in the darkness, until exhausted but flush with the success of his performance and the approval of the crowd, he pulled her into his arms and gave her a fierce and possessive kiss while she administered to him, wiping the sweat from his face and neck and clinging to him for dear life. He all but consumed her in that moment, and she secretly looked forward to it during every performance, much to the incredulity of the rest of the girls.

"Don't you want to be in the front row and watch the show?" asked once Stephanie.

"No. I want to be where Logan knows I'm waiting for him," was her simple reply.

Although, from time to time, she would watch from her reserved seat just to the right of where his mic was set on stage...but whenever the first strands of the final song would play, Tarni would rush to the sidelines and wave over security to allow her backstage and over to her spot...holding on to the towel and knowing in just a few more minutes Logan would go from belonging to thousands to all hers again.

"The party is going to be rad tonight!"

"Did you see the press? They went nuts! We are going to be all over the news!"

"Where's the candy? I need a boost!" Billy complained, massaging one arm. His drumming came with a side of ache that only a good dose of cocaine seemed to ease—or so he said.

"Got a fresh supply in from Ernie today! Time to party!" cried Cash, as he swept past Tarni still holding on to Logan, but not before he grabbed on to her, nibbling on her neck. "You need to stop keeping this one all to yourself, man. She's too scrumptious not to share!"

"She's that, all right. And she's mine, dickhead," laughed Logan, keeping a proprietary arm around Tarni's waist.

They took the party to the penthouse in their hotel, and it

went on for hours. Once the hangers-on celebrity set made their appearance then left, followed by the media and their endless need for interviews, the insanity multiplied.

The crew brought up selected girls from the hopefuls who'd waited outside the concert venue and were handpicked by the guys. The hotel's kitchen staff kept a steady stream of champagne, liquor, and delectable food flowing and didn't seem too upset with the goings-on. Even when Dave and Gunther started throwing items from the room off the balcony and into the pool below, the management was indulgent and looked the other way—and sent the bill to the band's attorneys with a smile.

Eventually, the revelry wound down and Logan, flush with affection and flying with the plethora of drugs coursing through his system, cocked his finger in Tarni's direction.

"Bedroom. Go get showered up and ready for my enjoyment. And Baby? Pick out a few toys."

Tarni gave Logan a lazy blink of her eyes and stood from the sofa she'd been lounging on.

"Your wish is my command, Master," she replied.

"Yep. I gotta get me a girl like Tarni," said Cash, as he passed by with three girls in tow.

"Can't," replied Logan. "She's one of a kind."

A few minutes later, freshly showered and lying on the massive bed all these penthouses seemed to employ, probably due to the host of rockers, movie stars, and VIPs who came to stay in them, Tarni watched while Logan entered the bedroom. Her eyes widened when she realized he hadn't brought a bevy of brainless beauties in with him for his enjoyment.

She'd witnessed his debauchery before, so she wondered at this lack of female companionship. Once, much to Tarni's amusement, Logan had three women stacked up on top of one another forming a tower of sex. Logan got to business, licking each girl going from the one on the bottom and working his way up, then positioning himself so he could perform the intricate maneuvers needed to service the girl on the bottom by sliding into her while munching on the girl on top. The one in the middle awaited her turn with a shift of hips and pouty complaint that she was being left out.

Tarni's hand wound up sliding down her body as she touched herself while taking in the sight of Logan's sexual escapades, and she couldn't believe how many positions he went through and what these girls were willing to do to remain in his good graces.

After a few hours—yes hours, thanks to the wonders of cocaine and its ability to keep a man at it for that length of time —Logan had quite the situation set up with two girls servicing him in a hungry, slurping battle of who would swallow the sausage whole, while he had the third riding his face in ecstasy.

He'd pushed the leggy blonde from her position straddling his face and rolled her down beside Tarni while thoroughly kissing the two who'd been working so hard to keep him rock hard—they needn't have worried about that.

Satisfied with his kissing administration of the other two, he positioned the first blonde near Tarni and ordered her to go down on her, much to Tarni's surprise. The blonde didn't need any prodding and began to lick Tarni, sticking her tongue into the soft folds of her lips and working her way to Tarni's clit. While not a regular occurrence, it wasn't the first time Tarni had this happen, thanks to her brief education with Monique and Stacey.

What was novel was the fact Logan began fucking the girl doggy-style, all the while staring deeply into Tarni's eyes. Not expecting the flood of lust that slammed into her at that precise moment, Tarni moaned in pleasure, but Logan immediately ordered her to keep looking at him.

"Stay with me, Baby. Ride it out, but look at me. Only me."

The other women all but disappeared. Tarni and Logan were lost in each other's minds. They become the props for the pair to amuse themselves with. Tarni startled when she felt Logan slide into her, so intense was her focus on his wicked black orbs, she didn't notice anything else as he rested his forehead on hers.

"Don't ever change who you are, Baby. Not for me, not for anyone. My God, you are incredible." The crushing ache in her heart was unexpected. Tarni didn't understand what it meant or why she'd reacted to Logan's words in such a way...yet even as she lost herself when his intensity and expert ministrations clouded her thoughts, a part of her filed it away to examine on another day.

So the last thing Tarni expected was Logan entering the bedroom now bereft of females.

"Baby. You look lonely. Lie back on the pillow and open yourself for me."

Tarni did as she was asked, wondering where Logan was going with this.

"Where are the girls?" she asked a bit breathlessly.

"Baby, you are the only girl. Perhaps, just this once, I can break the rules."

Right now, she was riding Logan's wave, and nothing would sway her from following along. He made love to her like a man drowning or waiting on death row for his final release from a life too difficult in which to remain.

They came together in an explosion Tarni was sure rocked the hotel to its foundations with its intensity.

That night, Tarni was awakened by noises coming from the bathroom. Thinking Logan had sneaked one of the adoring groupies in after she'd fallen asleep, she ran a frustrated hand through her tangled hair and crept to the door, her intention to startle her Lothario and freak out the bimbo.

What she found instead was a quietly sobbing Logan, his back bloodied and bruised, half insane from the pain he must been feeling.

CHAPTER 31

"Girls can't shoot."

"Says who?" Logan laughed.

"Says me," said Cash, and he sniffed when a cop friend of theirs handed Stephanie a revolver.

"You boys are crazy bored, aren't you?"

The officer had worked last night's concert in Phoenix, and now they were out in the Arizona desert shooting targets and drinking beer until they had to return for that night's show.

"Ten bucks says Steph blows a hole in the side of the tour bus."

"Done."

"Hey!" cried Stephanie as she pointed the gun at Gunther's foot. "I can shoot!"

Scrambling out of range of her fire, Gunther shook his head and said, "Women!" like that explained everything.

Logan looked at Tarni and winked. He'd seen her arsenal and was banking on her knowing something about weapons of the firing kind—or he was going to be hurting for money in about twenty minutes. He didn't let Tarni in on his side bets, however.

Logan refused to mention anything about the other night and his broken and maltreated back. When she tried to speak with him about it, he just shook his head and placed his fingers over her lips to stop any further questioning.

Tarni dropped it for now but knew she couldn't allow this to continue. It was time she discovered Logan's secrets and put a stop to the abuse being heaped on him by these unknown evil taskmasters to which he answered.

"Hey! I know. Let's set the bottles up on the fence and place bets. Anyone who can shoot ten in a row wins the money."

"You're on!" cried Billy and that was the most animated Tarni had ever seen the man off his drum set.

"I'm in." Dave threw a wad of cash down on the picnic table, and everyone followed suit.

Doing a quick count in her head, Tarni thought there had to be at least eight thousand dollars in play. She shook her head and sat back wondering if they'd go through with it.

"I'm going first."

Stephanie engaged the gun, a Glock 19, and aimed with wobbly hands.

Bam! Bam, bam, bam! Nothing. All ten shots rang out and she didn't hit a thing.

Everyone roared with laughter, and Deanna pushed her out of the way, grabbing the gun.

"Watch it!" Dave ducked and scowled at her and pointed to the fence railing and bottles. "Point there, dummy. Not at us!"

Deanna tried with the same result, although she managed to hit the road sign about twenty yards away.

All the men tried with varying degrees of success—or failure as it were.

Finally, Officer Jacobs, who'd watched indulgently like a proud Poppa witnessing his kids on their first shoot, stood up and retrieved the gun, slapping in a new magazine. "Let me show you how it's done."

He lined himself up facing the fence and let loose a stream of gunfire and got all but two bottles. "And that, right there boys, is how you do it!"

Reaching for the cash, Officer Jacobs was stopped by Logan's hand on his wrist. "Not so fast, man. Let my girl try."

Everyone turned to stare at Tarni who'd shook her head no, scowling like an irate cat who was sprayed with a water bottle. "No, that's OK. I'm good."

Logan stood up and walked over to the fence where he lined up a fresh set of ten beer bottles. "The bet was whoever could hit ten in a row. You got eight, Jacobs. Let's see if Baby can get all ten."

The men scoffed, the women laughed, and Tarni wanted to run away. She knew she could shoot like an expert, but did she really want to show her hand to this lot? Especially in front of a cop? What if he became suspicious and ran a check on her or something? She was about to decline, but then Logan came up to her and whispered, "Do it for me."

Ugh! This man! She thought as she stood and walked over to Officer Jacobs who held out his gun with a smirk.

"Anyone care to up the ante?" Logan called out.

"If your gal can hit all ten, she can keep that gun and a case full of bullets. It's unmarked. I was going to turn it in," said Officer Jacobs.

"I'll throw in another twenty-five thousand," said Billy. I'm good for it. But Baby isn't going to even come close to hitting anything. Right, darlin'?"

Tarni walked to the shooting line drawn in the dirt, let out a soft sigh, and took her stance. *Men! No... boys and their games!*

If she got in trouble with the law, she would personally murder Logan.

Clearing her mind, she let the stress go and allowed her inner predator out to play.

Bam! Bam, bam, bam, bam, bam, bam, bam, bam, bam!

Ten shots. Ten bottles shattered. Ten amazed faces turned in her direction...eleven if you counted Phil, their driver.

"Well, I'll be damned," said Billy and pointed to Logan. "You knew it all along, dirtbag."

Logan just smiled and winked at Tarni. "Actually, I didn't have a clue, but I know one thing for sure."

"What's that?" asked Dave.

"I'm not going to get this kitten's claws out if I'm naked and she has that gun. If Baby is mad at me, she might shoot my pecker off and feed it to the crows!"

You got that right, mister!

Tarni pulled the photo out of the envelope once more and stared at it, then read the note left with it: "I'm watching you. Always." She didn't know why she kept it to herself but winning the gun in the shooting contest made her feel a tad more secure. Witch magic, siren for backup and a gun...along with her hidden arsenal...Tarni was feeling like she could take care of anyone or anything that came at her or Logan.

Logan had enough to worry about without her adding to it.

Dumb, perhaps, but Tarni knew she was probably stronger than Logan despite his stellar display the day he'd dangled Todd off the balcony of her apartment all those months ago now.

"Do you think Gordon misses us?" she asked Logan the

next day as they were packing up their gear and moving on to Tucson.

"He's living it up with the lesbians, keeping an eye on our place with them. How hard can that be? They adore him."

"I know. But he probably thinks we're taking advantage of him. He's a good neighbor."

Logan just laughed off her worry and lit up a joint. Tarni hated that his drug use seemed to ramp up the longer the concert tour went on. She refused the pot, finding it stinky and nauseating, and only did the occasional line or two of coke which didn't make her very paranoid or awake. There was a new drug going around however, and the women seemed obsessed by it. Ecstasy, although Tarni had no idea what it did, nor did she bother inquiring.

She knew Logan upped his drug use to counter the pain from his back...and dull the constant worry that seemed to be building between them.

"I can't wait to do Tucson...after that it's a long, long drive to Dallas and three shows. We will have plenty of downtime." Logan seemed eager to get out of the bus and into a hotel.

That night, the concert in Tucson was fun and uneventful and the band was in high spirits when they climbed on board the bus for the long haul to Dallas.

"How long will it take us?" she asked Logan.

"Well...2 AM now. Tomorrow when we arrive, it will be late afternoon," Logan replied. "What? It's a huge state!"

Tarni couldn't imagine.

Hours later, having woken up and made her ablutions—and sharing a bus bathroom with five men notwithstanding, she was ready for that hotel room—Tarni couldn't believe they were still rolling along the Texas countryside.,

"This is Hell," she stated. "Cows, grass, and oil rigs. We haven't seen anything different since we left El Paso!"

"I told you."

That night, the sight of their hotel left Tarni and much of the band with the exception of Billy, gobsmacked.

"We're staying here?" Logan asked in wonder.

Tarni gulped and looked the massive, elegant structure and noted the name. "The Adolphus? This place is incredible."

Upon leaving their bus, the band discovered their manager, Chuck, waiting for them with a big grin on his face. "Things are changing for you boys. Get used to this from now on. We are making serious bank...oh, and your album just went triple platinum!"

To say the party that evening was long, loud, and boisterous would be an understatement. Forget for a minute that three other popular bands were in the area at the same time doing their own shows and all staying at the Adolphus. So were two big Hollywood producers, a director, several politicians and...

"Was that Jimmy Swaggart?" asked Tarni, biting her lip. "Isn't he going to like, I don't know, *implode* with all of us here?"

Logan laughed then looked worried. "With Motley, Aerosmith, and the rest of the bands in attendance, don't you let me see you get so starstruck you forget yourself, woman. Or I'll lock you in our room."

And what a room. They had one of the ten penthouses, and never had Tarni experienced such luxury.

The next few nights found her indulging in a little hundred dollar bill cocaine sniffing with Steven...hoping she'd not find herself on a permanent vacation after overindulging, a rousing and highly eye-opening game of drunken, naked Pictionary with the boys from OZ, and she realized that Tommy did have the world largest appendage since he'd run through the lobby flashing it at anyone and everyone he passed. By the time she saw Billy...platinum-blonde hair spiked to attention holding court with a bevy of beautiful women at his feet, Tarni knew she had well and truly experienced the rock and roll lifestyle.

Not even the scandalous appearance of a certain politician with someone other than his wife could phase Tarni at that point. And these people acted this way on a nightly basis. Insanity was the name of the game.

But after every good time had by all, there always seemed to be a fall—or a falling out, if you will, just waiting in the bushes to ruin the experience.

Tarni kept feeling things were slipping from her grasp and she was heading for a brick wall going well over one hundred miles an hour without a helmet on.

And she didn't know why.

CHAPTER 32

Up and down the United States they traveled. Days blurred into nights, the audience looked the same, the set list expanded and changed...each new city as forgetful as the next. But still the thrill of standing just off stage and listening to the screaming girls, the applause, Logan's deep, sexy voice, and the amazing music the band played, left Tarni begging for more.

There were always women, the girlfriends plus groupies, who wound up in bed with the band. Tarni remained by Logan's side through it all, nursing him back from the brink of insanity as he chose monogamy instead of coupling with a nameless face who would be gone the next day. Despite begging him to give up his brave attempt to stay hers alone, Tarni knew whoever was in control of Logan's life would be furious at his disobedience.

Logan didn't seem to care anymore.

Never once did she leave Logan's side, and when he overindulged in medication, she made sure he got back to his hotel or tour bus safely. Cleaned him up after the drug use, wiped away the powder or the newest drug paraphernalia to make an appearance, with needles and spoons and bits of tin foil. She mended costumes, chased away the underage girls always looking to sneak backstage, kept an eye on those who partied with the band in an effort to keep them honest, and did not allowing photographs or theft or the very many various things these wild hordes of women were wont to do just to be a part of it all. Be near the rock stars. Be a part of the glamour such as it was.

Every night his back grew worse.

Every night Tarni begged to deafened ears.

Until she could take it no more and cried herself to sleep wrapped around her lover, his blood soaking into the sheets.

On one break, when the band had two days of playtime in Las Vegas, they'd returned to her old place of employment, the guys enjoying the strip club and all it had to offer. Logan was buying drinks for everyone and offered to pay for dinner. No one stopped him. No one but Tarni. "You guys can afford to pay...chip in so it's not Logan alone carrying this crowd." The bandmates gave her a sullen look but agreed. There were fifteen or so hangers-on and the bill came to $4000—and that was just for dinner and drinks. Indulging in the VIP rooms with the strippers was another matter.

The next day they returned and did it all over again, but this time the band didn't need prodding to pay their share.

It started to become painfully obvious that something was up with Logan. The band noticed his lack of female companionship, not to mention his weakened state in the mornings.

Tarni, afraid the attention from the band would cause an incident or some revelation both she and Logan weren't prepared for, did the one thing she knew to put an end to such inquiries—she used her siren voice on everyone and convinced them everything was perfectly normal, and Logan was fine the way he was. She even tossed in some witch magic to cloud their minds and implant the thought that Logan had always shunned too much attention after a show.

No one questioned much after that when Logan refused to join the party.

After damaging the bands funds by spending too much time at the strip club, they all congregated at the place it all started for Logan and Tarni, The Peppermill, and much to her astonishment, upon entering, she ran into her youngest cousin, Adelaide Croy. Then Tarni looked over her shoulder to see Addy's sister Jessica, and their longtime pal, Charlie Sweet.

"Addy! Jessie! What are you doing here in Las Vegas?"

"We ran off together on an adventure," Jessica laughed but looked weary.

"I heard you were with Logan MacDuff!" gushed Adelaide. "Kimberly and I stay in touch. You can trust us, Tarni...we have our own secrets keeping us on our toes! I can't believe Logan is here on tour! We have tickets and everything."

"Here, let me give you upgraded tickets. They're VIP...you can come party with us afterward."

"Addy can't do much partying...she's pregnant!" cried Jessica.

Tarni looked at the blushing Adelaide then over to Charlie Sweet who looked at her tenderly.

"But you're what? Eighteen?" Tarni cried.

"And married!" Adelaide proudly held out her left hand and showed off a simple white gold band.

"Well. OK. Congratulations, then!"

Adelaide and Charlie shared a look with Jessica.

"Listen, Tarni. Just don't say anything to the family. We're keeping it under wraps for a bit. Look...we will have Kimberly call you and explain things in a few months. Just...pretend you didn't see us, OK?" Jessica implored then looked around the room as if she were being hunted.

Adelaide and Jessica were witches, just like Tarni, so their worrisome glances caused some alarm.

"Are you OK? Is something going on with the family?"

"When isn't there something going on?" grumbled Adelaide.

"Things are brewing—no pun intended, Tarni—just be careful. Our world is changing," said Jessica cryptically. "We will do the same for you. If anyone asks, we will remain silent. And Tarni? Your father suspects you might be out this way. Las Vegas has been on his radar as of late. Kimberly has been trying to reach you to warn you."

Tarni spent her time at the concert that night fretting about what her cousins had said and didn't want to ruin their visit, so she kept quiet when they showed up later at the after-party. It was good to see them, *some* kind of family, a link to her past, but as she had her own secrets to consider, she didn't pursue their troubles.

Later that night, Logan and Dave decided they wanted to keep the party going by hitting a popular dance club that went all night. Tarni followed along and remained on the sidelines observing the throngs of women vying to have a chance to dance with—or grind up against, rather—Logan. One in particular seemed to have her sights on her man...her friend making a bookend of sorts and keeping him in their orbit.

On a short foray into the ladies' room, she'd overheard the two women talking about Logan while fluffing their hairspray-stiff hair, teased to unimaginable heights. Girl Number One was speaking, "Well, I intend to slip him some of these babies and get him into the back rooms they have here. My doctor said I'm ovulating, and I want that man's baby."

"That's one way to keep him bound to you for life. Maybe I'll take your sloppy seconds...although with the amount of coke running through him, he might keep it up long enough for both of us to win the prize!" said Girl Number Two and chuckled while applying lipstick. They both wore skintight dresses they probably had to peel on and off and one had a tear in her fishnet stockings.

The first girl looked keenly at her friend. "Go after the lead guitarist. Leave Logan alone. He's mine."

"OK, OK. You better hurry up though, there's too many women around tonight, and Logan always manages to bang one or two then disappear. His reputation proceeds him! I'll go order them a few more beers."

Her friend gone, Girl Number One noticed Tarni for the first time.

"Hey, a girls gotta do what a girls gotta do, right?"

Tarni smiled and nodded, nonchalantly walking over to where the girl was about to apply mascara. Reaching her hand up, Tarni grabbed a hold of the party girl's hair, and slamming her head down as hard as she could on the marble countertop, she watched in satisfaction as the girl's eyes rolled back, and she was knocked out cold.

Or worse.

Didn't she let loose a bit of magic to go along with the fight?

Tarni decided she didn't very much like party girls...but realized she might have taken this a bit too far.

Rushing back onto the dance floor where she'd left Logan, Tarni tugged at his sleeve and murmured, "Logan, we need to go. Now."

"Why? We've only been here less than an hour."

"Logan! I can't explain. Just move it. We need to leave."

Groaning, Logan shook his head then called for Dave who was dancing with a freckled redhead is a shimmery green dress.

Turning back to Tarni he ground out, "What have you done now, woman? Did you shoot someone?"

"Not exactly."

"Not exactly? What does that...you know what? Forget it. Let's go."

Tarni spent the next few weeks scouring news stories for reports of a groupie found dead in a nightclub in Vegas but never found anything.

A pity.

The tour continued its grinding pace, and the party was going strong.

But all good things, and not-so-good things must come to an end. The premonition Tarni had felt dancing around the periphery of their lives was closing in on her faster than she could possibly realize.

As the tour moved toward the holidays and the end of one year and into the next, one thing became apparent. Logan was getting more and more popular as the lead singer, and the rest of the band was feeling left out. There was talk of a Grammy award. Even the MTV video awards came knocking. Directors and producers approached Logan, offering movie roles and solo projects and as in other bands going through the same growing pains, things became strained.

By January and the new year, the bandmates weren't even on speaking terms, and Tarni had had enough.

"I think I'm going to fly home and get away from this toxic for a bit."

"What? No! Baby...I need you here."

Seeing how her words brought such an instant change to Logan, Tarni backed down...but as the leg of the tour that would bring them into Florida drew near, she knew she couldn't stay and had to think of something to get her away and back to the safety of Los Angeles.

"Logan, I need a break from this insanity. And I can look in on the house and check the mail. I will only be gone for a long weekend. You guys do Florida, and I will be back when you hit Richmond. I promise."

Logan refused to speak further about her suggestion, denying that she ever leave his side. Yet Tarni knew she dare not enter Florida. Later that night when the distractions of the tour were over, she'd explain to Logan why she had to return to Los Angeles.

Only he never gave her the chance. Instead, he wound up in the hotel's bar with a bunch of minor celebrities hanging on to his every word.

Tarni was frustrated by Logan's behavior and became frantic with worry about her plight.

Her chance for escape came in the oddest sort of way and was totally unexpected.

"Aren't you Tarni Vanderzee?"

The man questioning her took Tarni by surprise. A suave-looking, older gentleman with an air of entitlement sat beside her at the bar in New Orleans where they were just off from another show.

"Forgive me, you must be startled since you don't know who I am. The name is Donald Bartleby. I saw you perform at The Belly Room, and I'd like to discuss a record deal with you." Donald smiled at her look of shock. "I'm a record producer, you see."

"Donnie! What are you doing in town?" Billy came over and slapped the man on the back. Logan trailed behind looking warily back and forth but obviously knowing who Donald was. Tarni relaxed a bit. She still found it odd he remembered her from one performance—even if it was incredible.

"I was just offering Tarni here a chance to record for me back in Los Angeles."

This was met with dead silence, especially by Logan who was now frowning.

"Tarni isn't interested..."

"I think that would be terrific. When would you like to meet up?" asked Tarni, hurriedly cutting off Logan's rebuff.

Jacksonville was the next stop, then Orlando, and Tarni, getting desperate, needed to leave now. This was not only a way to escape a return to Florida, but opportunity knocking meant a boost to her career plans—and a record contract. A way to gain the fame she coveted and the lifestyle that would provide a way for her to take on the sirens.

Especially in light of the last message she'd received back in Las Vegas when stopping in to see Buffalo Jim and informing him of Romano's demise. Jim not only warned Tarni to stay hidden for the time being, but cautioned her about pursuing anything further regarding her father and her plans to mete out damage to his dynasty.

"You'll need more money than I have on hand to pay the folks I have looking into your father, kid. Right now, it's best you let it go. These aren't nice people."

What Jim hadn't realized is how far from nice Tarni had become. There was no turning back now. And if she needed a ton of money? A record deal could be the answer.

"How about you fly back with me in the morning? I have my private plane, and we can discuss my plans for your career while riding in style. How about it?"

Logan, a look of fury clouding his face, and something else...fear? tried to appear nonchalant about the offer, but there was something else behind his demeanor...and Tarni tried to get him to look her in the eyes.

He wouldn't.

"I'd like that. Logan, I have a few things I need to do back home. Of course, I won't make any contractual decisions until you get back in a couple of months, OK?" Tarni stretched her hand out and touched his with her fingertips and she could feel him pull away ever so slightly.

"Would that be OK with you, Logan?" Donald asked.

Logan just jerked his head in a quick nod but didn't speak.

"Are you sure?"

"Tarni isn't a slave. She's free to come and go as she pleases," Logan ground out.

"Excellent. I will have my limo pick you up at the hotel in the morning, my dear. This will be an enjoyable flight now that I know you'll be on it. I must go now and tell my wife, Virginia. She does love to know when we have company coming along. See you tomorrow, Miss Vanderzee."

The mood that night back in their penthouse was chilly to say the least, and Tarni didn't know how to soothe Logan or placate him for that matter.

"Logan. Please understand. This is something I'd like to try and passing up an opportunity like this with Donald and his credentials...even Billy said I'd be an idiot not to go."

"Oh. So now Billy is your mentor. I see. Do you not even see what kind of man Donald Bartleby is?"

Panicked. Logan looked absolutely panicked, and Tarni grew angry because she jumped to the wrong conclusion in her fury.

"You see nothing! Logan! Stop it. You're making things up just to get me to stay. I'm not doing anything wrong, and it's only a few weeks. You'll be back home by early March, and we can celebrate my Birthday, and I will have stories to tell you and you'll have some to tell me, and I will water your orchids. This will be a good break...you'll see."

Logan regarded her quietly, his jaw grinding. "Is that what this is then, a break?"

"From touring. From the road. Logan, stop acting like this.

You know I am excited about trying for my own career in music. Please don't be this way. What is wrong with you? I don't understand!"

"Then go. I can't stop you from doing this. It's not allowed —to interfere. Just remember what I've told you. You do what you need to do...and I will do what I must. Take your break from me. Oh, and perhaps you should just leave my fecking orchids alone."

CHAPTER 33

Logan, 1987 New Orleans

I'm going to destroy her.

I never should have let her into my life when I discovered she was the one. All my life, I've been waiting for her. All of it. My destiny, everything that I've worked toward, all the planning, training, determination to bring about that which I was born to do, all of it now confronting me and I no longer want this.

How do I go on knowing what I know?

How do I continue this path knowing it's Tarni who will suffer?

And the damnedest thing is I can't change what's going to happen. Or can I?

If I grab her and run off to that remote island now and we could live our days away from the world, forget that it exists, would she be OK? Would the world follow and take her from me anyway?

They told me she would be a warrior.

They told me she would bring revolution and destruction.

They told me she'd need to hit the bottom before she'd climb her way to the top—and be an unstoppable force for change.

They didn't tell me she'd be gorgeous, intelligent, and perfect.

They didn't tell me my heart would soar the second I'd hear her voice, or she'd walk into the room. That I'd fall in love with the way she drooled on her pillow or wake with hair so tangled it would take twenty minutes to comb through to retain some semblance of neatness. That her insistence that three pieces of bread needed to be left in the front of a loaf and I'd have to dig in for the fourth or she wouldn't eat her sandwich. Or that a box of cereal could only be eaten the first day and she'd not touch it again—so Franken Berry or Count Chocula would have to be consumed in one sitting.

The little things that would upset me with anyone else—taking food off my plate, hogging the bed and shoving her ice cold feet in places they had no business being, stealing my favorite sweatshirt so she could wear it, her ridiculous need to dance in the rain or stop and save every fucking turtle wandering across the road—somehow none of it bothers me when it's Tarni.

No one warned me that I'd fall so hard the knowledge of what was to come would destroy *me.*

And I can't say a thing to her. Warn her. Protect her from these evil ones.

This will destroy us.

Or will it? Only time will tell.

Time...and my trust that Tarni will understand one day...

...and forgive me.

What do I do now? How do I go on?

Without her?

~

None of his bandmates questioned the reckless behavior Logan began to devote every waking moment to—nor did they ask what was causing him to do so.

The drugs went from smoking a blunt, doing lines of cocaine, and drinking Guinness, to injecting himself with heroin. But as long as he continued performing every night, who were they to complain?

The revolving door of women became a whirlwind of epic proportions and still the band chose to go with the flow. After all, it meant more to go around, and the boys certainly had no complaints in that department.

It was only when Logan began to act out and mess up the lyrics, storm off the stage, or ramble on incoherently to the disappointment of his fans and displeasure of his management and handlers that things became strained in Somber Sea.

And the cracks began to form that put a strain on the band...and their camaraderie.

Logan didn't care.

Logan stopped caring the day Tarni walked out of their hotel room.

Logan stopped existing the moment her scent was a distant memory he couldn't find in the many objects she'd touched or brushed against. He even stopped using a towel after his shows and would storm off to the showers, pushing anyone and everyone out of his way.

Rumors started he began hurting some of the girls he'd choose to be his bed partners after a show.

They all looked similar to Tarni.

But none could fill her shoes, it seemed.

Management paid them off and sent them quietly on their way.

Still, no one said a word or reached out to their lead singer, the front man. The face of the band that was heading to superstardom. The parties, the press, the interviews, the accolades—nothing mattered but the success of the band, despite Logan's indifference. Even though his acting out was causing a rift, a chink in the armor that protected the band and kept them together, it would blow over soon enough and they'd survive this hard patch.

Don't rock the boat unless it becomes necessary...Logan will snap out of it.

So, he's a little rough with the groupies. It wasn't the first time a rock star indulged in some hard-core action. It won't be the last.

Logan will bounce back.

He always does.

CHAPTER 34

Tarni, present day

Logan made love to me the night before I left like a man drowning. Then he went into self-destruct mode and he and the band decided mixing drinks and drugs would continue well into the wee hours of the morning. I packed my bag to leave, watching him cavort on the bed with four women surrounded by drugs, booze, and Polaroids. I guess the old Logan was back in full force, and I didn't understand at all.

Oh, I tried to speak with him. To explain my side of things and tell him I'd listen to his reasoning for me to stay, but he waved me off like an annoying gnat and told me to have a nice trip.

He didn't say goodbye when I walked out the door. I decided to wait for morning to come in the lobby of the hotel—I couldn't take another minute of Logan's behavior. He didn't notice me leaving.

He was too busy having lined the girls up in a row on our bed, faces down and asses high.

As I sat in luxury on Donald Bartleby's Cessna, it dawned

on me Logan had mentioned, "it wasn't allowed." What wasn't he allowed to do or say? I began to worry it might have served me better to have listened to him.

I didn't realize at the time I'd been spelled, my mind muddled with strong magic and my judgment altered for the worse.

I didn't know Logan couldn't interfere with what was about to happen. How could I? The game was devious and the players pure evil.

Two short weeks after I returned home to Los Angeles and found myself bereft and missing Logan something terribly, the rumors began to hit the airwaves and gossip columns that he was seeing someone. Wondering how anyone would know about me seeing as I hadn't signed any contract with Donald Bartleby, I nevertheless ignored the whispers and went about my business.

I still pondered Logan's words...couldn't make sense of them...and whenever I tried to reach him via his management, he never returned my calls. I was annoyed to say the least.

I was sad he'd chosen to go the route of sullen and sulking.

Our home was lonely without him there.

Donald Bartleby was pressuring me to sign on the dotted line, so much so, that I went out and hired my own attorney to look over the contract. He'd come highly recommended by Ernie and had a reputation as a top entertainment lawyer. All I needed was Logan home to see if anything seemed out of line, and I'd be ready to sign and start my new career as a recording artist.

Donald had big plans, and after several meetings, I liked where he saw my career going, so much so that I could taste success even before it hit. I celebrated my pre-signing of the contract by going out on the town with Ernie and his boy pals and we wound up in a nightclub that catered to the gay set.

The dance floor was packed, and the projector screens showed videos from MTV on rotation. It was loud, flashy, and fabulous and I had a grand time, for a while anyway.

"Look at her. She's a knockout. And Duffy! He looks like the cat who swallowed the canary!"

"Or is that the canary who got himself some high-end pussy! Meow!"

Laughter erupted.

Parker and Ernie instantly tried to distract me from hearing any more of the conversation as my head whipped around to search for where the two men at the next table were looking. That's when I saw the live feed from New York City and Somber Sea was being interviewed.

"Logan MacDuff and his girlfriend, Rebecca Felicity Mackenzie, are hitting the town and living large even as the band skyrockets into the stratosphere. Rebecca is the daughter of New York politico Rory Mackenzie and Deirdre Watkins of the oil magnate, Watkins dynasty."

The blonde reporter from Entertainment Tonight was gushing over the couple and fought her way to the front of the line.

"Rebecca, when is the big date?"

"Oh, I don't know. Duffy isn't the marrying kind. Right now, we're living in sin. But who knows? I'd certainly like to run off to Vegas and make it official!" said the leggy blonde with an elbow to Logan's ribs.

I felt the room go black and nausea threatened to take me down as my world began to tilt. I remember all sound leaving except for the grating laugh of that lousy heiress.

Ernie jumped up and got me out of the bar and into his limo where he instructed the driver to take me home.

Big mistake. He shouldn't have left me alone.

I remember very little about that night except I'd managed

to clear every item that was mine and a few that Logan had gifted me from his house and packed up my car, returning to my tiny studio apartment in West Los Angeles. But not before I consumed every drug he had hidden in his stash and polished off two bottles of wine. I also took care of his prized orchids for him. Just before I left, I took out the knife I'd held up against Cash's throat, something Logan stated he cherished and often had me pull out for him to examine, and waltzed into the living room where he kept the expensive collection of plants.

I proceeded to hack and slash every single one of them into a million pieces. It was a massacre in plant form...and even as I wrought my destruction upon them, I cried at their loss and mine, until I had no more tears left to cry.

As I was heading to the front door, intending to walk out of the beach house for the last time, I paused at the locked door that Logan never once opened for me. Fury overcame me and I busted it down with one well-placed kick and a bit of dark magic. I found a dungeon of sorts. A sex room. An S&M dream —or nightmare. Hundreds of photos of women and a few men doing nasty things to each other stared back at me.

I even found photos of Monique and Stacey...and one of Heather. All bound and all with some kind of kinky sex being done to them. Was I a joke then? Someone to laugh at, someone to pity? When did he have the time for all this depravity? Who were these people who were in the shots? Did they all know Logan, or did he rent out this room for their enjoyment?

I didn't care by that point and could barely contain my fury, stopping myself at the last moment from using my magic to flatten the beach house.

I arrived at my old apartment, and Monique handed over my spare key with sympathy written all over her face. Apparently, everyone knew but me. She didn't offer explanations or apologies. I didn't tell her I'd discovered what she'd done.

Irma and Clarissa were happy to see me back. Clarissa even handed me a flask of something that had to be pure grain alcohol and patted my shoulder before wandering off, her phlegmy cough trailing behind. Irma *tsk'd* once and told me I didn't owe them anything that month rent-wise. It seems they knew about my torrid affairs as well.

I didn't want to speak to them. I didn't want to see anyone. Not right away. Maybe not ever again. And in my misery, how could I know what was heading my way like a freight train off the rails?

I didn't sense a thing coming.

Tarni, West Los Angeles, March 1988

Tarni spent those first few days in a daze of drugs and alcohol. She finally discovered just how much she needed to become as messed up as the humans who indulged while she watched, amused and unaffected. Not any longer. Now she could numb herself with the best of them.

Her tears dried up.

She woke as if from a dream and found herself lying on a pile of shredded clothing, all the items Logan had bought for her and nothing she wanted to keep.

Tarni stumbled into the bathroom. Startled by her own appearance, she decided she needed to clean up and a plan of action.

She took the hottest shower she could handle and wondered that she didn't continue to cry, deciding she must be all out of tears by now. Tarni laughed to herself at that, knowing how powerful and precious her siren's tears could be —the magic in one tear alone was potent—as she gazed blankly at her reflection. Miserable and dripping water all over the floor of her bathroom, she didn't feel anything but empty.

Tarni didn't think twice before smashing her hands into the mirror to remove her face from view.

The blood and shattered glass must have been cleaned up by Monique or Stacey—or perhaps it was Heather. It was gone when she returned from her brief hospital stay—a nightmare of epic proportions since she spent most of her time altering the memories of everyone who tended to her wounds or tried to run tests.

Mustn't let them discover my secret and realize I'm a freak!

No one bore witness to Tarni's first attempts at taking heroin. She'd gone out to a well-known area of downtown Los Angeles to the Alexandria hotel and scored some along with cocaine. Shooting up the first time left her catatonic and motionless for hours, but then the drug harmlessly left her system and for the first time she cursed her siren existence.

Tarni then began speedballing—combining both drugs in a toxic cocktail—and went flying down the streets in her Mustang, breaking every speeding record but managing to avoid the police—and traffic, which was ironic in its own right. That too did little harm and was out of her system in a flash.

She even came close to sleeping with a guy who'd followed her home from a club she'd met Ernie at on one of her resupply missions—Ernie was concerned but not enough to stop selling her the goodies or counseling her that perhaps she was in an overindulgent mood due to her misery. No. Not in his wheelhouse to get too involved.

Then just as suddenly as Tarni's downward spin into obscurity started it was over. She picked herself up, dusted herself off, and hardened her heart. No one was worth losing sight of who she was and what her life's goals were. No one. Even though it felt like half her soul had been ripped from her body and shredded, now floating and drifting in the wind, Tarni knew she had to move on and leave her heart out of it.

Drugs would never affect her the way they did humans. No artificial substance would bring the light back to her life.

The light.

Logan.

In the back of her mind Logan's words played on a loop. He warned her he'd break her heart. He told her something like this would happen. But for some reason she couldn't quite shake the notion that something bigger was going on. Too many things didn't add up or make sense, and part of her, a very small part, kept the love she couldn't just remove from her heart for Logan packaged up in gossamer and tucked into a tiny compartment with her faith. Faith that somehow this was part of an elaborate scheme and things between them would once again be...what?

What did she hope for?

Tarni didn't have that answer. But she refused to let this break her down any longer.

I'm a dark witch, damn it all. And a siren. What's more, I am Vengeance, and I will win—no matter the cost.

Two weeks later, on Tarni's twenty-first Birthday, she sat in a posh office in Century City and signed the contract that would change her life and bring her fame, fortune, and she hoped, the power she needed to dominate the world.

Hollywood was abuzz over Donald Bartleby's newest acquisition and the fervor was growing about her upcoming freshman album.

Word reached her via Adelaide that Kimberly had gone missing...along with her new boyfriend. No follow up notes were forthcoming and Tarni was frantic her stalker had returned and taken Kimberly. Or perhaps it was her father and a way for him to lure Tarni back so he could capture his troublesome offspring, putting an end to her foolishness.

Part of her hoped this was some kind of elaborate scheme and Kimberly ran away and would contact her shortly. She awaited news knowing she dare not return to Florida to search for her sister.

That wasn't the only thing to reach Tarni's ears.

Through the endless paparazzi coverage, she'd learned Somber Sea had one of the highest grossing concert tours of 1987, but the band was on the outs since the members were at each other's throats. A breakup was in the cards was the consensus. Rumors also placed Logan MacDuff back in Los Angeles, and he and Rebecca in their Malibu love nest. Dear Becky had hired a decorator and started the process of making the place into her aesthetic. They were not giving interviews.

Tarni held her head high through it all and doubled down her efforts via Adelaide to discover Kimberly's whereabouts. Although Adelaide seemed to have her own troubles going on, and she and Jessica seemed distant. Perhaps family would always let her down and she needed to stand—and fight—alone.

She strengthened herself and felt her emotions slipping away—becoming detached, cold—like a statue carved of marble.

She wouldn't let anything get through walls she'd constructed around herself and her damaged heart.

Because she couldn't comprehend even remotely, anything that had transpired in the last four months of her life, she transformed, embracing the darkness within her, putting Logan and her time with him in that same box where she'd tucked her heart, closed the lid, locked it with a key, and sunk it into the deepest, darkest recesses of her mind.

She stopped considering his last words to her.

She buried thoughts about all the lessons he'd given her or

the words of caution he lobbed at her while instructing her in the art of fighting.

Tarni could barely think at all except to focus on her plan for world domination. Unable to feel the malevolent enchantment that surrounded her, clouding her judgment, and making her everything Logan schooled her not to become, Tarni barreled headfirst into danger.

Getting ready to go out that evening with Donald to meet her new musical director and the people who would be involved in her album—including her bandmates that Donald had handpicked to back her, Tarni knew her days at this beloved little studio apartment were numbered. Success was knocking hard and fast—she already had quite a fan following and made the rounds at the Hollywood events where people were meant to see and be seen.

Ironically, she was heading to Spago since that was Donald's go-to restaurant. She refused to recall the night Logan had shown up and insisted he would take her there for dinner.

Donald sent a limo, and she arrived at Spago in style. The 1920s façade and the line of people waiting to get in didn't faze her...especially since she was escorted past everyone and ushered to a prime seat in the center of the dining room.

Donald and his wife Virginia wined and dined Tarni and she remained distant but interested in all he had to say. People at nearby tables were making note of her, and she kept a supreme look of ennui on her perfectly-made-up face.

"Ah, here's the man of the hour now. Tarni may I present you with your new drummer and musical director. He used to be in the band Toxic Clover, but now Todd is in charge of you. We've decided to call your band Rogue Witch."

Her blood running cold, Tarni made to stand up and leave, but Donald clamped a firm hand down on her arm and leaned in even as Todd sat down on her right, effectively blocking her in the booth with a predatory grin. "Hello, precious."

Head reeling from seeing the man she'd helped Logan bury sitting by her side, Tarni glanced quickly at Donald and his wife. Virginia had arrived bedecked from head to toe in sequins and dripping jewelry Tarni could only wonder at how much the cost could be, so expensive looking did they appear.

That she gave Tarni an openly predatory look now, sent tremors coursing through the young woman and had her worrying her lower lip in dismay.

"I don't understand," murmured Tarni.

Virginia, sensing Tarni was about to make a scene, ran a blood red fingernail across Todd's arm, licking her lips. Giving Tarni a sly look, she explained in a way that made Tarni shiver with dread. "Better to hide right out in the open, wouldn't you say, my dear?"

Running her tongue over her teeth and leaning close to Tarni so only she could bear witness, the unmistakable sight of extended fangs made Tarni's blood run cold.

And just like that, whatever glamour Donald and Virginia cast on Tarni was shattered and she became self-aware once more.

Vampires! They are all vampires! They must be involved in some way with the stalker! Why didn't I let Logan know about the notes? It's too late now. What have I done?

Yes, she might be strong, incredibly so, but even Tarni knew she'd have a difficult time of it with three vampires coming at her. And by the looks of Donald, or more importantly, Virginia, she was probably dealing with two who were beyond ancient.

Logan's words from months past entered her mind.

"If something evil should come calling, play along, bide your time, then fight with everything you've got. You can only do that

if you refuse to let whatever is done to you break you. I might not be around to back you up in a fight for your life."

Tarni knew she had little choice, yet fear coursed through her body, and she started looking for a way to escape despite the futility of it all.

Noticing she was about to bolt, Donald reached out and squeezed Tarni's knee...hard.

Sitting there in his expensive suit and sporting a solid gold Rolex watch, the man oozed charm and power—the kind only someone who usually got his way and didn't fear anyone or anything, could pull off.

"There's nowhere to run, Tarni." Donald murmured with a smirk. "We own you now. But don't worry, you'll get the fame and fortune you crave...it will just be on my terms. You might be surprised to discover we both have a common enemy, and you will be my way to bring him down."

Then Donald stroked Tarni's cheek before giving it a small slap. "You have no choice, my dear. After all..." Donald placed his mouth gently up against Tarni's ear and whispered...

"I know what you did."

Thank you for reading! I hope you loved meeting Tarni and Logan and their harrowing tale of romance, mystery, and tragedy. The next book in Secret Sirens is Siren Star. Find out if Tarni can break away from the tyrannical hold her new handlers have on her and her career. What do these vampires want of her and will becoming famous under them mean an end to her ulterior goals? And what of Logan? Is he truly out of her life or is he playing a dangerous game that will help Tarni reach victory over her enemies and give her a chance at happiness...and love?

CLICK HERE TO READ SIREN STAR NOW>

Secret Sirens ties into my Lily Sweet World. Home Sweet Witch is Book One in the Lily Sweet Mystery Series, and A Tale of Two Sisters in part of the Fortune-Telling Twins Series. All of the connect in some magical way.

Won't you please leave a review on Amazon and Goodreads and anywhere else you'd like—authors need reviews! Yours would be appreciated.

You can also join my Facebook Group: Author Bettina M. Johnson's Team Wicked for exclusive giveaways and sneak peek of future books—and just plain silliness!

SIGN UP FOR BETTINA M. JOHNSON'S NEWSLETTER: http://eepurl.com/gZK051

Continue on for a sneak peek at SIREN STAR....

Siren Star

Living in Los Angeles in the late 1980s meant decadence, overindulgence, and excess—and movies about vampires, like

The Lost Boys, Waxwork, Fright Night, and *Near Dark*. Only in my case, the vampires were real, and I lived among them.

My name is Tarni Vanderzee and I am a siren, a paranormal being who can entice, enslave, and enchant humans with my voice—a vocal vampire, if you will. And now I am being used for that very purpose by men who would dominate me and take away all I hold dear.

I'm biding my time.

I've not given up.

I've been trained by the best...my former lover. And the man who I'd give my life for even if he's abandoned me to my fate.

Perhaps I am being too harsh. Too cold. I know I've become all these things and more. I've taken to drinking until I pass out and using drugs to dull the pain of my success. For I am successful. My orbit to stardom left a streak through the sky like a dark star, an angel who has fallen from grace only to land, not broken and damaged, but triumphant in a world of depravity.

They wanted a siren. They got more than they bargained for.

I'm a dark witch.

I'm vengeance.

And I plan to win... or die trying.

SOCIAL MEDIA LINKS

I write in my own style that may not be everyone's cup of tea—so if you enjoy my characters and humor, my plots, how the storyline is developing, etc. and are eagerly anticipating the next in the series, be aware that I am just as excited as you are—I've found someone who thinks my story ideas are neat! That is thrilling for any writer to know (or it should be). THANK YOU!

Visit my official website to receive updates, find out about special offers and new releases, or read my blog about writing and farm life - complete with photos - you might even catch me mowing my ten acres (seriously): http://www.bettinamjohnson.net

For more information or to contact me:
author@bettinamjohnson.net

For even more (if you just can't enough of me) follow my Social Media Links

Mailing List - https://bit.ly/2BvQXmP
BookBub - https://bit.ly/2Epejwj
Goodreads - https://bit.ly/3aTejQW
Author Page - Amazon - https://amzn.to/3lj7L2L
Instagram - https://bit.ly/2QpZa01
TikTok - https://bit.ly/2PQa6Hg
MeWe - https://bit.ly/36A2RcM
Facebook - https://bit.ly/3gOaFZY
Twitter: https://bit.ly/3jahMgY
YouTube - https://bit.ly/2Stvy2X

ABOUT THE AUTHOR

I always knew I wanted to write. As a kid, way before the technology age had hit, I'd be stuck in the car with the folks as we drove from our home on Staten Island, NY, where I was born and raised, to our family property in the Catskill Mountains. To drive away boredom, I would sit, staring out the window, and create adventures of daring thieves riding horseback along the road, trying to escape the law. Other times, I'd imagine a wild girl riding her unicorn into battle (I had a vivid imagination—we didn't have video games yet!).

As the years passed, I'd start writing a book, then stop, then start again only to let life get in the way, until one day I had an epiphany—a kick in the pants moment. If I waited any longer, all those wonderful characters in my head would never have their stories told, and that made me sad. So, I treated writing as my career. Once I started, it became apparent nothing would ever stop me again. YOU, dear reader, are stuck with me until I go off to that great library in the sky...or wherever writers go when they crumble to dust in front of their typewriters (or laptops...whatever!).

I live in the North Georgia mountains on what I like to call a farm, with my husband and almost adult kids, a Cairn Terrier, a bunch of cats, and fish. Occasionally other critters show up to keep things exciting.

BOOKS BY BETTINA M. JOHNSON

Secret Sirens

Siren Rise

Siren Star (Coming March 2022)

The Lily Sweet Mysteries:

Home Sweet Witch

Witch Way is Up?

How To Train Your Witch

Sweet Home Liliana

Witch Way Did He Go?

Revenge is Sweet, Witch

Witch and Peace

The Sweet Spell of Success

I Spell Trouble

Sweet Briar Witch (Coming soon)

The Fortune-Telling Twins Mysteries:

A Tale of Two Sisters

Double Toil and Trouble

Fire and Earth, Sisters at Birth

Kindred Spirits

A Djinn and Tonic

A Werewolf in Sheep's Clothing

A Pocketful of Pixies (Coming Soon)

www.ingramcontent.com/pod-product-compliance
Lightning Source LLC
LaVergne TN
LVHW040827090826
845145LV00001BA/292

* 9 7 8 1 7 3 6 5 1 7 6 8 0 *